# Woman

# of

# Valor

To Uncle Ernie
Happy reading
love Jane

Read Time Travel Romance at its best

Be My Valentine
by
Jane  Beckenham

Treble Heart Books
1284 Overlook Dr.
Sierra Vista, AZ 85635-5512
http://www.trebleheartbooks.com

ISBN: 1-931742-72-3

# WOMAN OF VALOR
## By
## Janelle Benham

## Treble Heart Books

## *Dedication*

To modern technology which brought us together despite being separated by an ocean and to all the women of valor who operate mum's taxi service while multi-tasking and deserve to be recognized and whom all too often aren't.

# Chapter One

For the hundredth time Samantha Pinkman pondered how she had gotten into this mess. She was strapped in a plane on her way to Tel Aviv.

Sam did not want to be here.

She wanted to be at the Louvre, visiting the galleries and museums, spending evenings strolling along the Seine. She yearned to spend the summer surrounded by culture as she improved her photographic skills and career, not slumped in an overcrowded El Al airplane.

Exhausted after hours spent trying to convince her father to change his mind and which failed miserably, Sam watched her fellow passengers' antics with mixed feelings. She wished she could claim her camera from the hold above. The scene begged to be photographed.

Although the flight was filled to capacity, the ultra-orthodox Jewish men had wasted no time before moving to the rear of the plane and beginning their incantations, swaying backward and forward on the soles of their feet, chanting in unison. Dressed in coal-black coats to their knees, heads covered with matching hats, their long beards and drooping curls made them look like some fashion relic of the 1960's. They reminded Sam of the Diamond Exchange merchants in New York and she found herself watching them with fascination. Their constant hum as they prayed set her nerves on edge and the aroma of percolating coffee along with the oily odor of sardines served up at meal time, permeated the whole plane, making Sam's stomach twist in rebellion.

For the umpteenth time, Sam punched a fist into her flight pillow and tried to sleep. With the continuous praying combined with incessant chatter from the passenger next to her, she resigned herself to a sleepless flight.

"Visiting relatives, dear?"

Sam twisted in her seat and sighed heavily as she looked at the elderly woman sitting next to her. Dressed in a nylon puce pink trouser suit, and with blue rinsed hair, the woman was a fashion nightmare nearly as grating as her Queens accent, the sound gravelly as if she was afflicted by nasal congestion. A whiff of her cheap perfume made Sam nauseous. She rubbed her temples. The acidic aroma of the perfume combined with the abrasive tones was giving her a headache.

"Spending the summer at an ulpan to learn Hebrew?" the woman asked referring to the language school for foreign students.

Sam shook her head trying to shut out the chatter.

"Volunteering on a kibbutz for the summer? Wait until you see those adorable Israeli soldiers." The woman sighed theatrically. "If only I was your age again."

She couldn't ignore the chatty woman. "Archeology dig," Sam mumbled.

"How marvelous. You lucky, lucky girl. What I wouldn't have given to do that when I was young."

"You can go in my place if you like," Sam offered with a wry grin. Embarrassed at the sudden prick of tears, she turned away.

"So you've decided to come to Israel?"

"It wasn't my decision. I should be going to Paris."

The woman clucked sympathetically. "What happened?"

"My father won and my chance to photograph with the best in the field in Paris lost."

A soft touch on her arm made Sam glance up. She caught the sympathetic affection from the stranger. The woman's worn face and kind gray eyes that crinkled at the corners, looked at her with genuine concern.

The promise of tears finally spilled over and sniffing loudly, Sam dashed the back of her hand over her eyes.

"Oh, dear, have I started the flood gates? I'm sorry."

Her mouth trembled and she bit down hard on her bottom lip, struggling for composure. The drinks cart was a welcome diversion. She accepted a plastic glass of brandy on ice from the hostess and took a gulp, choking on the taunting burn as it slid down her throat. "He said it was the only way."

"Why not tell me? Sometimes it helps to talk to a stranger."

Sam eyed the woman. Would unburdening herself of the whole sorry saga ease the ache in her heart?

"Paris was my dream. I'd worked so hard for it, but Dad had other ideas. It wasn't exactly my fault the job I'd had with Eric went wrong." She blushed furiously. "Eric was married." She sought the woman's compassionate gaze. "How was I to know the job had strings attached? I arrived for a photo shoot. I mean, I'm not that type. The man was a letch. Said he'd teach me technique. It wasn't the technique I had in mind." Sam heard her own voice above the drone of the engines. She was babbling, unable to stop the words flowing. "My father hit the roof."

"He sounds over protective."

"One little mistake and I ended up being shipped off." Sam looked at the passing clouds through small window. "He's got some idiotic idea I need to discover my Jewish roots," she muttered. "I'm an adult for heaven sake, but he treats me like a kid at times."

"I see."

"Do you?" Sam sighed wistfully. "What he wanted was to get me out of America as fast as possible. Finding our history is his dream. He thinks it should be mine, too."

"And it's not?"

"I'm interested, but not right now. I have a career, or I did have until he interfered. I try to be independent, but the Pinkman name always gets in the way.

"Pinkman, as in department stores?"

Sam nodded. "I want to make my own name. Samantha Pinkman, Photographer."

"It's a good dream. A woman needs independence," her neighbor nodded sagely.

"Tell that to my father."

"Did you try to change his mind?"

A wry chuckle escaped Sam. "You bet." Sam remembered her father's stony expression. The man had gone beet-red and his shirt collar tightened so much she thought it would strangle him. "He wouldn't budge an inch. All he said was that my antics with that stupid photographer were an embarrassment. I tried to make him realize he wasn't letting me grow up and solve my own problems, to manage my own life." She tossed her hands up in despair. "And so here I am...strapped to a seat, thirty thousand feet up, winging my way to the Promised Land." Sam rolled her eyes. "I suppose it's not his fault," she said grudgingly. "I love him, and I'm all he's got. My mother died when I was five."

"You poor thing," the woman cooed

Sam wished her father could understand as easily as this woman. She touched the woman's hand. "Thank you for understanding."

"Oh, shush," she admonished kindly. "Fathers can be overbearing with daughters. They want to protect and nurture their little girls."

"That's just it. I'm no longer little. I have a life."

"Next time, you need to choose more wisely.

Sam let out a heavy sigh. "I will." Silently, she vowed to be very careful who she would trust in future.

The woman nodded her head knowingly. "My dear, I have advice for you. You may not want it."

"Oh, but I do," Sam edged forward, eager to hear the motherly woman.

"A woman understands a woman." She tapped an arthritic finger on her nose. "You need independence, to show your strength of character and spirit, only that way will your father learn to accept his little girl has finally grown up. Go ahead and pursue your photographic career, carve out a niche for yourself. You may have not have wanted to come to Israel, but why not use the time here to your advantage and show him what you're made of."

Sitting back in her seat, Sam mulled over the woman's sound advice. For Sam, sleep proved elusive as her mind whirred with the possibilities of photographic shots, and the sepias she could produce of the orthodox men in their bygone garb. "A black and white show," she contemplated, visualizing the angles, textures and locations.

Resting against the small window, Sam spied the world below, the endless miles of ocean. She felt a burst of excitement as she thought of what she would see, remembering vivid memories of land and bazaars, the colors of the dry baked earth she'd read about in the National Geographic. Perhaps the kindly woman whom fate had seated next to her was right. She should look on this land and its people as an adventure.

The monotone ring of the bell from the in-flight sound system jostled Sam awake. "This is your pilot. We are flying over Tel Aviv and will be landing in a few minutes at Ben Gurion Airport."

Everyone around her craned their necks to gaze out the tiny windows at the view below and burst into spontaneous applause as the wheels bumped on the tarmac and the plane landed. A canned recording of Hava Nagila came over the loudspeaker system.

Sam started at their behavior. "You'd think landing a plane was some sort of miracle," she muttered.

"To many it's exotic, flamboyant even," the woman next to her advised. "But to those returning home, or arriving to the Promised Land, it is the way they show their delight at arriving safely. They had survived."

The flight was over. The over processed food had done nothing for her mood. She was tired and jet-lagged, but as she glanced at the woman next to her, giving her a grateful smile, Sam realized that listening to her fountain of sensible advice, was more important than anything.

Sam had already decided to take the advice of the elderly woman; it was what she needed to turn this negative experience into a positive one.

As the plane came to a halt her fellow passengers excitedly yanked open overhead bins and collected their belongings before descending steps to board the bus that would ferry them to the terminal gate. Sam hung back, staring down at the throng charging towards the bus. With grim humor she thought it resembled something from a tropical island, its sides all but non-existent.

Stepping through the plane's exit, a blast of heat from the notoriously hot desert winds, the hamsin phenomenon, sent her staggering back into the cabin. The blistering heat shattered any soupcon of cool and patience she had left.

"If it's roasting in April, what will it be like by June?"

Sam blew at a strand of hair that fell over her face. Even her breath was hot. The hair she'd so carefully straightened started curling, sticking to her damp, sweaty forehead.

A woman with a walkie-talkie told Sam to hurry, giving her a slight shove. Trapped by the crowd, she was carried along like a wave into the vehicle, but with standing room only, it was like being a sardine in a can and the smell wasn't a lot better either. The stench of sweating bodies turned her stomach and she had to force down the urge to be sick.

The bus lurched and Sam pitched forward against another passenger. She braced herself, and after two of the longest minutes she'd ever endured, the jolting ride came to an end at a terminal gate. Everyone was shepherded into the building to stand in line, while girls wearing military uniforms examined their passports.

Sam held hers out to a female soldier. The woman's long auburn hair, although tied back was the only feminine trace amidst the severe drab khaki uniform.

"Business or pleasure?" she asked courteously.

Sam blinked at the soldier who couldn't be more than twenty years old. "Pleasure, I hope," she answered wistfully, though she wasn't at all sure.

The soldier flicked through the document, typed into a computer and stamped the passport. "Welcome to the Land of Israel."

Sam followed the others into a hall lined with luggage carousel belts. Everyone crowded around, manhandling trolleys. Wielding her way through the crowd, she swung her leather bags onto the trolley and headed towards the exit.

A customs inspector directed her to another line, indicating she lift her bags onto the rack. Fighting exhaustion she snapped open the catches. Sam glanced around. The same was happening to most of the passengers and it made her realize the seriousness of the country's security. The hair on the back of her neck rose and the surrounding noise was drowned out by the thudding of her own heartbeat as fear caught her in its grip.

She wondered if she could capture this same sense of life on film. Did she want to? Perhaps she should stick to something less threatening—produce a book about cactus. This country was an incongruous mixture of nature versus man. It would require a complete mental shift, away from the glamour and architecture of Paris, to the stark reality of life. A desert world with an intricate mix of life and death. Could she rise to the challenge?

Waiting in line, Sam looked around the terminal. A conglomeration of Israeli, Arab, soldiers, orthodox, monks in flowing robes and Christian clergy hustled on their way. Tourists bedecked with cameras jostled for position, eyes wide as they spied automatic weapons waved airily as if they were nothing but a toy water pistol. The young soldiers looked as if life was for relaxing, but Sam knew this land was on alert. Excited, she realized she wanted to capture the sense of life on film for all to see. The possibilities were endless.

At the next table people were fighting with a customs officer about a cellular phone. Loud voices in strange languages rose all around her, a mumbo-jumbo of sound. It reminded her of a United Nations tour she had taken as a schoolgirl; a melting pot of colors and nationalities.

With a cursory wave of the hand, the inspector motioned Sam to the end of the hall. Resolutely, she strode forward. "Okay, I'm here. Let's get out and show the old man I'm my own woman," she resolved.

Glass doors opened and once more the heat hit her in waves. Her knees buckled and she gripped the handlebars of the trolley, thankful for its strength. Rolling heat coiled up from the black asphalt and she fanned away a fly, which stuck to her damp skin. Diesel fumes spitting from the waiting taxi and buses assaulted her nostrils. It was a heady mixture. Overheated sweaty bodies, the putrid aroma of tobacco and gasoline. Everywhere, people were shouting, rushing, arguing. It was a mad house of frantic activity and she was right in the middle of it, for better or worse.

Sam glanced in every direction. Where to now?

People lined a barricade, manned by uniformed police, eagerly awaiting friends and relatives. There was no limousine or anyone to meet her. A sudden bout of fear coiled in her gut. Where was she to go? Sam hesitated, unsure where to turn.

Behind the waiting hordes, a row of taxis waited by the curb. Sam was jolted by a passing soldier, the muzzle of his machine gun digging her cruelly into her hip. It was as if she'd stepped into a war zone. The whole scene was intimidating, although she was no novice at world travel.

"Jerusalem! Jerusalem!" The raucous shout of taxi drivers hawking fares added to the cacophony.

With concentrated effort, Sam pushed her trolley through the crowds and the barricades towards the taxi rank, but the jerky movement of the trolley over the uneven pavement loosened her bag, knocking it to the ground, snapping open the catches. A rainbow of expensive delicate lace and silk lingerie decorated the pavement.

Drained by the brutal heat, Sam stared at the case; sure she had closed it properly. "Obviously not," she groaned aloud.

She stooped to pick it all up, while the amused snickers from the crowd of onlookers added to her discomfort.

A man stooped to help.

Flustered, Sam looked up into coal black eyes, soft with compassion.

He handed her a flimsy pink bra and panties held between his forefinger and thumb, his rueful expression only adding to her embarrassment.

Sam didn't think it was possible for her color to get higher, but a scorching blush seared her already hot cheeks. Mortified, she snatched the underwear from his tanned hand and tossed it into the bag. She slammed the bag shut, clicking the lock forcefully; making sure it wasn't about to embarrass her again and escaped as quickly as she could into the blessed anonymity of the crowd

\* \* \*

Josh Ben-Sion watched the flustered traveler disappear. An amused grin lit his usually serious face before he turned back to scan the last of the disembarking passengers. He shook his head and paid attention to the last stragglers coming through the airport barrier. He'd scrutinized every traveler who'd come through the gate. Had he missed Sam Pinkman?

Mentally he replayed his boss, Professor Shapira's description. Red hair, twenty-one years old, and American. It was scant, but so far not one man had fit even this miniscule description. The man had probably missed the flight.

"What a waste of an afternoon," Josh muttered. Annoyed and more than a little frustrated he turned to the waiting taxis to catch a ride to Jerusalem and elbowed his way through the crowds to the *sherut*, the group taxi service. A loud argument accompanied by wild hand gestures, caught his attention. He shrugged sympathetically. Street arguments were commonplace. The hotter the weather, the more it fueled tempers. Two ultra orthodox men were shaking heads at the driver, their long curled sideburns dancing. The driver pointed to the front seat where a woman with her head covered was already settled, her nose buried in a prayer book.

Casually, Josh noted the lady with the silk underwear in the middle of the argument. Shouting in English, her mossy green eyes blazed as she gestured to the back seat of the vehicle. With her mint colored dress and flaming hair Josh thought it gave her a striking resemblance to a sea nymph. He ducked his head in amusement, listening to her complaints.

"What is your problem? Don't you want a fare to Jerusalem?" The woman's hands flexed and un-flexed with frustration. She brushed tangled curls from her face, fanning her hand for any semblance of cool air. "Five minutes in this country and my hair reverts to unmanageable," she scowled in the direction of the vehicle's empty seat. "What is wrong with this place?

Transfixed, Josh watched her.

"You," she pointed to the driver, "and those lunatic men are the final straw. I'm tired. All I want is to be clean again. A bath, a shower, a swimming pool, a trip to Alaska."

Josh could see no one was listening to her complaints. He strode forward and came to a halt between her and the two orthodox men. He pointed to them and spoke. "They can't sit next to you," he said gently.

"And why not? Do I smell or something?"

The two orthodox men moved as far away from her as they could. "Do they think I have the plague?"

"It's their custom not to sit next to a woman. They might accidentally touch you or brush against you, and that could lead to, well, to lewd thoughts. I realize it must sound ridiculous to someone who doesn't understand. While some are not observant like the ultra orthodox, we are mostly still raised in a traditional home where everyone's views are respected," he said with a serious undertone. "If more people listened to each other, we wouldn't suffer from so much hatred and intolerance."

"Well that's fine. So they get the ride and I'm stuck here."

He shook his dark head at her. "I can sit in between. Act as a buffer."

"I see," her lips pursed. "So you won't have any lewd thoughts?"

Josh's brows arched at the challenge in her voice. He looked down at her wrinkled linen dress, which clung to her body. Some challenge! "Never mind. Get in. Your bags?" He pointed to the brown leather luggage stacked on the trolley.

She nodded.

Josh slung the bags into the trunk. Acting as a buffer, Josh edged in between her and the others. Their quarters were cramped and he struggled to get comfortable, twisting his long legs in the narrow space. The car lurched into motion, taking the sharp curves at speed, flinging the woman across him. Her dress rode up her thighs and she brusquely shifted back into the corner.

This was going to be harder than he thought. He was starkly aware as the woman's legs rubbed against his and when he gasped she gave him a curious glance beneath those long hooded lashes of hers.

Josh swallowed hard. He was in hell. He was in heaven. As the woman's sleek bare legs chafed against his own, his thoughts went awry. He struggled to keep them in check and his eyes away from the hem of her skirt which rode higher and higher with every twist the vehicle took along the winding road. He could smell the faint aroma of her exotic perfume and it sent his senses reeling. The woman was intoxicating.

No one spoke, except the driver who hummed a mournful folk song—badly. He shouted over his shoulder at the woman. "Your first trip here, miss?"

"Mm," she muttered beneath her breath.

Unperturbed, the driver continued speaking. "Welcome to the Promised Land."

Seemingly disinterested at first, Josh noticed she brightened as the miles unfolded. She leaned forward to the driver. "How far is it?"

"About forty-five minutes, give or take a good or bad road," he chortled, and increased speed, throwing her back against her seat. Like him, she was squashed. Trying to ignore the woman's body pushed tightly against his, Josh's gaze returned to the passing scenery. Israel was a contradiction. Orange trees, armed soldiers, and water sprinklers made up the passing landscape; it was greener than most realized. People expected a desert, not the lush greenery and orchards of the country's center.

"Is it always like this?" Her singsong voice interrupted his meandering. He turned to face her.

"These colors are so bright, intense even," she enthused. Her green eyes glinted. It was the first time Josh had seen her interested in her surroundings.

"It offers such infinite possibilities for differing photos. I just wish I had kept my camera, instead of storing it with the luggage." Her voice drifted off and she gazed out the window. She was in her own world. Josh couldn't help but wonder what that exactly was.

As the driver shifted gears to begin the long ascent to Jerusalem, everyone lurched forward. They sped past forests and the occasional burned out tanks.

"Can't they haul away the rubbish?" she whispered.

Josh heard the sharp reproach in her voice. Mangled metal lay in a heap alongside the road. His jaw clenched and he shook his head sadly. He pointed to one of the burned out trucks. "These vehicles are our memorial to those who died trying to break the siege of Jerusalem during the War of Independence," he said more sharply than he intended.

"Sorry, I didn't mean to be insulting. It was a simple mistake. I didn't know a pile of metal was a memorial. It isn't as if it looks like a traditional sculpture or anything. More like that dreadful exhibition last month at the Museum of Modern Art," she muttered under her breath. "Who knew a pile of old metal was supposed to be a woman?"

"Simple mistake," he snorted. "Everybody in this country knows someone who experienced the siege, or died trying to break it."

The woman gulped visibly and flushed.

"You have a lot to learn about this country."

"Too true," she muttered. She refocused on the abandoned tanks. "Maybe I could set up a photograph with a couple of soldiers sprawled across it. Israel is famous for its women soldiers isn't it?"

Josh nodded.

"What a contrast to my life. Women who are treated as equals, instead of mollycoddled by fathers." She chuckled under her breath.

A broad smile lit her face. "I could send my father a picture of myself in uniform, toting a rifle over my shoulder. Now that would make a great photograph to send to him."

As if in a world of her own, the woman at his side settled in her seat. Josh struggled to ignore the sea green nymph in such close contact. Sour sweat trickled down his back as they were jostled every which way as the vehicle sped over winding roads.

A light groan escaped her lips. Josh gave the woman a sideways glance.

Reaching past her, Josh slid the small side window open. A cool breeze wafted in the gap and within minutes her eyes drifted closed, while Josh struggled to come up with a suitable excuse for his boss.

The city came into view. He nudged her. "We're near the city. It's high in the hills, much cooler than on the coast. Tell the driver where you want to be dropped off and he'll take you there," he instructed

She fumbled through her purse and handed a folded square of paper to the driver.

The city unfolded as the driver navigated evening rush hour traffic. Josh pointed out the Knesset and Israel Museum as they headed towards the city center. He caught a glimpse of a windmill and the walls of the Old City behind it. The setting sun lit the walls with a surreal golden light as if the entire structure had been crafted by gold. He smiled as he saw her wide-eyed response to the beauty. Gone was the annoyance and frustration he'd seen written on her face, as she was enchanted, like all visitors to the city.

"For the rest of my life, I'll remember this. Paris is nothing compared to this." She shot a hand out, pointing toward the rooftops. "Look," she chuckled. She was pointing to the sight of television antennas sticking above the ramparts.

Josh nodded. "It's an incredible sight," he agreed. "A juxtaposition of old and new."

"This would be great for photographing, maybe even good enough for a book," she enthused.

The driver turned down a large avenue and pulled up in front of an apartment building.

Sliding off the sticky vinyl seat, Josh was surprised when she followed him. He tried to ignore her. Some hope. He was sure those flashing green eyes were going to haunt him. He handed a fistful of bills to the driver, making the man grin widely while the woman struggled with her bags as she stepped towards the building.

He wondered whom she knew in the building, but shrugged off the thought. He had more important things on his mind. Like how to explain to his boss about not finding the American. He followed the woman into the building entrance.

"Are you following me?" She shot him a dark look.

"Of course not." He lifted one bag while she struggled with the others into an elevator, trying to ignore her grateful smile. She pushed the fourth floor button.

Josh frowned at the coincidence.

The ride took several seconds. The doors slid open and an elderly, bald man with bright blue eyes stood waiting. A broad grin lit his face. "My dear, Miss Pinkman, how delightful to see you." He leaned forward and lightly kissed her reddened cheeks. "I see young Ben-Sion had no difficulty finding you."

The bag fell out of Josh's hands, landing on the floor with a thud. He stared in horror at the rumpled, tired redhead. "Sam Pinkman?" he croaked.

"Samantha. Sam will do fine," she replied, fumbling in her purse. She handed him a crisp ten-dollar bill. "Can you carry the bags in please?"

# Chapter Two

Josh was afraid. An unusual experience for a former combat officer. Professor Shapira's greeting to the redhead sent a stab of fear deep into his heart. How was he going to explain the foul-up with the woman who dropped underwear in her wake? Thongs, and scraps of lace and silk that would barely cover a flea, let alone the lush redhead whose eyes shot daggers at him at the airport, had done little for his equilibrium. Sitting for forty-five minutes, jostled against the willowy American had sent his temperature skyrocketing on the lust meter. Okay, so he took advantage now and again, enjoying the contact as the van swerved around numerous bends. How was he supposed to know Sam Pinkman was short for Samantha? Absentminded Shapira never said look for a woman.

He groaned remembering his macho offer to sit between the other men and the pretty girl. How was he supposed to know she was the American whose father was funding the entire season? He'd seen enough over the years to realize that this was some rich American parent's idea for their child and not the other way round.

"Bring her bags in," Professor Shapira motioned Josh into the house.

Josh scowled. Both of them treated him like a hotel bellhop instead of what he was—a top graduate student, field archeologist and dig manager for the summer. Anxious, sweat broke out on his forehead and trickled down his back. His shirt stuck to his wet, clammy skin as he struggled with the heavy, expensive luggage. He'd made a big mistake. Huge. Upset her father and he could upset the entire dig. Then where would his career be?

"And the trip was a nightmare. I barely slept a wink," Josh heard the woman moan as the sympathetic professor led her into the cool airy salon. He followed the pair and spied a tray of cold drinks on a table that made him drool with need.

Professor Shapira poured an icy orange juice into a frosted glass and handed it to the young woman who sipped delicately. The older man glanced at him behind his back. "Help yourself."

Josh dropped the bags with a bang. Fists clenched at his side, he glared at the girl with dislike. Apparently, she was important enough to be offered a drink and the hired help had to fend for themselves. Josh guzzled his juice down in one gulp, aware of her disapproving glance. Tough. She could sip as genteelly as she liked. He had a raging thirst.

"Well, Miss Pinkman, I'm so delighted you chose to spend the summer with us."

"I didn't choose," she admitted. "My father insisted I learn something about my Jewish roots. I planned to spend the summer in Paris. This was definitely not my idea."

Josh frowned. Having an unwilling student did not bode well for a happy dig. Sam turned and faced the professor and gave him a dazzling smile.

"Nonsense, your father couldn't have chosen better. Digging in the past, discovering new insights into our ancient civilization will be the most memorable experience of your life. We'll see to it, won't we, Ben-Sion?"

"I'll be sure to make it memorable." Spoiled princess. She'll get the worst, toughest jobs that exist. We'll see how your royal airs and graces help you then, Pinkie. Josh forced himself to smile, flashing even white teeth at the restless girl. He was aware his attitude wasn't about to make things easy, but was unable to figure out why he was bristling at having to work with her. She was a gorgeous woman. Okay, so she was ignorant of dig life and her religious past, everything embedded in Josh from the moment he was born.

But she sure is sexy. Don't forget that.

How could he?

Maybe she'd give up, get on another plane and leave tomorrow. Then he could go back to his work and put this day behind him. Josh peered at the woman and felt his heart sink. Sam Pinkman's brilliant white smile and gorgeous face had clearly bewitched the Professor. His optimistic dreams were about to be dashed.

"Now, my dear, I'm sure you'd like to freshen up. Feel free to shower while I make arrangements for your transportation with Joshua."

She rose from the sofa. "Can you bring my bags in the bedroom please? Don't be too early tomorrow please; it's been a long flight."

Josh bit back a retort. He watched as she sauntered out of the room, her dress clinging in the heat to her luscious behind. One part of him thought she deserved a tongue-lashing like his mother gave him when he was little; the other part of him was dying to pat that adorable butt. See what silky fripperies did to his thinking, he groaned in silence. He needed to concentrate on dust, dirt, and digging. On bringing the past to life, not redheads with come hither lingerie.

Disgusted with his own wayward thoughts and her condescending tone, he opened his mouth to retort, but a warning hand on his forearm prevented him.

"Don't forget, her father is funding the entire season," warned the older man.

Josh forced his tense muscles to relax.

"He wants to be sure she's safe. And whatever Geoffrey Pinkman wants, he gets. He could fund the dig for the next ten years and never miss the money."

Shapira's innuendo was clear and Josh choked on his words, his throat suddenly dry, unable to form a coherent sound. He could see all he had worked for, strived for, evaporate before his very eyes. Unless...he looked after the dig's new benefactor's daughter. "As if I don't have enough to do," he managed to grumble. "Professor, we're nearly there, nearly down to the Roman era."

"Yes young man, I know. I understand your love of the dig, of finding the past." Shapira's gaze swiveled in the young woman's direction. "She's an only child. Over protected. Some sort of man problem in New York I believe. Her father wants her kept safe. That's your job," he ordered.

Josh stared back. "A babysitter? To her?"

"I'd hardly call it babysitting, but use the term if you prefer. Be sure to keep her happy and safe."

The threat to his career was clear. The dig needed the funds and Pinkman had them to spare. Josh would do anything for the security of the dig. It was his lifeblood. His life, his love.

He drew a deep breath and nodded to his superior, understanding. No pampered princess would ruin all his years of hard work. There would be no escape from this assignment unless he wanted to lose his job. Josh needed the job as dig manager. He'd swallow his pride and serve as nanny to the American if that would secure the dig's future, along with his own.

"That's fine. I knew I could count on you," Shapira beamed his approval. "I'll see you in the morning. Not too early," he reminded Josh, inclining his head towards the bathroom where the swish of drumming water sounded like paradise to the humiliated and sweaty, young scholar.

The Jeep rattled over dusty roads. With fierce concentration, Sam gripped the armrest. Strands of golden hair whipped across her face and swirling dust rose up around her, getting in her eyes. She stole a sideways glance at Josh. But the man's stony face told her nothing, except that he still wasn't pleased to see her.

Too bad.

She was here now.

As they rounded a corner, flashes of colorful fabric caught her attention. She gasped at the sight.

"Stop, stop. Oh, look at that." Jumping in her seat, Sam scrambled for her camera. She hadn't made the same mistake this time and kept it close to her.

The Jeep came to a screeching halt, throwing her forward in her seat. Her knees hit the dashboard and she let out a yelp. So she'd have a bruise later. That wasn't important. What was, was the wonderful tapestry of life settled at the side of the road.

Sam jumped out of the vehicle, not giving Josh a backward glance as she scrambled over the dung colored mound toward the Bedouin settlement. "I have to get a photo of this," she exclaimed.

"Sam!" Josh roared behind her, but she took no notice, riveted by the sight in front of her. Clustered together were several Bedouin tents with a television antenna poking out of the flimsy material. The sight perfectly expressed her impression of the country. Old and new jammed together.

A mahogany brown hand snaked around her wrist, stilling her. She spun round to face Josh. Dark, angry eyes bored down at her.

"What the hell are you doing now, Pinkie?"

Sam's nose screwed up in distaste. Already he'd labeled her.

"Taking a photo," she answered simply and took another quick glimpse at the wonderful ménage of life nearby.

"We can't."

"What do you mean we can't? It's right there."

"Sam, we don't have time. I've got to get back to the dig. I have meetings. Shapira wants those reports faxed tonight. Tomorrow we've got to be up early. I've already explained."

Frustration and disappointment warred inside her and she hesitated a fraction, but saw the firm set to Josh's jaw and realized she had no choice. "Very well," she grumbled. "But I'll make sure I carry my camera and plenty of film everywhere from now on. I might as well use my time. Maybe the university has a contest, or I could develop a calendar series." Excited by the sudden prospect of such a project, Sam followed Josh back to the Jeep.


Her first evening at the kibbutz was an eye opener. A meeting was called after the dinner hour. Sam watched as the kitchen staff cleared up in double-quick time, each person performing their own tasks, working as a team. Heat rose across her back and she felt the hairs on the back of her neck rise. Turning slowly, Sam caught Josh's intense dark gaze. She looked away. The enigma that was Josh Ben-Sion made her nervous. Not only was the man a war hero, but also he was a hero to the throng of volunteers who crammed the room, ready to listen to his lecture.

Josh's voice rang out. "Most of you have been here before and are highly knowledgeable, eager to learn, hence the series of lectures. Use this time to make notes, to learn."

Was he talking about her? Look, listen, learn. It was like the road rules, learning to cross the street.

"We are close to the Roman era, the time of the Roman occupation of Judea." Josh continued, but Sam couldn't concentrate. Jet lag had her in its grip. She'd had a day in Jerusalem with the professor, then the drive to the kibbutz, the heat, the strange voices, and food. It was all a bit too much. Sam shifted uncomfortably on her seat, trying to force herself to stay awake. It wasn't that Josh's lecture was boring. Hardly. It was riveting. The man was riveting. Shame she was so tired. Perhaps she could read it up later, go to the other lectures. Just not tonight. She wanted to blob out, relax under the sun, and perhaps try out the Olympic sized pool she'd spied earlier. Sam wondered if she could just up and walk out. Hopefully it wouldn't upset anyone. She looked around, everyone was engrossed. No one even blinked an eye in her direction.

Getting up slowly, she turned and stared to walk to the exit.

"Going somewhere?" Josh voice boomed.

She halted, her shoulders slumped. She felt like a kid being caught doing something naughty. Flush faced, she turned to face Josh, tilting her chin up, giving him the Pinkman stare. Like father, like daughter, she mused. If he could get away with it, perhaps she could too, just this once.

"I'm tired. I'm sorry." Exiting in a hurry, to the sound of silence around her, Sam dared not look back, knowing she'd see shock in her fellow volunteers' eyes that she wasn't staying to listen, devotedly, but also disappointment in Josh's.

The pool beckoned. Two hours, soaking up the sun, resting beside the water with the cool evening breeze for comfort revived her spirits and the admiring glances from the crowd of young male kibbutzniks and their attempts to humor her made the time fly by.

"So you prefer a pool to a lesson about your own history." Josh interrupted the young Danny who sat beside her, telling her of his army training.

"I..." was all she managed to stutter, before Josh spun on his heels and stormed off, not before giving her a blazing dark-eyed glare, of course.

* * *

Josh rose at three thirty the next morning to prepare for the day's work and to be sure all the volunteers were ready to be bussed to the dig site. Everyone stood around yawning, sipping steaming cups of coffee as the sun rose. He counted the work crew.

One missing.

Sam didn't want to be up early. Too bad. Although he had, in consideration of her long flight, discussed the necessity to start so early. Scorching heat and being out in the open, digging for hours on end wasn't easy. Starting early, like they did on the kibbutz during the blaze of the summer months, was the only option.

Sam had reluctantly agreed, but obviously his advice had gone unheeded. He didn't need this. He needed everyone to work as a team.

Josh rolled his eyes and he felt his jaw tense. He should have known who it would be. She couldn't even get out of bed on time. He stormed to Sam's room, yanking the door open. It banged open, hinges groaning at the attack. "Wake up."

"Just coffee and juice, thanks." Sam rolled over.

The princess was still in dreamsville, Josh scorned silently. He grabbed the jug of water and tipped it up. Water spilled over Sam's face. She bolted upright, gasping in indignation.

Josh towered over her, the empty plastic pitcher dangling from one hand. "Get up!" he roared. "I told you last night we needed an early start. Unless, that is, you want to work in the heat of the day."

Sam blinked in confusion.

"Get dressed. Now." Josh averted his eyes. Dowsing her with water wasn't smart. Clad only in a skimpy tee shirt and ridiculous lace panties that barely covered anything, the early morning downpour gave a whole new meaning to the wet tee shirt look.

Thick curls tumbled down her back. It was more than any man should have to bear. "Everyone's waiting for you. Move your backside."

Josh pivoted and strode out the door, shaking with rage. It had taken all his control to stop himself from physically hauling her out of bed. First day and already late getting started thanks to Sam Pinkman. He wanted to get going. He wanted to dig. Princess Pinkie was getting under his skin and the aggravation she seemingly caused so easily more than annoying. Everything she did disrupted his organized world. However, a niggle wormed its way into his conscience. Was it just him she annoyed, while all the men stood about, mooning over the sexy young woman? Josh scowled. It wasn't something he wanted to think about.

Standing with the other volunteers in the quadrant, he searched their faces. They'd come from all over the world, competed and paid for the right to win a coveted spot on the dig. All, except one. Josh's foot tapped with impatience, his lips grimaced in annoyance.

Her door finally opened and Josh's eyes narrowed as he watched her wander casually over to the group. Perhaps she didn't care for his fashion sense. She certainly wasn't wearing the drab work clothes he'd given her.

Long, slender legs drew all the men's eyes, including his own, like magnets. Sam Pinkman may be the bane of his life at present, but she was definitely more than cute. She was a sexy woman, Josh acknowledged, though he'd rather not.

She wore a khaki shirt tied around her narrow waist, accentuating her lovely curves. An expensive looking camera dangled from her shoulder. "She looks like she's going on a damn safari," he muttered.

Sam caught Josh's brazen scrutiny. "The shorts just weren't my style," she shrugged. She saw anger flush across Josh's face, but she wasn't about to walk out in the clothes he had thrust at her. She'd had no choice but to reject the khaki shorts. They were hopelessly too big, falling down around her ankles twice. All the other female volunteers had already headed to the bus and Sam had no one to ask for help. She had tried to keep them up and that's what had kept her so long. Figuring she would annoy him by spending most of the day hanging on to her pants, she had pulled on a pair of denim cut-offs, screwing her nose up when she realized how brief they were, more conducive to an exotic resort than a dig where dust, heat and sweat would be the order of the day. Oh, well, she sighed. Better half covered, than not covered at all. That, she knew, wouldn't go down well with Josh Ben-Sion if his reaction to her underwear on the pavement was anything to go by.

She patted her pocket with the spare lenses. Even exhausted, she hadn't forgotten her camera. One never knew where a great shot might suddenly appear. Yesterday she'd learned her lesson.

Brightening at the thought, Sam trotted docilely towards the rickety bus, struggling to cover her yawn.

"Everyone on the bus. Now. We're late." Josh barked, glaring at her. "Going to a dig and you carry a blasted camera like some tourist."

Sam heard his scorn, although no one else seemed to have. She chose to ignore it and lifted her chin in defiance. "Got out of bed on the wrong side this morning," she taunted. She saw him grit his teeth, fists clenching, but said nothing.

"I didn't want you here this summer, Pinkie. I have work to do. Ensure you do yours."

Sam gasped. "Of course."

It appeared that now, thanks to her, everyone was late. The early morning group of volunteers shot her a curious look, their resentment at being kept waiting obvious.

An older man in his seventies offered a hand to her. "Allow me," he gestured politely with a sweep of his hand. His gray eyes twinkled at her disheveled hair.

Sam took his hand gratefully and stepped into the bus.

The man took the empty seat beside her and turned to her. He offered his hand. "Permit me to introduce myself. I didn't see you last night at the volunteers' meeting. My name is Jan de Vries, from Amsterdam."

"Sam Pinkman from New York."

"Your first time on a dig?"

She nodded sleepily at him.

"Student?"

She shook her head, red curls bouncing as they jolted along the rough road to the site.

"Feel free to ask any questions. I've been coming on digs here for over forty years."

Sam's eyes opened wide. Forgetting her fatigue, she stared at his wrinkled, placid face.

"You're surprised," he teased.

"I had no idea people were so... addicted to this stuff."

"Stuff," the old man chided. "But you're right, it is addictive. I was a child during the Second World War. I still remember the Nazis and what they did to our Jews. My family hid a Jewish family during the war. They live here today and their son became Professor Ben-Sion, a prominent scholar. We always stayed in touch over the years and from the time I was a young man, I wanted to help build the new country. I come to the digs as a volunteer every year. I was at Masada and Hazor with the great Yigal Yadin," he added casually.

Sam tried to absorb the information. He paid to come every year to live like this. Ben-Sion. Wasn't that the tyrant's name? "Did you say Ben-Sion?"

Jan nodded. "The little boy in the family became a professor. His son," Jan inclined his head to the front of the bus, "is well on his way to a similar ambition. A very gifted young man. Shame about all the trouble." He bent his silvery head in thought.

"What trouble?" Sam's interest was piqued.

Jan lowered his voice. "I've known Joshua since he was a baby. A delightful child, full of curiosity. He went on his first dig when he was fourteen." The old man's eyes misted, lost in memory. "In this country, all the boys and girls go off at eighteen to serve in the army for several years. It's common for friends to go to the same unit. To make a long story short, our dig manager joined a combat unit with many of his school friends, including his best friend, Avi. Those two boys were inseparable. More like twins, than friends. Both went into the paratroopers, both went to officers training. Towards the end of their service, their unit was ambushed. At least half the unit was killed. The rest were saved by Josh's cool action. Wounded, he still managed to carry Avi's body back to medics, but it was too late. Avi bled to death. Josh was decorated as a hero, but he's never been the same since. He never laughs. He blames himself for all those dead boys, though there was no way it could have been prevented. Josh feels guilty for surviving."

Sam sat in silence, trying to digest the story. For the first time, she felt sorry for the bully who treated her so badly.

"Listen to an old man ramble," Jan smiled guiltily at her side.

"It does put a different perspective on things," she mused, her gaze shifting to Josh who was at the front of the bus, speaking intently to Sam's blonde roommate Lindsay.

"It does," Jan agreed. "Time, and those around us heal. You'll find this out for yourself," he said, his voice a mere whisper amidst the cacophony of excited chatter.

About to question Jan's ambiguous remark, the screeching of rubber and loud brakes thwarted her chances. Everyone started shuffling off the bus to be greeted by a waiting group.

Jan explained. "These are the experts. Field archeologists. Some specialize in pottery, coins, geology and so forth. We also have a photographer and an artist to capture everything in situ before anything of importance is moved."

"What do we do?"

Jan grinned at her. "The dirty work. We dig carefully with small spades so nothing is damaged. Occasionally, we get to brush away dust with a tool around the size of a toothbrush."

Realizing how ignorant she was of what actually happened at a dig, Sam watched dazed as Jan accepted his tools and instructions for the day. All hope of getting any photographs, let alone aiming for a book, vanished as the bus disappeared in the dust and she and the other volunteers walked through the maze of dug out troughs in the ground to start their morning work.

Sweat, always constant, dribbled down Sam's back, neck, and face, stinging her eyes. She wiped her forehead with the back of her hand and glanced up at the fierce golden sun. Roasting alive in the nightmare heat made her feel sick to her stomach. Covered in a thin coat of dust, her casually pinned up hair escaped its metal clip and fell around her face in loose tendrils. She licked her lips and winced. They were cracked and dry. She felt as if she'd spent days, instead of a few hours, patiently digging in the ground like some mole. Throbbing pains coursed through her head. In her early morning rush, she forgot to wear a hat and could feel her skin burning to a crisp. The spare cap they'd tossed at her was sadly useless. A child's size, it barely covered her head and fell off every few minutes.

"Freckles will be popping out all over my shoulders like a rash," she muttered, stabbing at the baked earth with the small pick.

Jan offered her a drink of water from a canteen clipped to his waist. "You must drink more."

"I'm trying," she answered. "I feel like I've drunk gallons of the stuff. Right now I'd prefer a Diet Coke."

The old man smiled at her words.

Sam arched her back and shuffled to stand. Around her, the others beavered away. Jan continued tapping patiently at rock and earth, his concentration intent, while Josh examined the work and dug with another group in a second trench.

A shout went up to stop for breakfast. No one said anything about the unusual meal of cucumbers, tomatoes, and some thin yogurt. Nothing surprised Sam any more. During the meeting the night before, Josh had said this would be their standard breakfast, typically Israeli.

She bit down on the crisp, fresh cucumber, mumbling to Jan who sat beside her on a boulder. "At least I'll be healthy. Burned like a lobster, but full of vitamins. Remind me next time to listen," she said realizing the consequences of her own admission.

The older man chuckled, his lips curved in a knowing smile.

Sam pounced on the coffee thermos. One sip and she nearly spat it out. It tasted thick, mud-like and revoltingly sweet. "This is awful."

"Turkish coffee takes some getting used to," he said, with a sympathetic smile.

Sam took another tentative sip, letting the thick, overly sweet flavor of the coffee nicknamed 'mud' coat the insides of her mouth. "Okay, so it's not a double latte, but it has a distinct bite," she smiled ruefully.

A fifteen-minute break and it was back to the dig. By ten o'clock the blazing sun felt like Dante's Inferno. Even Jan had stripped off his shirt. A curious birthmark on his shoulder attracted Sam's attention. He noticed her interest.

"It's supposedly a sign of great wisdom. Of course, I am living proof that it isn't so."

Sam chuckled. The man was a mountain of information and had given her a running lecture about archaeology all morning. Even the trained professionals admired his knowledge from forty years of experience.

"Oh-oh," Sam muttered. Josh walked towards Jan's pit. He beamed with admiration as he examined the old man's work, already three times as deep as hers. "We need to speed up," he said, not looking at anyone specifically. But it didn't fool Sam. She knew he meant her. She was trying. Israel was a different world from Manhattan.

Totally, but excitingly so, she recognized. She wanted to be independent and knew that this was her chance. Sam spied Josh examining a piece of pottery, turning it over repeatedly in his long bronzed fingers.

He may be a hunk, but he was also a hard taskmaster.

Sam buckled down, but before she managed to settle into a pattern of dig and dust, Lindsay sidled up to her.

"What'd you do to get the boss man so angry?"

Sam blinked, shading her eyes from the fierce onslaught of glimmering heat.

"Nothing."

"Doesn't sound like nothing. I've never seen him so grouchy."

Hearing Lindsay's accusations, Sam noticed a few of her co-workers nods of agreement. Her gaze flickered toward Josh who stood beside Dr. Navon, examining a pile of broken artifacts.

"He doesn't like me," she said simply.

A young Swedish worker chuckled. "You think so? Think again. Josh Ben-Sion doesn't know what love and hate is right now. He's too confused. He oggles you when you're not looking."

That brought Sam up sharply. "Why then, does he shout?"

"He's got a lot resting on this dig."

"He could at least be human."

Lindsay bent and whispered in her ear. "Tell me when you want our room to yourself. I'll move out and you can do the kissy-kissy with the leader, though I doubt it will get you anywhere. I've tried often enough."

"Kissy-kissy," Sam shrieked, horrified at Lindsay's suggestion. She jumped up. Bad move. Hours of unaccustomed stooping in the tortuous sun finally took their toll and she swayed, squinting in the sunlight at the form glowering at her. "When did the place turn into a ballroom?" She smiled graciously at the man and held up her arms. "Why, I'd love to dance," she said and she promptly pitched forward into Josh's arms.

Her head ached and there was a decidedly nauseous feeling

in her stomach. Josh gazed down at her. "What happened to the ballroom?"

He held her in one arm, Jan's canteen in his other hand. "Sam? Princess? Can you sip some water?" He urged her quietly to swallow the hot, unpalatable water. Handing the canteen back to the other man, Josh pressed one palm on her forehead. "She's burning up. We have to cool her right away. Lindsay, bring the bucket," Sam heard him shout. "I should have seen this coming. Made her drink more."

"It's not your fault," Jan commiserated.

Sam tried to nod her agreement. "I drank the foul stuff. I did, really I did." She didn't want to tell him she'd only sipped at it, not downed gallons like she could have. "Stupid. Sorry Josh. I know I should have listened. Don't worry, your cash-cow won't bow out just yet," Sam tried to appease him.

Josh's dark eyes glimmered with humor, despite his apparent concern. "You're saying sorry to me. That's a first, Pinkie."

She tried to smile, and failed. She felt awful. She wanted to be sick. Lindsay, scurrying to carry out Josh's orders, handed him a bucket of water. Unceremoniously, Josh dumped it over her head.

Sputtering, she sprung up. "How dare you!" But moving quickly was a mistake and she swayed precariously.

In one swift movement, Josh scooped her in his arms and cradled her against his chest. "That's enough for one day, Princess. You're getting out of here, now."

Barely able to comprehend what was happening, Sam lay in his arms as he strode to a parked Jeep. Gently, he lowered her onto the front seat and vaulted to the driver's side. He started the engine and pumped the gas a couple of times, ignoring her protests. She had no energy to argue and the Jeep took off, roaring down the road

Fussed over by the kibbutz nurse, by evening Sam had recovered from dehydration and mild heat stroke. She was burned to a crisp, however, and moaned as she spied her appearance in the mirror. "A lobster. And wait until it peels," she groaned. Although she felt more than a tad sorry for herself, she had already accepted blame, even if only to herself. She should have listened to him. Should have taken her hat, should have kept the water intake up, instead of sipping at the brackish tasting water. Should have, didn't. And here she was, baked, blistered and thoroughly miserable.

"A lesson in life," she said aloud. One, she decided, she had learned once and for all.

The door opened and Sam spied her roommate Lindsay's reflection in the mirror. The blonde sauntered in followed by a sandy haired young man. She snatched up a change of clothes. "Got plans," she intimated, winking at Sam. "Gee, Sam you're smarter than I gave you credit for." Lindsay stopped next to her. She leaned over and whispered. "I've been on a couple of digs and no one ever got anywhere with Josh before. You should have seen his face when you fainted. He never gets involved with anyone. Never. Very slick, Sam, very slick." Lindsay's gaze turned to the young man with her. "He's okay, but Josh, well he's in a class by himself." She sighed theatrically. "Take it easy. I won't be back tonight." The man and Lindsay's eyes met. Understanding passed between them.

Sam sighed deeply as Lindsay left.

No one mentioned love. Maybe Lindsay had the right idea. No complications, just lust, though somehow, Sam couldn't see herself doing the same.

While Lindsay and everyone else on the dig socialized, probably beginning half a dozen romances, if the behavior she had noticed last night had been any indication, she lay back against the mattress, resting her burned arms behind her head. What she wouldn't give for the softest down filled mattress right now.

As moonlight filtered through the linen-covered window, Sam stared at the stars. She wondered how Lindsay did it. Rumor had it that the woman had all the young and not so young men traipsing after her and managed all her relationships like a breeze.

Sam wished she could manage just one.

Mind you, it was only a rumor. Sam was used to rumors, often the victim of gossip herself. Toffee-nosed, stuck-up and a snob were words used to describe her. She knew she was none of those things and was determined to make her own way. She was going to concentrate on her photography. No man was going to cause her such turmoil again.

# Chapter Three

The first two weeks on the dig were the worst two weeks of Sam's life, far worse than the summer at Camp Minni-Ha Ha when she got poison ivy. Worse than the summer she was shipped off to a boring aunt's house in Provence, where there was no one under the age of sixty in the entire village. This was ten times worse. The heat, dust and monotonous and painstakingly slow digging seemed interminable.

Two days after recovering from her episode of heat stroke and dehydration, her sunburn had transformed into a becoming, soft golden tan, Sam was back at the dig. Up early, invigorated with excitement— she'd heard the heated discussions that they were close to the Roman period. All night she'd been unable to sleep, her mind whirring with the possibilities of what they might find, how she could photograph it. The idea of a book had firmly taken root. She was a determined woman. Grabbing her sun block and hat, she exited her room, filling her bottle from the dining room water dispenser on route to the bus.

She'd learned her lesson. Now she drank religiously every fifteen minutes, reminded by a beep on Josh's watch, which although it made her at first feel like a child, it was, she admitted ruefully, a positive. It made Josh happy that his staff was healthy, and she sure didn't want another episode of sunstroke. Once in a lifetime was enough.

"Time for your water," he intoned solemnly.

Hearing the snickers around, Sam screwed up her nose.

"Can't you remember for yourself, Pinkman?" Lindsay's whiplash tongue snickered as Josh handed her a fresh bottle of cold water, taking her empty one.

Sam fumed inwardly, embarrassed. Once again it seemed a man was in control of her, telling her what to do, and here she was trying to be independent.

"I can remember."

"Yeah, right," Lindsay taunted.

"It's merely concern," she snapped back.

"Whatever." Lindsay sauntered off.

Concern or control? Sam's gaze searched out Josh. He was over by another of the small groups, engrossed in conversation with one of the volunteers. Lindsay plastered herself up against him, eyes flashing, smile brilliant white, as she flirted audaciously. Josh didn't seem to notice.

Sam sighed. She hoped it was concern. She'd had control. Her father snapped his fingers, she jumped. But not now. Now she was her own woman she determined, tilting her chin up. "I'll show you Josh Ben-Sion. Daddy too. I've had it with men ordering me around, making a fool of me." Sam resolutely decided. "It's time," she admonished herself, "that Sam Pinkman made a stand, took control of her own destiny once and for all."

The trouble was it wasn't a smooth path. A hiccup to the new and improved Sam Pinkman plan occurred on their first outing, the next day. She still had to learn to listen. The one and only outing to the beach as a reward for all the hard work was disastrous.

Josh seemed happy. Everyone listened intently, hanging onto every word he said, despite the scorching heat. No air-conditioned coach, they relied on the flicker of breeze through the bus's windows. But the stupefying heat and incessant roll of the bus lulled her into a drowsy stupor. With an earplug of her walkman in one ear, and trying to listen to Josh, though only hearing a smattering of his warnings about dangers, she dozed for a while, smiling. Josh was like a mother hen, an old worrywart.

When the bus rolled to a halt beside the glistening waters, Sam couldn't wait to hit the water. The sight of the golden sand, the softly rolling surf, and blue sky was too much to bear. She threw off her tee shirt, revealing a clinging, flesh colored maillot which created the initial impression of nudity, earning the enmity of the other girls and admiring glances from the men. But Sam only had eyes for the cool water. She ran into the water like a happy child let loose from school, ducking under as she swam out into the waves.

It was paradise, waiting to be enjoyed.

Even paradise can be deceptive.

The first few minutes were glorious. "This is great. Time off from work," she called out to the others still walking toward the water. "This is what I need," Sam lay back and floated in the vibrant blue crystal clear water, warmed by the intense heat of the sun. She stretched out, letting it soothe the muscles she never knew existed, and others that hadn't actually been invented yet.

Letting her gaze travel up and down the beach, Sam spied a group of camels at one end, herded together by a young Bedouin boy. She smiled. Here again was the fascinating contrast of ancient and modern. She noted the Nike sneakers peeking out beneath the boy's black robes and mentally visualized the photo, with the sun glinting down across the hills in the backdrop. The time worn craggy cliffs had shed most of its foliage, leaving behind a scarred hillside. The colors were lustrous. Deep earth tones, russet and grays and every shade in between, blended under the heat of the golden disk shining above. Sam couldn't wait to begin her photography in earnest, right after her swim.

A sharp stab assaulted her feet, her legs, her ...Sam's piercing shriek echoed around the silent cove. It was too late, she found out why she should have listened to Josh instead of Whitney Houston.

Lying in the shallow beach beneath the silky water's edge lurked sharp edged fire coral. The stuff attacked her mercilessly. On and on it stabbed as she thrashed about in the water. Coral was meant to be that beautiful stuff, all colors and something kids collected. There was nothing beautiful about this stuff. It hurt. It was agonizing.

Sam's shrieks brought everyone running to her aid. Josh was the first and wrapped his arms around her waist, taking no time in the niceties. "Shut up. Stop moving Sam. Now," he ordered.

Sam stopped squirming immediately. It was a command. It sounded like her father ordering his staff and no one questioned a Pinkman command. Sam obeyed but her quiet sobs continued. The pain attacking her lower limbs was excruciating. Her face contorted in agony as fiery welts began erupting on her legs. "It hurts, it hurts," she moaned.

Several strides away from the rolling surf, Josh placed her softly on the sand. Others in the group rushed round her, offering advice. Lindsay handed Josh a towel and stooped and whispered in Sam's ear. "Nice going. He's all over you again. You've got to teach me those moves Sam," she smiled laughingly down at her.

Gently, lifting her head, Josh placed the towel under her tangled hair and lowered her head against it. He issued sharp, staccato commands to several in the group. Sam, for once was thankful that he was here and desperately hoped he knew what to do.

"Josh, take the pain away, please," Sam pleaded. "Do something."

He started wiping down her skin with a towel dipping it in cool water from the ever-prepared Jan who handed him a canteen. Sam let out a sigh. The water was like a magical balm to her heated and now itching skin. The others started moving away, the drama over.

Quietly, Josh murmured. "I know it hurts. You're being very brave. Settle down and let me help you."

As her skin cooled, Josh opened up a jar of cream. Rotten eggs couldn't smell worse.

Her upturned nose wrinkled in disgust. "You're not putting that stuff on me." Sam struggled to sit up, but Josh's firm grip on her shoulder put a stop to that idea.

"It's either this or the pain Sam. Your choice."

Sam eyed the bottle of thick glutinous cream. Choice? There was no choice.

"Next time remind me to put in some Chanel. Sorry it stinks, but it does work." Josh scooped out a glob of the stuff, holding it up for her to see. "Sam?" he questioned, brows furrowed with concern. "We've got to get this on, fast. Do you know what just happened to you? You've been stung by fire coral. If you don't put this cream on those welts that are rising rapidly, well..." and Josh's voice trailed off.

Sam could clearly see what he was talking about. The fierce red swellings were rapidly covering her legs and feet and there were even some on her arms. She definitely knew there were some on her buttocks. She flushed, keeping that detail to herself.

"Now, Pinkie, let me play doctor, hmm?" Josh smiled at her mischievously.

Sam couldn't stop him as he began spreading thick glutinous cream all over feet and ankles. Carefully, with feather like touches, surprising for such a strong man, he smoothed the cream on her damaged skin. Higher, and higher, his fingers massaged it up her calves and thighs.

Sam was never sure when, but sometime while he slapped the awful stuff on her, she forgot her pain. Her senses began and ended on the sensation caused by Josh's fingers as they continued their path up her legs, the cream quickly dousing the fiery heat from the coral. But his fingers re-ignited another kind of heat as they traveled upwards on her thighs.

"Now turn over." Josh looked down at her, his jet black eyes watching and waiting for her response.

"What do you mean, turn over? Whatever for?"

"For the last five minutes, princess, you have been squirming like mad. Unless this is some new American dance, if I'm correct, I would guess that you have a few large coral stings on that pretty little behind of yours. Now over you go."

Fuming, Sam had no alternative. He was right. Her derriere as well as her legs had been hit by that blasted coral. She rolled over, her humiliation complete.

Josh gasped.

Sam swiveled and saw concern etched in his eyes. "What's the matter?"

But he said nothing. Instead he gathered her up in his arms, and strode, silently, toward one of the ramshackle cabins at the edge of the beach. With a swift kick the door flung open and Josh bent down and entered the small doorway.

The cabin was more like a grass hut, a safe refuge from the heat of the day and cool desert breezes at night, for the myriad of backpackers who hitch-hiked up and down the country all year round.

Gently, he placed her on a grass mat. The dry plaited reeds scratched at her swollen wounds. Sam winced. Outside, she could hear laughing children, their chattering remarks in words she didn't need translated.

"Turn over Sam."

She did as she was told and with infinite care, Josh slipped her bathing suit aside as he dabbed the soothing cream on the afflicted area. Sam wanted to die of mortification. Her cheeks burned. Holding her breath, she dared not move. The electrifying touch of his hand was unbearable as it smoothed over her buttocks. Her body vibrated from the contact. The awful smell forgotten; Sam could have spent the entire afternoon feeling his magical ministrations. She had no desire for it to end. A small moan escaped her mouth.

"Still hurt?"

Speechless, she twisted her head to look at him. The sight of his bare, golden chest made her heart lurch. Why hadn't she ever noticed how terrific he looked? Strong powerful arms and corded muscles. Sam drooled at the incredible sight.

"Are you thirsty? You can dehydrate even in the water. You're drooling," noted the worried man. Silently, Sam sipped at the canteen as he slipped a supportive arm around her back. What must he think? Even going to the beach was a disaster. And here she was trying to be so self-reliant. She knew everyone referred to her as the princess behind her back, except Jan.

Back at the dig, Josh assigned her a new task. Sam was determined to get it right and headed to the room where the pottery fragments were cleaned. Each day, hundreds of fragments were recovered. They had to be carefully cleaned and laid out for the pottery expert, Dr. Navon, to date and assign a time line. An expert in her field, she could determine if the object was a perfume bottle, oil lamp, or container of some sort. Sometimes, she could piece them together and give a better picture of the way the object might have looked. However, the work couldn't proceed until the pieces were washed.

Sam sat at a long rectangular table adjoining the dig's staff kitchen and recreation room with a television set and ping-pong table. Today had been an incredibly successful one as the dig gave up its lost treasures. Now, it was time for her to get to work. Her heart sank at the sight of the hundreds of pieces to be cleaned. It would take all day and most of the night, she sighed. At least she was out of the hot sun and could make an instant coffee whenever she wanted one.

She set to work, a radio blasting in another room in a language she couldn't understand. The hours dragged as she sat hunched over the fragments, zillions of them. She'd never get finished.

The pottery expert ambled into the room and tsked at the work. "You should work faster. This needs to be done today. I can't get my work done if you move at the speed of a snail." Dina Navon slammed the screen door and marched out.

Sam glanced at the clock. Eight p.m. She'd been at it all day except for a short lunch and dinner break and she wasn't even half way through. Her shoulders and back ached and it was lonely working all by herself. At this rate, she'd be up all night. She went back to work, listening wistfully as voices rose in the recreation room. People had been swimming in the kibbutz pool, and playing tennis on the courts. Everybody was having fun, except for her, because Josh had put her on pottery duty.

Sam worked on for hours. Whereas some kibbutz were on the tourist routes, others agriculturally based, her kibbutz was associated with the university and the dig. As Jan had said, "If you want to find artifacts, you might as well dig up the whole country."

Jan's silvery head poked in the door. "It's close to midnight, Sam. You can't stay up all night."

"I have to finish this today. That pottery lady, Dr. Navon said so."

Jan sighed. "Stubborn," he muttered. "No one expects you to go without sleep."

But Sam wouldn't listen. She was much tougher than Jan or anyone else realized.

"Try to get some rest," he had said as he left, the door shutting behind him.

Sam stood and stretched her arms over her head. Her shoulders ached terribly. More than one hundred pieces still to go. She walked into the staff kitchen, made a cup of coffee and gazed around. Her eyes opened wide as she noticed the little dishwasher next to the microwave. Of course, how stupid of her! No wonder everyone finished pottery cleaning quickly, except for her. Small wonder everyone thought she was stupid.

Sam raced back to the pottery room and scooped up fragments into a basket, returning to the kitchen. She laid them carefully on the dishwasher racks and shut the door. Which temperature? Would they break at a high temperature? Sam pushed the cold-water button for a quick rinse, smiling smugly at her cleverness.

Josh couldn't concentrate. He was still writing daily reports for Professor Shapira late into the night. He never slept much. Sleep only brought on the nightmares, the blood and screams and bullets flying past. And Avi. Wandering into the kitchen, he was surprised to find Sam still at work. "What are you doing up?" he asked casually, pouring hot water into a cup with a tea bag.

"Still washing pottery," came the reply. "I was so stupid I didn't realize I should have used the short cut," she admitted ruefully.

What was she talking about now? "What short cut?" he asked, almost disinterested.

"The dishwasher." Her voice was triumphant. A victorious smile shone on her tired face.

"The dishwasher?" Josh nearly choked on his tea. He yanked open the dishwasher horrified to see dozens of pottery fragments laid out on both racks. With shaking hands, he gently pulled out the racks, while his heart raced. Dr. Navon would have a fit. He quickly scanned the racks. Miraculously, nothing seemed damaged. "What the hell did you think you were doing?"

"I..." Sam stumbled on her words."

"Didn't you listen?"

She nodded. "I did," she said defensively. "This was such a slow job, I thought maybe a quick dip in technology would help."

Josh ignored the mumbled speculations of onlookers who shuffled, sleepy eyed into the room, their mumbled speculations coming to a halt when they saw the incredible sight of Josh holding Sam firmly over his thighs with one hand, while he whacked her bottom with the other. "Spoiled brat. Big baby. Pampered princess." Insults spilled out in rage. His hand halted mid-air. My God what was he doing? He couldn't believe his own actions. He was a monster.

Sam squirmed and wriggled, desperate to get away from him. Finally, his temper cooled and a wave of guilt washed over him. He sat her up like a rag doll on his lap. Moist green eyes glared back at him, her full, rosy lips quivering. "Congratulations. I never hit anyone in my life until you."

Rage overtook Sam as it had Josh. Tearfully, she shoved her way off his lap. One hand rubbed her sore buttocks. Her gaze took in the crowd that had formed. But everyone looked away and Sam saw their embarrassment at having walked in on the scene.

"I hate you, Joshua Ben-Sion. I hate you."

"You're not the only one," Josh agreed, eyes downcast. He couldn't look her in the face. Sam ran past the audience, tears blinding her way as she stumbled from the most embarrassing scene of her life, far worse than the incident with Eric and the naked model. As she dashed through the crowd Sam admitted she had failed again. She gulped in abject misery. Why did everything turn into a catastrophe? First one boyfriend, then another and then Eric. Sam lowered her head in shame as she remembered how she had thought she had loved Eric, only to be betrayed by him and her father's outrage at her embarrassing antics. Now Josh. Even he raged against her. Every man around her turned against her. Failure. Always failure.

Despite her hysteria, Sam remembered her camera. It was her one saving grace. She could take photos. Good photos. She had won prizes at college for her work. She would find a way to succeed using the only thing she was good at.

# Chapter Four

Sam raced toward her room, past the astonished volunteers. But Josh was right behind her and one quick glance over her shoulder told her that he was repentant. His face flushed, eyes dark with misery. He caught up to her and grabbed her arm. Sam kicked savagely at his ankle. "What do you want now? Haven't you had enough?"

Josh cursed and released her. "I'm sorry. I'm sorry I lost my temper. It's just those fragments are priceless. I could lose everything over something like this."

"And that's all that matters, isn't it? You and your precious job, your precious pride." Sam spoke through clenched teeth, before pivoting and walking away.

Josh continued to follow her. "I'm sorry," he repeated. "I'm sorry I hurt you."

Sam turned on him. "It isn't the hurt that matters. You humiliated me. Are you going to apologize in front of all those people?"

Ashamed, he nodded.

"First thing in the morning?"

Another nod.

"I won't have any trouble getting up tomorrow." Sam said.

She felt a frisson of triumph. She was in control. At last.

"I've been a fool."

"True," Sam agreed. She was enjoying seeing Josh humbled for once.

He gave her a sheepish smile. "It was far nicer rubbing that cream on your backside at the beach than ..." the words died on his tongue and Sam saw the spread of color across his cheeks. "I was concerned about you after the fire coral," he admitted, looking her directly in the eye. "But sometimes, Sam..." Josh ran a hand through his disheveled hair, frustration flickering in his eyes.

"Sometimes," she prompted.

"Sometimes you get under my skin. You're so—"

"Useless?"

Josh's eyes widened in shock, "No. Not that. So..." But he didn't finish and Sam felt a distinct disappointment. What had he been going to say? Instead, he walked silently beside her until they reached her room. He opened the door and flicked on the light. "I am sorry. I mean that." His gaze wandered around the tiny room. Sam had covered the walls with photographs. Palm trees, setting sun, kibbutz children's faces. There were several portraits of Jan and pottery fragments. The pictures had a wonderful texture, some were sharp, others softer, with a dreamy quality to them.

"Yours?"

She nodded. "I wanted to spend the summer photographing Paris. I love Paris," she admitted wistfully. "I wouldn't mind getting a chance at Jerusalem either. That one sight of the walls bathed in gold was incredible." She sighed with pleasure.

Josh's fingers stroked his jaw. "Maybe you should help the photographer. Do you know your way around a dark room?"

Sam snorted. "Of course. I have a degree in communications. I did several courses in photography. I even won a prize for one of them," she admitted shyly.

Josh beamed. "It's all settled. I've found the perfect job for you. It'll keep you out of harm's way, away from the dig. No more sunburn, no more washing fragments."

A crimson heat flushed her cheeks.

Josh continued. "You can work with the photographer. And he's British, no problem with misunderstanding instructions. Rob will be happy to have an assistant with some knowledge instead of having to explain everything all over again every day." Just then Josh glanced at the empty bed. "Where's Lindsay?"

"Oh, she has quite a collection of admirers and never sleeps here," Sam mumbled. "I'm not bothered. I quite enjoy my privacy."

Josh frowned. "I had heard. She has quite a reputation," he admitted.

Sam felt Josh's intense scrutiny. She flushed deeply. "I hope you don't put me in that category."

Josh shook his head. "If anything, Pinkie, you keep yourself aloof from advances."

"And that's why I get called the ice princess behind my back." Seeing Josh's embarrassment, she couldn't help but laugh. "Don't worry, I know what they say about me."

"And you ignore it."

"I try," she admitted.

"It can't have been easy. You're like the new kid on the block. Kibbutz life is so different from anything you've ever experienced."

Sam couldn't speak. Everything Josh said was true. Overwhelmed by his understanding, she averted her face so he wouldn't see the tears that welled in her eyes.

Suddenly, Josh bent and brushed a light kiss on her forehead, like he would to his little sister. "Goodnight. Try to sleep."

Reddening at his action, Sam was glad the dark hid her face. She felt nothing like his sister. Without another word, Josh spun round and walked off. She stood and stared at his retreating form. His kiss, albeit a peck, was a complete surprise. Her forehead was still warm from the touch of his lips. However, she could still feel the sting of his hand on her backside. She tried to harden her heart despite the confused feelings he stirred in her.

No men.


The volunteers shuffled uncomfortably the next morning as Josh gathered them together. "Obviously rumors have gotten around," he started. He looked directly at her. "I have an apology to make," he declared, eyes dark and earnest. "I shouldn't have acted like I did. I'm sorry."

Seeing Josh's embarrassment, Sam stood quietly triumphant, her broken and damaged morale boosted where men were concerned. However, his unexpected apology was soon forgotten as the volunteers got busy with the day's activities and her buoyant mood was short-lived as guilt nudged at her conscience and her mind replayed Josh's apology. Okay, perhaps she shouldn't have tried a short cut, knowing it could possibly damage the artifacts. Thank goodness it hadn't and Navon was still busy examining the loot.

But the day had to continue and Sam trotted over to Rob, ready for a day in the dark room. The photographer was leaning against the door, a strange expression on his face. For an instant, Sam felt uncomfortable. The man reminded her of the letch she'd left back in New York. However, she was determined to make good with her photography and pushed all thoughts of men out of her mind. Determinedly, she squared her shoulders and focused on her job.

"I have to go out to the site for the morning, but I'll be back with the afternoon film. Can you do the prints for today?" Rob questioned.

Sam nodded. "Tell me which paper, which size and how many of each to produce. Would you prefer a contact sheet for each roll?"

Rob raised his eyebrows. "Josh was right. You do know about film," he said.

"Of course."

Swiftly, he issued instructions before climbing aboard the bus to the site, cameras dangling around his neck; a bag of film and a tripod tucked under one arm, leaving Sam to get on with the job.

As the morning ticked by, she worked diligently in the dark room. The work was easy and she enjoyed playing with the different kinds of paper, working out the best texture for the prints. She fiddled with the time, trying to get the best clarity and definition.

A knock on the door startled her. Rob was waiting outside. She was surprised he was back. She had been absorbed with her work and hadn't noticed the time. It was already afternoon.

Rob glanced over the prints hanging from a twine clothesline with pins holding the curling paper to dry. "Nice job," he grinned. "Maybe you know about other things, too."

Sam frowned, hoping she'd misunderstood his insinuation, but as he busied himself, preparing the negatives, Sam's professionalism took over and she concentrated on what had to be done.

"Lock the door, willya, Sam. I need to develop some negatives right away."

Obediently, she bolted the door and flicked off the light.

Rob clicked a switch and an eerie red light glowed in one corner.

"Interested in learning some technique?"

"Of course. I'm always interested in learning." Sam saw Rob's outline as he groped through the dark.

"Oh, excuse me," he whispered when his hand cupped her breast.

She went rigid and a cold chill went up her spine. He was right on top of her. She inhaled his sour breath.

"Come on, kid. Don't be so naïve."

"Naive," Sam snapped. "Here I was thinking you were more professional than to try for a grope in the dark. Haven't you grown out of school boy pranks yet?"

Rob merely laughed, a sickly chuckle that sent goose bumps shimmying up and down her spine. "I can give you work here the whole summer. Just the two of us." His other hand groped up her thigh feeling his way inside her shorts, fingering past the elastic to her panties.

Sam let out a bloodcurdling scream and at the same time lifted her bent knee and aimed for his crotch. She missed. So much for self-defense lessons, but before she had time to re-aim, Rob grasped at her leg, yanking it so hard that she lost her balance. Roughly, he grabbed her around the waist and covered her mouth. "Shut up. We just have time for a quickie today. I promised the film would be done by five o'clock, so stop playing games." His rough hands tore at her cotton shirt and the flimsy material ripped. Sam righted herself and took aim. Her knee connected with his groin. Rob screamed in pain, releasing his hold as he doubled over.

Her screams rent the air. Frantic to get out the door, she scratched at the lock. It burst open, the bolt smashed. Bright light streamed into the dark.

Josh Ben-Sion stood glaring at the scene, arms folded over his chest.

Quivering in fright, Sam pulled at her ripped shirt, trying to cover herself.

"She started it all, the tease," Rob whined.

Sam spun round to face a sweating Rob. She looked at him in disgust. "You jerk," she snapped. Sucking in a lung full of air, hoping to steady her riotous nerves, Sam took a step toward him. She saw fear etched in his eyes and it bolstered her confidence. "You call yourself a professional. You're a letch, a sleaze bag who thinks they can hit on any woman around them. Well, let me tell you buster, I am not one of them." Giving him a last disdainful look over her shoulder at the sniveling heap on the floor, Sam strode to the exit. Once outside, she stopped and she started to shake. She leant against the wall afraid to move, afraid if she did she'd topple to the ground in a heap. She turned to face the scene inside.

Josh strode over to the Englishman. He lifted him by the throat, eyes wild with rage. "She didn't do anything. Don't try to fool me. I heard about the trouble with you last season in the desert. We can get another photographer if we have to. Don't ever touch, talk, or anything with Sam ever again."

Josh turned toward her. Gingerly, one arm went around her narrow shoulders, he cradled her against his broad shoulder. His gentle fingers stroked her back. "Shush, don't worry. The letch is history."

Sam sniffed.

"You must have been terrified. I can see why your father wanted someone to watch over you."

Sam pulled back, eyes narrowed as she glared at Josh. Angry red whorls fused her cheeks. "I don't need a babysitter. I handled that creep, even before you entered the scene Josh Ben-Sion," she fumed.

"You sure did."

But Sam wasn't sure what she saw on Josh's face. It wasn't relief, or happiness. More like guilt. What did he have to be guilty about?

"I'm sorry. I thought you'd be pleased being assigned to work with Rob. Instead you nearly got raped." Josh averted his gaze "One more thing to be guilty about," he muttered.

"Shush," Sam soothed. "It's not your fault." She gave him a tentative smile.

"The only person I'm angry with is that heap of a man. You? Never. If he ever comes near you ever again, I'll throttle him. I'm sorry this happened. I wanted to give you a job you wanted to do. This was my fault. I'll arrange for you to use the dark room whenever you please."

As minutes ticked by, Sam became aware of the enormity of what happened and what could have happened. Rob had been intent on sexual play, with or without her consent. Waves of nausea washed over her. She thought she was going to faint. Shivering, she tightened the gray blanket that Josh handed to her around her shoulders.

"It's all like a repeat movie. Over and over again. Always the same. Every time I trust a man, they betray me. Eric, Rob. All the others. Why can't I get it right?" she muttered to herself, unaware that Josh eyed her with deep concern.

"You did good Sam," he confessed.

She smiled up at him. "Yes, I did, didn't I?" But despite of being proud of how she'd handled the creep, doubt still insinuated into her confidence, chipping away.

Instinctively needing security, Sam buried her face in Josh's chest. There was something wonderfully safe about feeling his arms around her. It was much nicer than having him angry with her. She leaned against him as he walked her protectively away from the dark room.

# Chapter Five

It was Friday afternoon and everyone had cleared out to go home for Shabbos, a time to give thanks, a time for family and to visit relatives. Sam lay sprawled on an old blanket under the shade of a palm tree. Silence hung over the kibbutz like a shroud, surrounding her in its peacefulness. Resting, she welcomed the break from the backbreaking toil of the dig.

Jan de Vries slung his knapsack over his shoulder. His long lean body outlined by the sun, shadowed Sam. She looked up into his bright eyes.

"I'm visiting friends at another dig in the north, Sam. You're more than welcome to come with me. I'd enjoy the company," he urged.

Sam shook her head. "No thanks, Jan. You go. Have a great time."

With a wave of his hand, the older man set out down the road to catch a bus.

Sam's gaze returned to the thick book she hoped would last all weekend. It was the story of an archaeological dig interspersed with history and fascinated her. Oblivious to the passing of time, Sam looked up when a shadow covered the page. Looming over her was Josh Ben-Sion.

"Still here? Everyone clears out early on Friday." Josh cocked his head to one side inquisitively.

Sam turned a page. "I'm not going anywhere," she said and turned back to the book.

Josh squatted down next to her. He took the book out of her hands. Idly he gazed at the title. Sam could see the irony wasn't lost on him.

"Don't you have any family or friends here?"

She shook her head and reached for the book. She wanted to find out what happened during the Roman occupation of Judea.

Playfully, Josh held the book out of her reach as if to tease. "No family. Nowhere to go for Shabbos? All alone?" he questioned. A slight frown creased his forehead.

Sam could see he still felt guilty over his treatment of her as a deep crimson stain spread across his face.

"You deserve a break; you've improved tremendously in recent days. Awake early," he added.

"And no complaints," she teased.

Josh smiled down at her, his lopsided grin made her heartbeat quicken.

"You mean I'm not playing princess-like?" Sam tried to joke. "I know what everyone thinks of me. Aloof, above others, are a few of the remarks I've overheard," she said simply.

Before she quite realized what he was saying to her, Josh pulled her to her feet. "Go pack a bag. You're coming home with me."

Her eyes flew open in surprise. "You? What for?"

"Maybe I'm feeling sorry for you, but then if I told you that, you'd run a mile, Pinkie." Josh spoke seriously. "Shabbos is for family. Mine is a big one. Hurry up and bring a dress for tonight." He stood impatiently glancing at his watch.

"Thanks, but you don't have to feel sorry for me. I'm used to fending on my own. My father was always away on business trips." The truth of her statement surprised even her. Her father was always occupied with business matters. She was never able to talk to him, ask his advice, and discuss a problem, so she usually acted on her heart instead of her head. Trouble was, most of the time, this sort of thinking landed her in hot water. Her heart at this very moment was fluttering from Josh's closeness. Sam was having trouble reminding herself of her vow of non-involvement. She bit her lip and looked down at the grass.

Josh stared at her for a full second before he pulled her by the arm to her room. "Pack," he ordered, though Sam saw the corners of his mouth quiver with the vestige of a smile. "I don't feel sorry for you," he said, but Sam noticed he averted his gaze. "I have a big family. You can avoid me if you want for the weekend. You'll hardly see me if you don't want to."

Sam gave in without any further objections. Besides she could see some more of the country, use it to gather ideas for her book of photographs and, as Josh said, she could avoid him if she wanted to.

But, did she want to?

Not giving herself time to contemplate the question, Sam quickly threw clothes, toiletries and her camera into a bag. At the last minute, she snatched the book from his hands and threw that in on top of the pile.

As Josh tugged her towards the door, she stopped, picked up a large reprint of her photograph of the setting sun, pink and gold over the amazing green hills and laid it carefully in the bag with tissue paper around it. She smiled as she snapped the catch and looked around the room. She had been brought up never to arrive without a gift to her hostess. "Let's go."

Sam walked at his side toward the Jeep.

Josh stowed her bag in the back and started the Jeep. "It isn't far," he said conversationally. "My family lives in Jerusalem, in the northern suburbs. They all speak English, so don't worry."

Sam listened to his descriptions of his parents, his two married sisters, their husbands, and children and the youngest sister, Ruthie, just released from her army service and about to begin university. Sam wondered about Ruthie. She had heard from Jan that Ruthie had coveted a place on the dig, but had been required to complete her military tour first.

Josh drove along the road leading past the Mount of Olives overlooking the golden dome of the Mosque, its glittering roof reflecting the thinning evening sunlight.

Entranced with the sight, Sam begged him to stop so she could photograph the incredible panorama. Dutifully, he pulled over and as she considered angles and light reflection, she and her camera became one, absorbed by the surrounding scenery. After a while, Sam became aware of Josh's intent gaze on her.

He glanced at his watch. "I'll bring you back tomorrow. We can walk through the Old City," he offered.

Reluctantly, Sam climbed back in the Jeep, her face flushed with pleasure. As Josh expertly navigated the vehicle around the Old City, Sam stared wide-eyed at the unfolding scene. Arab men in keffiyehs, young boys leading donkeys and more of the ultra orthodox men in long black coats all thronged the streets heading through the ornate Damascus gate with its curlicued ramparts.

"Do you like my city?" Josh asked her. For some reason she felt her answer was very important to him. He need not have worried. "I..." Sam hesitated, her gaze traveling over the panorama unfolding around them. She turned to him, whose dark eyed stare rested on her, and smiled broadly. "I love it."

Filled with a sense of calm, she sat next to Josh as he drove them through modern streets filled with people carrying packages. Jewish Jerusalem was preparing for the Sabbath while their Arab counterparts were already celebrating. They stopped in front of a large stone house nestled against the backdrop of a craggy hillside. Along the front of the house was a *merpeset*, a verandah, to take in the cool evening breeze and in the distance was a grove of olive trees.

Bright red bougainvillea covered the stone walls, a stark red slash against the white of the quarried stone. He jumped out of the Jeep, opened a wrought iron gate and shouted. *"Ima, Ani babayit.* Mom, I'm home."

A petite woman with dark hair and flashing jet eyes like Josh's, ran out the door wiping her hands on an apron. "Joshie!"

Josh stooped to hug his mother. Not wanting to intrude, Sam held back. Then Josh turned and motioned her forward.

"Ima, this is Sam," he said in English. "I brought her home for Shabbos."

Nervous, her fingers twisted in her hair.

"Sam, we're thrilled to have you here. Come right in. You must be dying for a shower. Maybe some lunch." Chana Ben-Sion hooked an arm companionably through hers. "Josh, bring her bags in."

Laughing at his mother's instructions, Sam stole a glance at Josh over her shoulder.

He scratched his head in amazement. "My mother treats me exactly like Professor Shapira did the day you arrived," he said giving her an amused grin. "Maybe I'm heading down a new career track. Bellhop," he shrugged his shoulders and winked at her. "I get enough practice. Funny how it doesn't matter so much any more," he said cryptically.

Once inside, a full hour of questioning from Josh's mother seemed to satisfy her.

"My son does not bring his friends home any more," she sighed wistfully while Josh was upstairs showering.

"Is that...um...since his friend?" Sam asked.

A sadness flickered across Chana Ben-Sion's face. "Yes. Since his friend died. You know of Avi?"

Sam nodded.

Mrs. Ben-Sion averted her gaze, dabbing at her eyes. "Look at me, sitting here when I have to…" She rushed off to another room in the house and closed the door behind her just as Josh walked back into the room.

"Where's my mother?"

"She said she had something to do," Sam said mystified.

A frown creased Josh's brow. He walked to the closed door and stood close as he could. Sam watched fascinated. Josh was snooping.

But he needen't have bothered, his mother's hushed tones, still reached outside the closed door. "Reuven? Come right home," she insisted. "Josh brought home a girl."

There was the click of the phone and Josh silently moved away from the door as his mother exited the office, a satisfied smile on her face.

Sam couldn't believe what they'd heard, but she had no time to question Josh. He turned to his mother. "I'm off to visit Avi's parents." he said quietly. "Can you mind Sam for a while?"

"What a question," his mother admonished. "Sam is absolutely charming. Don't stay too late. You know how it always upsets you after these visits."

Quickly, he explained to Sam where he was going. She gave him an encouraging smile. "Good."

While Josh's mother attended to her preparations, Sam wondered about the melancholic and somber man, remembering Jan's words.

Guilt.

Josh carried a heavy burden.

Sam's heart lurched for the man whose self-induced burden could only be lifted by his own efforts, yet he seemed paralyzed to do so.

Evening descended upon the household. Josh's father, Reuven Ben-Sion beamed, delighted to have Sam as their guest and her offer to help with the meal was politely refused. Although Josh hadn't returned, she decided to give his parents the gift of the photograph, rather than wait. They were such lovely people, welcoming her without a fuss. The gift of the photograph met with excessive thanks by both parents.

"Sam, you did this yourself? What a clever girl you are!" Chana admired. "Such artistic talent. No one in our family is artistic."

Sam blinked. The photograph was nice but not anything fantastic. Both parents gushed like it was an expensive original by Ansell Adams. Still, it was wonderful to feel admired, especially by members of Josh's family. Her only regret was that he disappeared during the afternoon and missed hearing their words of praise.

The house began to fill up with family and the loud voices of children echoed around the rooms.

"I'd better go change." Sam excused herself to allow the family to greet each other. Josh still hadn't returned. The sun was setting. Even Sam knew it was almost Sabbath. She was nervous. This was virtually all she knew. Her family, although Jewish, didn't abide by the strict code. She couldn't remember the last time she'd been present at a Friday night meal, surrounded by family and prayers.

Not wanting to keep them waiting, she changed into a simple periwinkle blue linen dress and matching short-sleeved jacket. She ran a comb through her thick curls and peered into the mirror. Freckles. Nothing but a mass of freckles. Sun-kisses. She remembered a day at a class picnic, the one and only her father ever managed to attend. Her face was awash with tiny brown dots too. Her father, laughing as she skipped toward him, her pigtails flying had hugged her tightly, calling her freckles kisses from the sun.

Fidgeting with her hair, Sam also remembered another day with her father.

"Don't forget it, Sam, honey. Impressions count. Gotta make a good first impression."

Sam screwed up her nose as she stared at her reflection. What would they think of her sunburned appearance? What would they

think of the so-called sophisticated New York girl, who knew nothing
of her culture and felt out of place?

Quietly, Sam walked into the room and the loud chattering
came to a halt.

"Come meet the rest of the family." Chana took Sam by the arm
and introduced her to everyone. A jumble of names, smiling faces,
and handshakes greeted her, while several sets of eyes exchanged
glances, accompanied by little, knowing smiles.

She saw Josh slip in quietly. He leant his large frame in the
doorway, staring at her, a look of surprise registering on his face. Sam
gave him a warm smile.

"You look lovely," he said as he walked up to her.

Sam preened, seeing the admiration in his eyes. Josh was
accustomed to seeing her in shorts and a tee shirt. "I can scrub up
well at times," she joked.

"Too true." His dark eyes twinkled and a warmth spread
through her veins.

"Oh, no, don't look now," he chuckled, "but my mother is in
full swing tonight."

Sam turned to see Chana staring at them, a broad grin plastered
on her oval face.

"I know that look," he advised.

"Look?" Sam didn't have a clue what Josh was talking about,
but gave his mother a smile anyway.

She walked up to Sam.

"Sam, girls, come with me. Time to light candles."

Obediently, Sam followed the other women and girls. A long
table in the dining room was set with a snow white cloth, beautiful
china, crystal and the symbols of the Sabbath; the twisted loaves
of bread and wine cup and the two candles representing male and
female, to remember the Sabbath and keep it holy.

Food covered every spare spot on the table. A side table
held a hodge podge of candlesticks, all with white candles ready

for lighting. Giggling, the girls, from Josh's young three year old niece to the older women, lined up, each before her own set of candlesticks. Sam hesitated. She had never done this before.

Chana pulled her to the table. She struck the match and showed Sam how to light the candles.

"You can repeat after me."

Sam repeated the words, understanding she was blessing the arrival of the Sabbath. In New York she would have been preparing for an evening at the theatre. Tonight, this simple act touched her heart, giving her a sense of home and family she had never experienced before, filling her with an overwhelming gratitude towards Josh for inviting her for Shabbos. Never had she experienced such a profound sense of family, so different to life in New York with her father.

The rest of the family took their places at the table. Josh sat next to his father, Sam on his left. All the men now wore skullcaps on their heads. Patiently, Josh explained in an undertone, the blessing over the wine chanted by his father, the bread, the hand washing, and the special Eshet Chayal, the poem describing a woman of valor recited to his mother. A woman of valor, her price is above rubies.

"How beautiful," Sam whispered.

Josh's mother nodded. "True. It is a great source of beauty dating back thousands of years."

"Just like our own history," her husband added solemnly.

Sam felt tears in her eyes as Reuven Ben-Sion called his children to his side, placed his hands on their heads and recited the customary blessing.

"May God bless you and keep you and cause his face to shine upon you."

The meal was a loud, noisy affair full of jokes, singing, laughter and catching up with the family. Josh whispered into her ear during the fruit dessert. "Do you like them?"

Excited by the familial atmosphere, Sam nodded. Reuven Ben-Sion was a scholarly man and it showed in his gentle, lined face. He had the same dark, smiling eyes as his son. Ruthie was a mirror image of her mother. Petite, feisty, caring. Earlier, seeing Ruthie in her army garb, rifle slung over her shoulder as she arrived home and now, in a soft flowing romantic dress, it made Sam realize the constant opposites there was in this ancient country. She sighed. The whole family was very kind and the thought brought the prick of tears to her eyes. Throughout the evening Chana Ben-Sion fussed around her, constantly asking if she'd had enough to eat, tut-tutting when Sam let slip that she didn't follow traditions back home.

Now as the family talked until late into the night, while children dozed on their parents' shoulders, Sam wondered why she and her father hadn't. She let her gaze wander around the gathering, soaking in the atmosphere, enveloped by a deep sense of contentment.

But as the evening came to an end, she felt real regret as they bade her a good night and promised to return the next day. Sleepily, but very contented, Sam made her way to her room.

Josh followed. "Sleep well. At least you don't have to be up at four."

For no reason she could think of, Sam stood on her toes and kissed his cheek.

Josh rubbed his cheek as Sam disappeared behind the closed door. He could still smell the lingering aroma of roses from her perfume, his cheek tingling where her lips touched him as he turned away from her door.

Some time later, he took another look at Sam's gift to his parents. His fingers trailed over the photo. There was so much life in it, it was as if he could feel the heat radiating from the sunset, smell the dust and sweat. It was astounding. How was it that he had looked at the same view and never seen it that way before? The colors came alive. Sam's eye had captured the landscape in a way he had never imagined, opening his eyes anew to her talent. He could see her enthusiasm and artistry deep in each line of the photograph, the light and contrast. There was a need within her that seemed to cry out from her work. Did she have any idea what a great gift she possessed? He had never heard her brag to anyone, modestly keeping her work to herself. With a start, the photo slipped from his fingers, falling back to the table. He stared at it for a few, long, drawn out seconds. He understood. At last. For Sam, her photography was her passion and life's interest in exactly the same way archeology was for him. "She's a different woman altogether behind that lens," he marveled aloud, delighted with his discovery.

Exhausted, Sam fell into a deep sleep within a minute of crawling into bed, thankful for the high ceilings that allowed the cooling breeze to circulate, when a loud clattering in the kitchen woke her suddenly. Disoriented, tiptoed into the kitchen. Josh sat at the kitchen table, elbows leaning in front of him, eyes faraway in thought. He sipped at a cup of tea as he looked up at her.

Sam covered her mouth and gasped. Josh wore only a pair of shorts. The sight of him bare-chested sent her pulse racing. But as she stood in the bright fluorescent light, she caught Josh's embarrassed gaze as he looked away. She glanced down and swallowed nervously. Her own nightgown was nearly transparent. "I heard a noise and woke up," she said feeling foolish.

Josh stood and walked over to her. "Sorry, I don't sleep very well. I didn't mean to wake you. Go back to sleep, it's only gone midnight."

Sam grinned sheepishly. "I'm used to waking up early now. Though I admit midnight is a tad early to go digging."

Josh smiled, but said nothing. She studied his face to avoid looking below his neck. "You're awfully tense. Nobody can sleep like that. You should stop worrying so much about the dig," she ordered. "Come with me. I can fix that."

"Pinkie, somehow I can't see you imitating Lindsay," Josh frowned.

Sam halted. She turned to face him, whorls of scarlet staining her cheeks. "I should be angry with you Josh Ben-Sion. Two insults in one breath." She punched him playfully in the chest with a pointed finger.

"Me?" Josh held his hands up in defense. "It's the insomnia," he admitted.

"Well just so you remember Ben-Sion, the name's Pinkman, not Pinkie."

"Ah," he grinned. "Pinkie suits you. The nickname matches that sweet blush you have."

Sam pursed her lips. "And another thing. I'm nothing like Lindsay," she snorted.

"Definitely not," Josh agreed formally.

She led him into the salon and pulled him down on the sofa next to her. "Put your head in my lap," she whispered quietly.

Cushioning his head on her thighs, Josh gave in without an argument. Sam's fingers began to work his knotted shoulders making him gasp with pleasure.

"Close your eyes," she ordered. Her fingers worked patiently at his scalp, her touch light.

"You're really good. Photography is your passion isn't it? I saw the photograph, the one you gave to my parents. The colors, the tone. You have a knack that brings your work alive. You have a great talent, Sam," he whispered as her fingers continued.

"That's high praise. Do you have any idea how much those simple words mean to someone who never gets anything right?"

Josh went to turn, but Sam gently pushed him back and increased the tempo of her massaging. Within minutes, he succumbed to the slow, rhythmic pressure as all the stress which constantly welled up inside him like a coiled spring, started to unwind and he fell into a deep, dreamless sleep.

Sam smiled down at the sleeping Josh, letting her fingers stroke across his back. She let her head slip back against the sofa and with Josh still cradled in her lap, she was asleep minutes later.

\* \* \*

As Sam stretched lazily, her eyes blinked open and she stared at Josh's head drooped on his chest. She smiled sleepily at him. Her fingers were still in his hair.

"That's the best sleep I've had in years," Josh confessed.

As her gentle fingers stroked his scalp, he leant against her, relaxed and comfortable.

Josh looked boyish, his face heated with the flush of wakefulness. Dimples creased his smiling face, making him look very young. It brought a joy to her heart as she recalled Jan's explanation. Small wonder he never smiled. "I'm glad you think I'm good at something." She smiled softly, full of pleasure, the heat of awareness prickling her skin as she bathed in the glow of his smile. "Good at massage *and* photography. I'm on a roll," she chuckled. Sam rubbed her neck, stiff from the awkward sleeping position.

"Here. Let me reciprocate," Josh eased her down on the sofa. "I'm not as talented as you are, of course," he offered. Large hands worked her narrow shoulders and neck muscles and as his face leaned forward, his stubbled cheek brushed across the soft velvet of her cheek. She was alive…alive with awareness, alive with a new found sense of desire. As his lips grazed over her lips, she grew weak all over. The taste and feel of his muscled body all at once was overwhelming, the male smell of him intoxicating, teasing her already sensitized nerves. Sam felt the same way she did the day she fainted and found herself in his arms.

From the corner of her eye she saw Josh's mother, Chana, and stiffened. "Your mother," she whispered, but already Chana had withdrawn from the doorway. "Such nonsense the boy tells. Not his girlfriend," Sam heard Chana sniff disdainfully. "They're all over each other. A mother can always other. A mother can always tell about these things. I tell you, Rueven, it's good to see the boy happy.

As Chana's whispering reached her ears, heat scorched her cheeks. She looked over her shoulder at Josh, but his eyes were closed, lost in thought as his body swayed with the motion of his massaging. She prayed he hadn't heard his mother's words, but as his fingers threaded their way over her aching muscles, she was lost to his touch and nothing else mattered.

Sam jolted awake. She twisted round on the couch and found Josh's dark humorous gaze staring down at her intently.

"I've finished."

She jumped up, yanking her bathrobe around her; aware her body exhibited what her mind was thinking. Heat flushed her cheeks, scolding her body with an aching awareness.

"How long have I been asleep?"

"Long enough," he said, giving nothing away.

Sam frowned. "What on earth will your family think? First we end up falling asleep downstairs all night, then your mother spied us...."

"Us?" Josh teased. "What were we doing?"

"Nothing," Sam snapped.

"Exactly." But he smiled at her nevertheless, though it did little to settle her nerves. Her sense of decorum was badly dented. A Pinkman was never an inconsiderate guest.

Josh continued. "Don't worry, Sam. I had the first good night's sleep in years because of your massage. My mother will thank you for it."

"She will?" Sam wasn't sure she believed him.

"Yeah. Now go on, time for that *mud* you like so much."

Sam screwed up her nose, and flung a cushion playfully at him. But she did as she was told and went into the kitchen. It didn't seem to matter that she was in her nightwear. Formality wasn't part of the Ben-Sion household, it seemed.

Relaxed, Sam ambled into the kitchen. "Good morning. *Boker tov,*" she tried in Hebrew.

Everyone beamed at her efforts. Chana poured her coffee and bustled around the kitchen.

Josh wandered into the kitchen several seconds later, a sheepish expression on his face.

"Sleep well?"

He nodded, smiling.

His parents exchanged looks. "A good thing. No nightmares at last," Chana intoned, lifting her eyes to the heavens in silent prayer. "Joshie, you'll go to synagogue with your father this morning? Sam, you'll stay home with me? All the family is coming for lunch again today."

"I thought I would take Sam to the Old City after lunch. She's hardly seen anything and it's an easy walk."

"Privacy. They want to be alone," Chana whispered to her husband, giving him a knowing look, making Sam's cheeks color.

Shabbos was a lovely day. One of the nicest in her memory. The family all poured in again like the night before. She noticed their eager intent. "It's like being the bait," she moaned to Josh.

"Yeah, my family loves to meddle. Just ignore them."

"I wish," Sam laughed playfully. "How can I? They're delightful." Her gaze shifted toward Ruthie who sat studiously drawing in one corner of the room, head bowed in intense concentration, a firm set to her jaw, while at the edge of the room, heading toward the kitchen his mother, Chana, spoke, hands waving in the air, a few quick glances over her shoulder toward her and Josh, giving them a flicker of a smile.

"Like lambs to the slaughter," Josh laughed. "Never mind. We'll escape later."

Sam's interest was piqued. "Where to?"

"Secret," Josh smiled, tapping his nose. "Just wait and see."

A while later, Josh stood up, held out his hand to her. He made his announcement. "We're off to the Old City."

"But Sam promised to play cards with me," whined Keren, Josh's niece.

Sam hesitated and she saw a flicker of worry crease Chana's brow. She crouched down to the child playing on the floor and held up the cards. "How about we play later."

Chana interrupted. "I'll play with you now, Keren." She waved her hands at her son. "Shoo, you two." The worried woman nearly shoved Josh and Sam out the door. It closed very firmly behind them, not before Sam heard Chana let out a heavy sigh of relief. "Privacy. They need to be alone," she heard the older woman tell the family.

Jewish Jerusalem had shut down. The shops were closed, workers having gone home before the busses stopped running and a sense of peace had descended on the city. Gone was the heady smell of the thick 'mud-like' coffee brewing in the coffee houses, the hurly burly conglomeration of Arab and Jew, Christian and tourist mingling in a city that means so much to so many.

It was a clear, cloudless day, overwhelming Sam with a sense, for the first time she could ever remember, of belonging. Hand in hand, Josh led her through the ancient Jewish Quarter of the Old City, walking down the Cardo, the excavated Roman shopping street leading down the heart of the quarter. Over the uneven cobbled streets, where every rut and craggy stone could tell a million stories.

Wide eyed, Sam gazed at the kotel, the crumbled Western Wall of the Temple. Separated by a partition, men and women prayed. Many swayed mumbling silently oblivious to their surroundings. Some caressed the ancient stones. Many were dressed in the same black orthodox clothing that she had seen those on the plane wear. But when Sam truly looked, it was a myriad of visitors. Army, male and female, their riffles dropped to their sides, old and young alike, all praying, all believing. Hundreds of people, hundreds of prayers, but all around only a soft murmur, as the believers chanted and prayed in silence. "It's time, Sam."

Sam jolted. Her intense scrutiny of the unfolding culture broken as Josh interrupted her thoughts. "They're leaving the customary note in the cracks of the wall," he explained. "You can do this."

She could? Sam wasn't so sure. "Visiting, looking on like a tourist is one thing, but being well...Jewish, really doing, acting, being..."

Josh gave her an encouraging smile, squeezing her hand for added assurance. "I'll be waiting for you when you finish on the women's side."

She approached the wall with awe and pressed her forehead up against the ancient stone, smoothed from thousands of caresses and kisses over the centuries. Closing her eyes, she prayed silently.

"Hey... God, I don't know too much about this sort of thing," she admitted, her voice slightly shaky. She hesitated a moment, turning sideways watching the other woman. But they were so engrossed in their outpouring, their lips murmuring to the stones, no one was taking any notice of her. Do you grant wishes? If it's sort of your thing, I would really like to wish for a family like the Ben-Sions. Large, loving, full of joy in each other. And I wouldn't mind if you could help Josh find something admirable about me, too. Could you manage that when you have some spare time?" she prattled on. Sam pulled back from the wall, realizing she had been hugging the ancient stones, feeling a warm glowing energy from them radiate through her body.

Weird.

She turned and looked back over the conglomeration of women in their separated area. Many had left. Others just sat staring, or resting their eyes.

She turned back to the stone, and her eyelids faltered, closing. Sam let out a heavy hearted sigh. "I hope you're still listening. I, um, realized it could have been a tall order. You know—too big, impossible. But maybe, just maybe, even my father might be encouraged to loosen the reins a little. Let the tight control slacken off a bit so I can manage life on my own mistakes and achievements."

Realizing she'd recited a list a mile long, Sam laughed quietly and turned and left the praying women at the wall to meet up with Josh. He took her hand and led her back through the bazaar, wandering through narrow alleys, some with roofs; others open to the azure sky, giving her a detailed description as they went. She could almost imagine how the city must have looked two thousand years before.

"It's almost as if you knew what it looked like."

"That's my job. I dig; I resurrect the past, so that we may learn, Sam. Learn and understand."

Sam sighed with pleasure. "This has been such a perfect day Josh Ben-Sion."

"Glad I could oblige." He stopped at a merchant's stall and bought two ice cream cones.

Enjoying the ice cream, Sam licked at the thick creamy vanilla with gusto, a white icy ring circling her lips like a white moustache.

Josh grinned and traced a single finger around the edge of her lips, the ice cream coating his finger. For a fraction neither moved. Then he bent down and with the flick of his tongue licked his ice cream coated finger like a cat with a bowl of cream. His dark eyes searched her face and Sam felt a shiver of excitement spiral through her limbs. In a sudden burst she was of aware of him as never before, aware of the powerful potent force that was Josh Ben-Sion, the leader of men, the hero and loyal family man, loyal to the core. Loving.

He leaned forward.

Sam's breath caught in her throat, her pulse erupted in an erratic beat, eyes locked with his. She waited. She...

Josh wrapped her in his arm so swiftly that her cone fell to the ground. He pressed her back against the ancient stone walls. The chill of the hard, marble-like rock dug into her back. She didn't care a hoot. She was in Josh's arms.

"Am I forgiven?"

"You mean for being autocratic, bossy, manipulative, and a pervert who likes the wet t-shirt contest look?" Sam added for good measure.

Josh grimaced. "They're strong charges."

"They are." She wasn't about to let him off too lightly.

"Truce?" Josh prompted.

Sam smiled. The tip of her tongue wiped over her suddenly dry lips. "I was pretty awful too," she mumbled.

"Yep," he added playfully.

She nodded, reluctant to leave his embrace. "Truce," she whispered in his ear and felt his heated shiver as he crushed her against his body.

"Boy, perhaps if they have truces of war like this," she mused, "then maybe wars might end a bit faster."

But what was nearly over was Shabbos. In the diminishing moments of sunset, as the golden rays of the sun mingled against the bronze and scarlet colors of the hillsides in the distance, Josh led her back to the Ben-Sion house. Above, stars appeared in the sky which turned rapidly from deep rose to indigo and the loud sounds of traffic again filled the street. The peace of Sabbath was over and it was time to go back to work.

Josh loaded Sam's bag into the Jeep. He kissed his parents, who in turn, hugged and kissed Sam.

"Be sure to come again," ordered Chana.

# Chapter Six

Josh seemed to be in a contemplative mood as he drove her back to the dig. "I'm going to re-arrange the work list," he informed her.

The thought of being next to him in a trench set Sam's mind whirring. The team had already dug through several civilizations. Pottery shards, a glass bottle, coins and a Crusader plate with the fish design confirmed they had passed through Byzantine and Crusader years. "I suspect we're very close to Roman civilization," he added as they arrived back at the dig.

Sam knew this was Josh's own area of expertise and his suspicions were confirmed the next morning.

"Josh, look!" Sam's excited voice rang out drawing his attention to her pointing finger. A small piece of bronze glittered in the light. Josh bent and carefully eased the piece from the crusted dirt, dusting away the debris. He held it up to the light. "For the freedom of Zion," His voice came out in a rush, eyes bright with excitement. "This clearly marks the coin as minted during the failed revolt against the Romans." Grabbing her, Josh kissed her in front of everyone else. "Clever girl," he grinned. "We're entering the Roman years now for sure. Here's our confirmation."

Sam beamed with pleasure. Between the compliment and the kiss, she was sure life couldn't get better. She finally had done something right. Ever since their visit to Jerusalem, a new peace and sense of unspoken understanding had existed between them.

As the day progressed, everyone's attention was now focused on the trench. Digging proceeded at a frantic pace with all hands aiding in the task. Towards the end of the day, it became apparent that they had uncovered either a burial cave or crypt. Human bones gave Sam the shivers as Josh descended to inspect the findings and for the first time, a sense of regret washed over her as the day's work ended.

She followed the small crowd over to the new opening in the ground. Josh was only letting a few volunteers down at a time. She watched with a jealousy she couldn't quite understand as Lindsay pressed herself against him, breasts rubbing against Josh's chest.

Finally it was her turn. Josh preceded her down the primitive ladder, holding her around the waist with his large bear like hands as she reached the last two rungs.

"I am not helpless, you know," Sam snapped at Josh. His touch confused her sending heat waves through her body. "Sorry," she muttered. She was. She just wasn't sure why she was acting like a shrew.

"Damned if I do and damned if I don't. I can't figure you out, Pinkie." His hands dropped immediately away from her, making Sam trip on the last rung.

Narrow clay colored walls barely four feet wide towered either side of them. Sam trotted promptly after Josh, worried she would lose sight of him. Still broad daylight above, down here there was an eerie gloom and a distinct earthy and dank odor. Goosebumps dotted along her arms and the hairs on the back of her neck stood out. She shivered. Stumbling into hard rock, she pitched headlong into Josh's back only to hear him scold her about her carelessness.

Josh quietly began pointing out the simplistic stick figure drawings and the scriptures etched into one wall.

A cold chill made Sam shiver. Something she couldn't explain sent a premonition of fear through her. Trying to pull herself together, she turned and examined the small pile of urns stacked against some stone squares. Ready to leave the creepy crypt, she spotted a shiny object out of the corner of her eye, hidden at the back of a group of smaller pieces. Sam bent down and picked up the piece, carefully shielding her actions from the group. She didn't really need another dressing down from Josh, especially not in front of the other volunteers, she thought, remembering the dishwasher catastrophe.

Lifting the piece up, she realized it was no scrap like Dr. Navon pieced together, but rather a beautifully crafted chalice, intricately carved with whorls like flames of fire, and stick figures holding swords ready for battle. "How peculiar," she mumbled. As her palms glided over its surface, worn smooth over the centuries, she felt an inexplicable warmth radiate from the chalice. She turned it over in her shaking hands and noticed a large circular chunk was missing from its center. The front was quite different from the other side too. An inscription, similar to a kind of hieroglyphics was etched into the chalice's surface. She wondered if it might be Hebrew, a squiggly looking language to her untrained eyes. Maybe Latin? Josh said they were in Roman times.

Placing it carefully back in the pile, she quickly made a decision to return later in the evening, when it was cooler. The heat in the narrow chamber was stifling at present and she desperately wanted to photograph the chalice and all the other items in the crypt before they were taken away. Seeing the artifacts in their natural habitat sent her imagination soaring and an idea took shape in her fertile imagination. "Spartacus, here I come," she giggled. Josh would be thrilled if she could photograph their wonderful finds in situ. Determined to return after dark with her camera, she began to mentally make a list of the items necessary for the night shoot.

Still lost in thought, Sam climbed up the ladder. Josh put his arm around her waist companionably and chatted animatedly. Sam was relieved that her outburst was forgotten.

"You know, quite a few years ago they discovered a crucified body outside Jerusalem. Absolutely amazing. They even found out the man's name. I wonder what surprises this cave will hold for us," he told her as they reached the top of the crypt.

Sam wondered about the chalice. She opened her mouth to speak, but changed her mind. She wanted it to be a wonderful surprise for Josh. A reward, for all her mini-disasters. She knew she could do a good job of it. Instead, she scurried to the showers, changing into a short cotton dress. Pink and blue sprays of flowers dotted the material, giving her a dainty and feminine look. Thrilled with her idea, she burst into her room and stared open mouthed.

"Pardon me." Sam hardly knew what to say. Lindsay and a young male kibbutznik were in bed together. "I'm off to the darkroom," she stammered, snatching her camera and backing out.

Casually as he could, Josh strolled to Sam's room. He raised his hand to knock and froze. Muffled laughter echoed through the door.

Male laughter. Who did she have in there? Filled with jealousy he burst into the room and flicked on the electric light.

"What is this, the central bus station? People come and go as they please around here?" growled the man.

Josh stared at two naked bodies, neither of which was Sam Pinkman's. Relief washed over him. He didn't understand why his relief was so paramount, only that if he saw Pinkie sprawled across the bed with some strange male, he would turn murderous. "Sorry," he mumbled. "You should lock the door. Where's Sam?"

"Something about a dark room," came a mumbled reply. "Turn out the light. We could use a dark room, too." Lindsay's throaty laugh made Josh burn with embarrassment, while the man was already occupied, nuzzling her tanned neck.

Striding towards the darkroom, Josh observed a pink figure slip furtively behind a vehicle. Keys were always on a board, making it easy to snatch a vehicle without any suspicion.

"Josh is going to be so proud me." Sam's voice echoed through the clear, soundless night.

He watched as Sam stored her gear in the seat next to her. She looked around as if trying to make sure she hadn't been seen.

He scratched his head watching her attempts to sneak away. For the former combat soldier, it was a ridiculous, amateur endeavor. "What's the little sneak up to?" He thought she had changed, especially since their wonderful weekend. He frowned. Maybe not. Once a princess, always a princess. At least she was alone and not running off with some man. Josh's blood boiled at his wild, irrational thoughts. Head bent, hiding in the shadows, he decided to follow her.

# Chapter Seven

Awry smile lit Jan de Vries face as he kept a safe distance behind and watched the furtive behavior of Sam and Josh. They were so busy; neither of them had noticed him. All these weeks he had kept a keen eye on their actions. Hurts, angers, and frustrations; they had felt them all. But now, Jan knew instinctively, they were about to walk a wavering path to the future and it was their actions that would consume his interest and concern him as to whether they learned the route they must travel. Accustomed to walking in his native country, he quickened his pace as he headed down the road to the dig site, arms swinging in rhythm. He had an appointment with fate, the fate of others, not his own. It was his duty to aid them, but he couldn't accomplish their tasks, only they could do that. "It is time, young ones," Jan whispered into the silent night. "Time for you to meet your destiny and discover your heart's true desire.

Still trying to avoid being seen, Sam arrived at the site, adrenalin racing in her veins. This photo was going to be her outstanding achievement. Josh would be so pleased. For some reason she couldn't fathom, pleasing Josh and making him proud seemed the most important thing in the world.

Groping for the flashlight, she armed herself with camera and tripod. The lack of noise and complete darkness was quite eerie, making her flesh crawl. "Get a grip on yourself, Pinkman," she whispered.

It didn't take long to find the crypt again. A large tarpaulin covered the entrance. The ladder was in place. Getting down backwards was a feat in itself, but she managed it. No broken bones yet. Josh wouldn't be able to call her Calamity Jane again. Not this time.

Creeping down the pitch-dark passage, Sam's free hand edged the now damp walls of the crypt to help guide her, the beam of her flashlight the only comfort in the eerie burial chamber.

Deep in concentration, she never heard the creak on the dilapidated ladder, the soft footfall behind her, until it was too late. A huge, rough hand spun her around, just as she bent to replace the chalice.

"What the hell are you doing? Fancying a bit of history for the private Pinkman museum collection for Daddy? Antiquity theft is a serious crime in this country." Josh pushed her against the wall. "I thought I had begun to understand you. Obviously, I was wrong," he said.

Sam heard the disappointment in his voice. Barely able to hold onto the piece of history, she had no desire for another breakage to her credit. She knew that it would be the icing on the cake as far as Josh Ben-Sion was concerned. "Who are you to creep up behind me like that? I'm not doing any harm. Merely taking photos."

"Merely photos?" Josh mimicked her reply. "Why go skulking around at night? You could have taken photos during the day." His head swiveled. "Whom are you meeting here?" Josh towered over her, hands resting on his hips. He glowered at her, making the sharp angles in his face even more etched in his mahogany skin, the darkening shadow of stubble outlining his jaw.

"Don't be ridiculous. And besides, why do you always think the worst of me, Josh Ben-Sion?"

Josh's mouth opened and shut. He said nothing.

"I didn't have my camera this morning, and you know it." Sam flung back at him. "If I had told you I wanted to come and do this, you would have said no. You always say no. I..."

"You wanted what, Sam?"

"Having to account to you for all I do is like having a babysitter. So I decided to do it anyway."

"Do what?" Sam heard the rising panic in Josh's dark tense tone."

"Don't panic. I'm not about to ship your sacred goods off to the antiquities market," she teased, but nevertheless heard a sharp hiss of relief from Josh.

Sam looked up at him. "Did you really think I would?"

He shook his head.

"I'm here because this place is perfect for photos. I wanted to give it to you as a present," she whispered, disappointed in having to admit it. "I could have made a print for my father. He would have paid for next season. You could have been dig manager then too." She wanted to do it for him. For Josh. All she ever wanted to do was please. Why did it always go wrong?

Reminding Josh of Geoffrey Pinkman and the power the man held over his future, brought Josh to a standstill. Sam knew Josh couldn't afford to jeopardize anything. The muscles in his neck stretched to the limit, pulses pounding as she watched him struggle to control his anger, his fists clenching and unclenching, as he calmed.

"Okay, Pinkie, so explain what you want to do here."

"Do you have to call me that? The name is Pinkman." Sam stamped her foot. She hated it when he called her that awful name. Her first boyfriend had called her that. Even princess, another insulting name he used was better. Marginally. The worst was Princess Pinkie. Why couldn't people take her seriously?

Disquieted by his quick change in mood, Sam took a few seconds to regain her composure. Here, cloistered in a narrow dimly lit space, he appeared even more intimidating than normal. Sam quietly explained the photos she wanted to do, the angles, the slow film, and the technique involved.

Josh nodded. "So far I follow you." He held the torchlight closer, defining the chalice as Sam pointed out the features of the item she had wanted so much to capture. "Be careful," she instructed Josh. "No sudden moves. I'm terrified of breaking something else. Dr. Navon will murder me and make sure I'm turned into kibbutz cow fodder if anything else is broken."

A deep throated chuckle leapt from Josh's throat. He leaned forward over her shoulder, his stubbled chin scraping the side of her face. "Let me see," he whispered.

Sam swallowed hard. She could smell his breath, still fresh from the minty toothpaste, his closeness bringing tingles to her neck as the hairs at the nape of her neck stood on end. Why did he have to stand so close? It always disconcerted her. She couldn't think straight when he touched her. Couldn't concentrate on photos. Couldn't concentrate, period. When Josh's lips brushed softly down her hair, tracing her jaw, arms around her middle as he pressed her back against his chest, Sam nearly bolted.

"I like Pinkie, by the way. A perfect description of those lips. Pink. Ripe. Luscious."

Sam pivoted in his arms and stared up at him. Dark exotic eyes gleamed back at her. His immense body, magnified by the shadows playing on the wall, made her knees feel like water. "Lips?" Her voice was a silky whisper.

"Don't you like it?"

"Like what?" Sam looked up at Josh, trying to be cool. She felt about as cool and collected as the hot desert wind. He was standing very close.

"Pinkie. It sounds like a pretty good nickname to me. Goes with your lips." Josh's finger traced the outline of her mouth. "Yeah, your pink lips. Perfect. Just perfect." Without warning Josh bent his head, his mouth seeking hers. He pressed her up against a wall, and for Sam, the photo, the anger and confusion were forgotten as she opened her mouth to his, accepting his probing tongue dancing with hers. His kisses were incredible and for a moment she thought the tremors were her heart beating from the sensation he sent through her. But the tremors strengthened, jolting her against him.

Josh's arms tightened around her as loose stones rained down from the packed earth. "I've got you," he shouted, one arm over her head to protect her from the rocks falling around them as the tremors died off.

Loud voices above, made her sigh with relief. "At least there's someone to help us out," she said.

"Are you hurt?"

Dumbly, Sam shook her head. She clutched Josh's arms tighter, nails digging into his flesh. He pressed her against the wall again, trailing soft kisses on her frightened face.

"Earth tremors. We're on the Jordan Rift. It happens a lot. We should get out of here. There could be another one and it's very dangerous," he said, his tone tinged with regret.

The voices were getting louder and a beam of light from a crude torch flickered into the hole. Hands were extended to help her up and Josh followed closely behind her.

Once out of the crypt Josh halted. "I don't recognize any of the people," he said. "They must be kibbutznik."

Sam looked at the flaming torch. "There must have been a power failure."

Everyone eyed them suspiciously and as the crowd was shoved back a column of soldiers dressed like extras from Ben Hur marched past.

"Are they having a pageant of some sort? I had no idea the kibbutz planned anything like this."

But Josh cocked his head to listen to whispered conversations and although Sam didn't understand what was being said, the sharp toned remarks sent a shiver up her spine.

"Pinkie, I don't know why, but something is very wrong."

"What could be wrong? It must be a celebration of some sort. A torchlight parade. I'll try to photograph it." As Sam turned to fetch her forgotten camera from the crypt, Josh's hand griped hers.

"There's something very wrong. The words. The verb structure is odd. Sam, these people are all speaking ancient Hebrew."

"Don't be so silly Josh. Did you hit your head down there? Look, there's light over there." Sam pointed out into the darkness where flickering orange flames danced on the horizon.

Josh didn't want to alarm Sam. Half an hour ago that hillside had been ablaze with lights. Now it was just a few clusters of burning torches. Doesn't she see the difference?

He gazed warily at the people again. The crowd was getting larger. Everyone was speaking exactly the same way. Not modern day Hebrew, but the words of ancient days. Archaic words Josh only heard in synagogue during a Torah reading. His stomach twisted in knots of fear and he struggled for control. Sam was completely dependent on him. He tightened his hold on her slender waist, pulling her closer into the crook of his arm as a young child came up to them. Wide-eyed, the child pointed wildly at Sam's clothes and in quick succession the crowd's attention turned from the passing soldiers to them, all muttering and pointing at their appearance.

"Who are you?" said one.

"Look at her." An old woman began pointing.

Josh glanced down at Sam's dress. Her long slender legs stuck out below the shortened hem for all to see. His heart tightened. The crowd edged menacingly closer as the seconds ticked by. Where on earth were they? What had happened? Questions crowded his mind. A shout from further down the cobbled street grabbed everyone's attention, quickly giving Josh the diversion he needed, thankful for the first time in many years for his military training. He had no time to be afraid. Besides, fear was an emotion that got you killed. That he and Sam were on their own, in a dangerous world was without question. His military instinct was never buried far. He had failed once before in protecting someone. He wouldn't fail again.

"Come on. Let's get out of here." Tugging Sam forcibly by the arm, his other hand sharply covered her mouth as he dragged her in the opposite direction. Sam struggled, twisting in his grip. She was like a child trying to fight an adult. They halted in front of a massive wooden gate at a fortress's entrance.

"What's wrong with you? I wanted to watch the parade." Sam groaned with disappointment. "Josh, you can be so macho and presumptive at times. This is an incredible spectacle. I never dreamed they could do something like this in the kibbutz. You're a real party pooper, Josh Ben-Sion," she pouted. Yanking her arm from his grip, she rubbed the red stinging marks where he had grabbed her. "Though I must admit, they could at least have bathed before the parade. Look, that old lady there, she's disgusting." Sam screwed up her nose as several people strode by, their body odor an assault on her nostrils.

"For heaven's sake, Princess, can't you shut up. Don't you see what's happening?" he growled.

"For an intelligent man, Josh you are talking in riddles. Sometimes you talk to me like I'm one of your soldiers in the army and you're the big shot officer," she snapped.

"This is not a joke, Princess," Josh answered, unable to keep the flicker of worry from his voice.

Goosebumps rose on her bare arms. She was unable to shake off the beginning seeds of concern. Trying to ignore a rising sense of panic, she turned back to Josh.

"Something is wrong. I know it. Please let me be wrong." Josh reiterated.

Seeing his frown lines deepen, her heart sank. "What is happening?" she repeated. "It's a parade of course, isn't it?" Hope rose in her voice as her fingers stroked Josh's jaw. A soft, sympathetic expression slowly played across her face. "You poor darling; you didn't go to parades as a child. Didn't they have them Israel when you were little?" she asked, flabbergasted at his lack of childhood education. "Okay, so it's not exactly the Macy's Thanksgiving Parade with giant balloons. Pinkman's always had a float in the annual event," Sam blustered. "I played a fairy once, though heaven forbid I'd have to wear costumes likes these," she said, trying to laugh, but not quite able to. "Still, a parade is a parade," she said, stretching up to whisper in his ear. "Some day I'll remedy this dire lack of parades in your life, Josh Ben-Sion." She gave him her brightest smile.

The motley crowd of marchers trudged toward them. Josh roughly pushed both of them against the dark dank walls of the fortress, flattening her against the cold stone. Sam vaguely wondered how they had constructed it so quickly, but her attention was drawn to the passing actors. She turned to the crowd, unable to ignore their rousing anger as it sent a sense of impending disaster spiraling around them. Children shouted and adults were hurling insults at the soldiers. Even without understanding the language, Sam could see the rude gestures. It was all very realistic. This was incredible. What an experience! Wait till Daddy hears about this! He's going to be so amazed. She was actually beginning to like this place. After the first battalion passed, torchbearers came next, holding long wooden sticks, wrapped in rough cloth. She could smell the pungent odor of olive oil from the flickering wooden poles.

"Look Josh." She pointed to the soldiers, their metal-skirted armor flapping at each step, the spears and bronze shields, all carved with crests gleaming in the full moon. Armed archers in light clothing came next, followed by a small cavalry contingent of mounted men on horses. The clip clopping sound of the horses drowned out the sound of the restless crowd.

A chill tingled up and down Sam's spine. "It's so realistic and visual. Someone has put a lot of time and energy into this pageant." Sam's pursed her lips in irritation. "Damn, my camera's still back in the crypt. There are wonderful photographic opportunities here. It's all so authentic looking."

"Sam, just quiet down, won't you," Josh murmured in her ear. "This is weird. I can't figure it out. Shut up, please. Stop pointing and shouting. Stop speaking English too. These people are already baying for blood, if I guess right. Here you are yelling and carrying on, and in a different language too. Be quiet. Please!" His dark eyes pleaded with her.

"Josh, don't you get it? It's clearly a parade or maybe film being made. A Roman epic of some sort and it's a night shoot. That must be it. Why didn't you tell me about this?" Her finger poked his chest accusingly. "I wonder who's starring in it. Wouldn't it be fun to see a celebrity? Maybe Michael Douglas? Like father, like son. I saw Spartacus three times on cable."

Overjoyed at working out the sudden, inexplicable appearance of all the crazy props and costumes, Sam smiled with satisfaction. Gazing over the surroundings, she wondered where the director and crew were hiding. No bright lights either, which seemed strange. How do they film without the lights? Where are the cameramen? Still trying to solve the puzzle, her emerald eyes narrowed as she turned her gaze to Josh.

A strange frown appeared on his face, jet eyes squinting at the passing menagerie of people. He was such an enigmatic man at times, Sam thought. Josh was right though, the crowd was shouting a lot. It was worse than a New York Rangers hockey match. This crowd was shouting for blood the same way they did if Wayne Gretzsky failed to score.

Sam squirmed uncomfortably as a crowd of passersby gathered to stare at them. Noise and crowds always made her nervous and this one was getting out of hand. Her eyes scanned the area for the cameras she knew had to be there, but nothing resembling a film crew was in sight. Kids kept looking at her legs, pointing. An elderly woman with long, stringy, gray hair hanging nearly to her waist stepped out of the crowd, her high pitched screeching aimed at Sam as she pointed at her bare legs. A bony, gnarled finger poked her roughly in the chest.

Sam couldn't work out what she was supposed to do. Did they think she was an extra and should react in some way? The thought cheered her and she grinned back at the still screeching woman who wore a weirdo costume, swathed in layers down to her calves.

*"Zona!"* The woman shouted. Her face was barely inches away from Sam's and her foul breath made Sam draw back. Then the old woman spat, leaving a thin trail of saliva trickling down Sam's face. Satisfied she made her point, the old hag walked back to the crowd, head held high. Sam started to chase after the woman, but Josh held her in a brutal grip.

Fuming, she wiped the spittle from her face with the back of her hand. "Did you see that? She spat at me. She spat at me!" Thoroughly distraught by the disgusting, primitive act, Sam couldn't believe it actually happened. "Wait until I get a hold of the director," she muttered. "I'll have a few choice things to say to him."

"It's your legs." Josh's voice was quiet and assured. He didn't have the heart to tell her the woman called her a whore.

"My legs. What's wrong with them? You don't seem to mind ogling them." Sam snapped back at Josh. "I've had enough of the movie business. Things like this never happened at Pinkman's Department Store."

"They're uncovered. Look around you. Everyone here is covered head to knees, and longer on the women."

"They're only costumes, right?"

He detected the start of uncertainty in her voice. Sam still didn't get it. He started to sweat, wondering how to explain to her, without making her faint again like she did the first day at the dig. "I don't know. I'm not sure. I do know we need to get out of here. Fast." He placed a protective arm around her waist and pulled her tightly against him in an obvious gesture of protection and began to walk toward the fortress entrance. He stopped without warning. Coming past was another group at the end of the parade. Slaves.

Manacled wrist to wrist, ankle to ankle, slowly shuffling. Occasional moans echoed in the silence. All were male, all bare-chested, primitive loincloths their only covering. Faces black with grease and dirt bespoke the misery they felt. A pungent odor of sweat, unwashed bodies and dried blood filled the still night air.

"Give me some warning next time, would you?" she snapped.

Josh heard the frustration in Sam's voice. She was getting bored and irritated.

"This night shoot is a disaster and your continual erratic behavior this evening is becoming just a tad too much to bear, Josh Ben-Sion. You seemed so nice recently, and now this. Maybe you're having psychiatric problems. All the stress from the dig must be adding up." Sam whittled away.

But Josh barely heard her. He stood hypnotized by the slaves still struggling past them. His jaw muscles tightened as a soldier rushed up to the exhausted men; whip in hand above the poor souls. He lashed out at the group indiscriminately. The sharp crack of the thick-corded leather thong made the men cringe in terror. One slave fell to the cobbled ground. The parade stopped. All eyes were on the slave. A man, so dirty his age was indiscriminate half knelt on the filthy stones, knuckles scraping across the cobbles as he tried valiantly to push himself back up. He twisted toward Josh, hazel eyes staring directly at Josh. A flicker of recognition passed between Josh and the slave. Mesmerized, Josh left their secluded spot against the wall and walked directly through the parade.

"It's Avi," he repeated. He elbowed aside the solders in his way and strode to the fallen man. White puss filled sores oozed across his back, the stench stomach-wrenching, making Josh want to gag. He lifted the man up, leaning him against his arms. Dry cracked lips could barely form words and his eyes were dull, lifeless. Josh turned left and right, seeking a cloth, anything to use to wipe the spittle and caked blood. Avi's loincloth was barely a ragged covering.

"Josh, what are you doing?" Sam called.

Avi. Josh's dead friend. This couldn't be the famous Avi. So dirty. What a disappointment. Josh certainly must have hit his head in the rockslide. He's bonkers if he thinks that fellow is Avi. Better get him to the doctor as soon as we get home, Sam decided.

"Josh, don't. It can't be Avi. He's dead."

Josh didn't listen. He wrapped his arm around the man, oblivious to the dirt and smell.

"Josh, what are you doing? Let the parade go on. You're making a fool of yourself. Come on," Sam pleaded.

A soldier prodded Josh with a metal tipped spear, yelling at him in Latin. The words brought back long forgotten memories of Miss Madigan's Latin class. All four boring years of it. She could still remember the disastrous performance of The Aeneid, all in Latin, for their parents. Half of the doting families fell asleep ten minutes into the thing. Geoffrey Pinkman said it was a better sleeping pill than Valium. Who speaks Latin? Sam felt bile rise in her throat as she struggled to come up with a feasible explanation for all the odd language and increasingly realistic Roman Empire props and extras working on this film.

Josh wasn't moving. If he doesn't move, he's going to get hurt. Stupid man. Sam went into action. Springing forward, she didn't pay attention to the looks she received as she jerked Josh away from the filthy actor. "Come on, Josh." She didn't know what else to say, or do. Josh was stupor-like. As she led him away and the parade moved on, the slave lifted his hand in a salute to Josh, thanking him for his help.

Josh startled. "Did you see that? Did you?" His voice rose. He grabbed Sam by the shoulders, shaking her, as if this would help her see. "It's Avi," he continued ranting. "His hand. Avi had a crooked little finger on his right hand. Whenever he had to salute, this little finger wouldn't co-operate. Always stood out. Avi always got into trouble for it, but couldn't do anything about it. A birth defect." A warm smile spread across Josh's face. "Sam. That was Avi. I'm sure of it."

But before she could open her mouth to protest, Josh hauled them off in the same direction as the parade, following them into the fortress.

A few minutes later, the pitted wooden door was pulled firmly closed behind them with a resounding thud and the parade and its followers disappeared down the myriad of winding alleyways. The silence was eerie.

Sam stood with Josh at her side, alone in the square. "Well, what now, Sherlock? I'm getting cold, I don't fancy going on some wild goose chase."

"Will you shut up, Pinkie? Let me think," Josh said.

"Think away, macho man. I'm going take a rest." Sam sauntered away, finding the nearest step she could. Feeling as grimy and dirty as the slaves who walked past, she brushed away as much of the soot and grime she could, plunked herself down, resting her hands on her knees. Chin cupped in her palms she watched Josh. Slowly, he turned around in a circle. "The man's flipped," she muttered watching him suspiciously. Definitely serious damage, she thought. The man is so eaten by guilt he imagined his dead friend was alive again. The head injury must have precipitated his odd behavior. They talked about this sort of thing in her psychology classes at college. Conversion or something it was called, Sam admitted in silence. She gave Josh a sad glance.

"Dead men don't come back to life Josh," she all but shouted at him." She tried again, knowing full well something was very wrong. "Josh, this is not Biblical time. You've been working very hard and pushing yourself to the limit. You're overworked, stressed out," she explained, grasping at any solution but the ridiculous explanation Josh had given her.

"Don't you see, Sam?" Josh gestured. An outstretched arm pointed into the darkness around them. "There, there, and there. That's the Lower City and there's the Upper City. Don't you think I recognize them from the models? Pinkie, we're in Jerusalem."

He was so adamant that Sam decided to go along with him. Perhaps he could turn violent if she disagreed with his fantasy. "Yes, of course we are, Josh. The dig is just outside Jerusalem. Right now you're very tired, dear." She patted his arm gently. "You need to get some rest and so do I. Let's go back to the kibbutz."

"Don't you see it? The people, their clothes, the language. Well, I admit you mightn't notice the language, even your modern Hebrew isn't too good. But the soldiers. Surely you can see it for yourself?"

"Sure I can. It's a great show. We'll go to the movie when it opens. We might spot ourselves in the crowd scene. Great costumes. Certainly looks real." But for all her bravado, Sam couldn't negate the furtive disquiet that lodged itself in the pit of her stomach. The '*What if he's right*?' part. Appalled at acknowledging the outrageous statement, realizing parts of it were making far too much sense and she really, really didn't want them to be, Sam bit her lip. "I wished I'd never had the bright idea of photographing the chalice in the crypt. Then at least we'd be back at the kibbutz. Heck, I don't think I'd mind cleaning those million and one bits for Navon..." Sam's voice trailed off as she slumped against an icy cold stone wall.

"Sam," Josh said her name with such softness, and sadness, she twisted round to face him. Dark, mournful eyes stared down at her. She could see the reality in his face, the dark circles under his eyes, and the slump to his shoulders. "It is real," he said with a surety Sam had never heard before. And didn't want to hear.

"I want to be sick," she screamed. "Josh I want to go home. Now. Please." She blinked. Once, twice. Nothing happened. The night sky was still pitch black, dotted with millions of stars and no electric light.

# Chapter Eight

They wandered around for hours through the narrow, dark winding alleys, the stench of refuse, human and animal droppings and the stale air putrid.

Sam covered her upturned nose in disgust. "Phew. You would think they would think of hygiene at least," she commented, disdain apparent. "There are parts of this country that *are* like Biblical times."

Josh saw a realization wash over Sam's face as she spoke

More and more, things indicated this was no movie set, and she was at last seeing this for herself. Blatant fear had her in its grip, evident in her mossy green eyes as she surveyed everything around them.

He knew she was struggling to come up with a feasible excuse for the realistic scenery, the ragged crowds and their dung-colored clothes. Nothing could douse the dreadful smell, just as nothing could douse the reek of his own fear—concern for Sam, concern and mounting fear for their predicament.

"Josh, I can't walk any more. My feet are aching and it's getting chilly. I only have a thin dress on."

He took pity on her and hugged her even closer into his body, hoping he could transfer some of his heat. Dazed, his mind overflowed with unanswered questions as they walked along the cobbled streets. It was so familiar, but different at the same time. He was certain they were in Jerusalem, but it wasn't the modern day Jerusalem he knew so well. Outside the city walls he'd seen several large groves of trees. Today, modern Jerusalem, beyond the walls was urban. The buildings were similar, the same quarried stone, even the myriad of winding alleyways, were familiar. It ate at him. The Cardo, running north-south lined with shops, the wares totally different, the stone smooth, not as pitted and ground by several thousands of years of foot traffic, as it was when he and Sam spent Shabbos rambling around the city.

Looking down at Sam, he could see her face in the moonlight glow. She was so worn out, the skin stretched around her eyes and mouth. It was such a beautiful cherub of a mouth. He couldn't resist. Bending down he kissed her gently on the lips.

"Don't worry, Pinkie. I think we are lost, but I'll take care of you." Josh tried to make his voice sound light, not wanting to scare her. "Let's head down this alley." He pointed down the street directly in front of them. It was a short alley, marginally cleaner than others they'd seen. "We'll have to sleep rough tonight, Pinkie. I'm sorry, honey I know you aren't used to that sort of thing. Until the sun rises I really can't figure out how to get back to the dig. I learned a lot about topographic navigation in the army, but the best I can tell you is that these are the same stars I always see from my parents' house."

Josh lifted Sam in his arms. The poor thing was exhausted. He stopped at the edge of a stone dwelling sheltered in a dead end. He laid her down carefully and sat down, cradling his arm around her.

He could see realization was beginning to sink in for Sam. Fear, previously unbridled and haunting in her eyes, was no longer there when she opened her tired eyes wide. There was a sense of resolution about her.

She was struggling to stay awake and try to talk him out of what she thought was his dreadful delusion. "Maybe in the morning things would be different," she said.

As her dark lashes fluttered shut, Sam snuggled into his arms and curled her long legs, resting her head on his chest. His body heat enveloped her and she sighed with pleasure. Within seconds she was asleep, her delicate snoring humming in the silent night.

Cradling her, Josh leaned against the cold stone walls. He felt fiercely protective of Sam Pinkman. Ruefully, he admitted to himself he understood her father's demand for a babysitter for the beautiful girl. The last few weeks Josh had noticed a change in her though, or perhaps, he had become more observant as she obviously was, through her camera lens. Sam was single-minded and passionate about her work and despite his increasing sense of terrible danger, he wondered if she was as passionate about other areas of her life. His face reddened at the thought.

Josh glanced tenderly down at her. Sam's hands still clutched the chalice, its elegant gold etching glinting in the moonlight. He let out a heavy sigh and decided to let Sam live in her fantasy world, believing they were safe for a little longer. Bad news could wait for the morning. He didn't have the heart to tell her. How on earth was he going to explain they had somehow traveled back in time over two thousand years? He could barely believe it himself.

Night fell, and the heavy silence enveloped them like a blanket. In the distance, a dog barked occasionally. Thankfully, no one came near them. The populace was more than likely controlled by a curfew, Josh reasoned, which would be why the streets remained empty. It at least served to protect them. Huddled in the alleyway, he marveled, as he looked skyward toward the stars and the golden glow of the moon surrounded by the black inky darkness of the night sky. There was nothing else. No planes flying overhead, no antenna. Nothing.

The emptiness answered all his questions.

# Chapter Nine

Dawn slowly crept into the still black night and gradually awoke the earth as the birds began their morning chorus.

He'd arrived in time.

Jan knew the pair was to travel a path; his job was to merely guide. At least his journey to the past was unencumbered by fear. Thrust back into history too many times, he'd become seasoned in the art.

He studied the confused pair as they slept in each other's arms, sprawled in the corner of the modest stone dwelling, unaware of his presence.

The sound of barking dogs not far away disturbed Sam's slumber. Such a lovely dream. A double room at The Ritz with an enormous, soft bed covered with thick quilts.

Her eyes fluttered open and closed. In a twinkling, her lashes flew open wide. She shoved her snoring companion roughly on the shoulder. "Josh, Josh wake up. It's Jan. Oh, Jan, am I glad to see you. We were in the crypt, then the earth shook and rocks fell and we came up and then there was this parade. It was so very strange."

She drew a deep breath and stared. Jan was dressed for some masquerade. He certainly never wore clothes like that at the dig. However, she was too happy to see his face, she disregarded his odd appearance. Maybe it's something Dutch! She'd sure seen enough odd clothes in the last few hours.

Obstinately, she refused to listen to the warning bells ringing in her head and she babbled on, words running together. "Jan, I'm so worried. I'm sure Josh got hit by falling stones." She lowered her voice to a conspiratorial whisper; hand over her mouth. Her tongue licked over her dry, chapped lips as embarrassing noises rumbled from her empty stomach. Her face flushed at the sound. She glanced quickly at Josh and spoke again. "He thinks he saw his dead friend dressed as a slave in the parade. There's some movie or celebration going on here and Josh is terribly confused. The poor thing thinks we're in Jerusalem. Jan, please talk to him. Make him see sense. We have to help him." Sam pleaded.

The old man looked directly at Josh, waking next to her. "So you haven't told her, have you? You've figured it out I presume, Joshua Ben Reuven?"

Josh nodded, unable to speak. He looked flabbergasted. But the odd thing Sam noted was that Jan addressed Josh in the ancient manner, Joshua, son of Reuven, something he would only hear in synagogue.

Irked, she couldn't understand a thing. She scowled at the two men in frustration. It was driving her mad and Jan seemed to be taking Josh's side. "Jan, what are you talking about? You of all people should see through this silly charade. Josh needs help, medical help, for goodness sake. He thinks Avi is alive." Anger at the two men surged through her. "How typical of men, always sticking up for each other," she muttered under her breath. She threw up her arms, pleading, but to no avail. Frustrated, she walked away from the duo.

Josh sat up, rose to his feet and stepped forward and shook the old man's hand. "Sam still doesn't understand," Sam heard him agree.

She gave him a scathing look.

But Josh ignored her and carried on. "Somehow, during the earthquake we've been hurtled back through time. I stayed awake most of the night trying to make sense out of the events."

"Ridiculous," Sam muttered, "the man's hit his head, hard." She eyed Jan, but the old man remained silent, and gave nothing away.

"I know it in my heart. It seems ridiculous, something that happens in novels written by fanciful authors, but the dwellings, clothes and speech all leads me to believe it's true," he addressed Jan. "I'm a man who spends his time digging in the past. Jan, this is the ultimate field trip. Instead of digging in the past, we're living in it." He slumped down, a look of awe mirrored in his eyes.

It sent goose bumps up and down Sam's arms. She didn't want to see Josh's excitement; she wanted him to say they were going home.

"My guess is we're sometime in the first century CE," Josh said, using the term for Common Era, otherwise known as AD. He brightened slightly. "What an opportunity! To actually see how accurate all the theories were. To see if the models were correct. To see The Temple in all its glory!"

To Sam's horror, Jan smiled indulgently at his fantasizing. Josh's eyes glowed like burning coals.

"To worship at The Temple!" he whispered.

Jan nodded. "Don't be afraid. I am here only to aid you in your tasks. Within a short time you will require my services," he addressed Josh, as if she wasn't there. Sam bit her tongue, and said nothing. Let them play their games.

"Josh, please explain to Sam why we need to avoid English in public places."

Josh's gaze turned to her. "You're going to need the mother of all crash courses in ancient Hebrew, Sam. At least you understand Latin."

"Latin," she exclaimed. Sam gaped wide-eyed at Jan. "You're both wacky." She shoved a dirty strand of hair off her face. "Is every man around me going nuts? Maybe I'm the kiss of death with men, and drive them all mad." Sam rose and walked away a few steps, rubbing her calves. "I need some space." She stepped away, leaving Josh to talk with Jan.

She heard the two men talk in hushed tones.

"So I was right then?" Josh queried Jan.

"Yes, you're correct. You and Sam have traveled in time. You're now in 69AD."

Sam didn't want to listen to this. But her mind buzzed with a zillion questions. How did they get here, really? Why was Jan here? Where exactly were they? Why were they here? And of more importance, how would they get back? She shuddered at the thought. Could they go back?

Jan began ushering them to the end of the alley. "Hurry along, follow me. The legionnaires will be here shortly and I really wouldn't want Sam to be seen by them. Especially not in that dress."

The older man took hold of her hand and gently led her through a narrow stone doorway in the last house in the street. Josh followed. The door led into a small paved courtyard. A large metal pot sat at the center. Two donkeys brayed a greeting from another section that functioned as a sort of stable or barn. Next to them were several penned sheep.

Still not wanting to accept the mounting evidence, Sam grabbed at any possibility. "Josh, perhaps this is part of the kibbutz outer buildings. You know, way out back where livestock is sheltered. Maybe after the earthquake we came out through a tunnel at the other end of the crypt?" But Josh's stony silence killed that idea instantly, and anyway, even she didn't really believe her optimistic thoughts.

They passed through the courtyard into a room bare of furnishings other than a crude wooden sort of bench with a back. In a corner, was a fire pit. Several earthenware jugs and a bronze container were scattered near the shallow pit. A rolled mat was tucked neatly in a corner. Sam caught sight of a wooden ladder similar to the one at the crypt. It lead up to a second floor. Sam wondered what the ladder was doing here in this building. Nothing made any sense.

Jan pointed to a wooden bench. "Take a seat both of you. You must be hungry."

As quietly as a cat, a young woman entered the room. Slender, with doe like eyes, her silky black hair hung to her waist. She cast her eyes down, keeping them fixed on the floor. Jan spoke to the young woman. It surprised Sam that it wasn't in any language she knew, and certainly wasn't the guttural Dutch he used when swearing in annoyance. The young girl left the room as quietly as she entered, shutting the door with a soft click.

Clasping his hands behind his back, Jan turned and faced them. "I suppose you want some explanations?" The question was really directed at Josh, who so far had remained quiet since they entered the house.

"Yes," he murmured.

Sam looked at Josh. He had turned quiet again. I must remember to get Jan to call a doctor for him, she thought. She frowned in worry.

"Firstly, I am not Jan. My name is Yigal. Nobody in this time knows me by my other name. Sam," Yigal looked directly at her, "you must refrain from speaking English, at least not loudly and certainly not in public."

"Yigal? What are you talking about? Why can't I speak? I've got quite a few things I want to say." Sam rose, hands on hips. "What a nerve. All you two do is tell me to keep quiet," she shouted, eyes blazing as she stepped up close.

Josh roared with laughter. "Like a fire breathing dragon." He turned to Yigal, unable to hide his mirth. "Do you know what you're asking of Pinkie? To be quiet! That is an extremely tall order. Probably impossible," he chuckled.

A serene smile lit Yigal's face, his eyes crinkling at Josh's humor and deepening the wrinkles in his face. Their male camaraderie at her expense annoyed Sam and she punched Josh in the arm in frustration. How dare he? "Of course I can be quiet." She snapped at the pair. "Mind you, I don't know why I should."

Yigal's silvery eyebrows rose questioningly at Josh. "Shall I? Do you want me to tell her, Joshua?"

Another silent nod from Josh.

Sam looked from one man to the other. "What is going on here?" she demanded.

"Sit down Samantha, dear. What do you remember of yesterday?"

"Everything, of course. What a silly question. Why wouldn't I remember?" What were they getting at? Why was the old man asking her if she remembered yesterday? A band of fear tightened its grip on Sam's heart and she slapped a hand to her mouth in horror. Some people insist everyone else is nuts. Was she was the one with the problem? What's it called anyway," she mumbled to herself. "Obsessive compulsive? Schizophrenia?" No, it wasn't her.

"I told you, Yigal. She'd have a hard time keeping quiet. See, she even talks to herself. I hope she finds it interesting, at least."

"I can recall everything. It was Josh who was hit on the head. Not me," Sam said indignantly. She shot Josh a murderous look. "I went to the dig to take photos of the chalice. Josh arrived. We didn't finish the shoot. Then there was a small earthquake and …" She stopped and colored, her cheeks stained a bright cherry red. She cast her eyes down and peered furtively at Josh through sooty lashes. Purposefully, she avoided any mention of the kiss, embarrassed to say anything in front of Yigal, although she knew she wore her embarrassment on her face.

"So the last thing you remember before seeing the parade," Yigal coughed as he hesitated, "was the small earthquake while you were down in the crypt. Am I right?"

"Yes."

"Ah, I thought so." Yigal looked down at the chalice, still clutched in Sam's hand. He reached for it, studying it thoughtfully for a few minutes in complete silence. "Let me get this straight. You were holding this chalice. Am I correct?"

"Yes." Sam's curly head nodded vigorously.

Josh interjected. "We both were."

"What has the chalice got to do with anything?" Sam's brow wrinkled. "You two are talking in riddles. What is going on? Will someone please tell me?"

"Listen to him, Princess." Josh spoke quietly, but firmly to her. It was his authoritative voice that made her obey instantly.

"Let's put the scene together. We have you both in the depth of night, down in the crypt, in the burial passage if I am not mistaken. This passage and the drawings on the walls were completed sometime during what we call the first century of the Common Era. They describe a variety of subjects but the ones you are concerned with are about love, hate and war. By any chance were the two of you touching in some way and holding the chalice together at the same time?"

A rush of blood reddened Sam's cheeks as she remembered Josh's kisses in the crypt. They were holding the chalice, too. "Yes, Yigal," she said using the name he said he preferred.

"You're correct on both counts," replied Josh.

Sam noticed Josh didn't elaborate on exactly how they were touching and was thankful for his discretion.

"Well, there's your answer then. That's the reason."

"Would you two stop talking in riddles?"

Yigal took pity on her and walked towards her, putting his arm on her shoulder. "My dear child, you and Josh have traveled through time. The fact that you were touching each other and the chalice at the same time is the catalyst that caused this to happen." He paused to allow the statement to sink in. "Well, that is how. Quite why, is for you to find out. But there is always a reason, a purpose behind the travel. Unfortunately, I cannot aid you in discovering the reason. My path is that of a guide, but not a leader. You must lead yourselves." He coughed briefly as Sam stared wide-eyed at him. "The figures on the wall in that chamber tell a story, a story of love and hate, how the two are entwined. Usually the recipients of this travel adventure, like the two of you, dislike each other. That's what mystifies me, the hate part. You and Josh will need to interpret the chalice's code. You are now in Roman occupied Jerusalem."

Hate.

The word hung in the air. How many times had she uttered the word in regards to Josh, let alone thought it. I hate you, Josh Ben-Sion, she had screamed more than once, especially in her early days at the dig, when everything was so strange and she felt isolated and ignorant. It had all been so hard, so different. But time travel!

"I don't believe you. Are you bonkers?" She turned to look at Josh, but neither man said a word, their faces somber as they looked directly at her.

Fear, and an undeniable realization crept up on her. She looked from one to the other. "That's impossible." Icicles clamped around her heart. She wished fervently she could wake up from this terrible nightmare.

Both men continued staring at her.

Sam's eyes darted around the crude, plain room. She walked with determination to the door. Early morning risers were already preparing for the workday. Donkeys with loaded packs moved along the alley. Several women stooped over heavy pots. Young children hauled water in heavy containers. In a corner of the alley, a potter squatted, fashioning containers from red clay. His quick hands worked confidently over a charcoal fire.

"I must have dehydrated again." Sam whirled around to the two men. "I'm hallucinating," she mumbled, swaying as the black void in her brain sucked her in, drowning out all hope. Desperately she tried to ignore the truth she already knew in her heart. She turned back slowly to the street, blinking her eyes, so clouded with confusion, wishing away the donkeys, the carts, the huddled groups in their odd garments. "It can't be true." She turned to Josh. "Please, Josh." She longed to see his face light up. "Josh, say something, please. Tell me it's an elaborate joke, a dream, a hoax, *anything*..." Sam's words trailed off to nothing.

Josh came up beside her and stood silently. One hand rested on her shoulder.

Time travel? Slow and painfully, reality sank in. Her knees wobbled and she swayed violently. Josh's grip on her tightened. She tried to smile her thanks, but her lips wouldn't move, her voice soundless.

"The Bible. Finding my Jewish roots," she muttered. "It seems a bit excessive, even to a Pinkman. My father sent me on the ultimate Jewish studies tour." She let out a thin piercing screech. No matter how crazy the words sounded, the people, the animals, and the street, it was her reality. Sam's mind flashed back to her outing to the Old City with Josh. They wandered in an alley just like this one. Rushing to the window, she glanced up at the skyline, hope rising in her heart. She studied the roofs. No television antennas. She remembered them so well from her first sight of the ancient city. Everything was gone. She cocked her head. No vehicles, only animals and carts. The hubbub of the people was the same, but the clothes, the language so different. Gone was every modern convenience, the heady odor of diesel from the buses, the cacophony of blasting horns from erratic drivers. All gone. Everything.

An enveloping blackness snaked through her, sucking her down into an empty vortex. She took the only option left at the start of the worst day of her life. She collapsed into the arms of the waiting Josh.

A cool breeze wafted across her face like an elixir. Anything to keep cool in this stifling country. Sam's eyes fluttered open and reality flooded back with a vengeance. She tried desperately to focus on the two concerned faces peering down at her. She looked from the silver eyes to the dark ones. Jan, no Yigal, no Jan. Her mind fought for control, trying to make sense. Memories washed over her tired brain. Israel. I'm in Israel. Not in the twentieth century, according to the two men in front of her.

Sam squeezed her eyes shut once again as the enormity of hers and Josh's situation flooded over her again. She wanted to sink away, just go to sleep and when she woke up it would be all gone, and they would be back at the dig.

"Sam, Sam," Josh's concerned face loomed over her.

Her eyes shot open. Nothing had changed. The three were still there in this near empty room. Yigal was still dressed for a masquerade party. Sam shivered, watching Josh's face. She could see fear in his expression no matter how he tried to hide it. Poor boy, he looks scared out of his wits. Temporarily forgetting her own terror, she pushed herself up, Josh aiding her with an arm under her elbow.

"What a mess to be in!" And, Sam realized, there was no one to ride to the rescue. She was stuck on her own and had to try to solve the problem. "This makes the crisis with Eric seem simple in comparison," she grimaced. But if there is one time she needed to use her head and not be ruled by her heart, she knew this was it. Sam continued. "Okay, if I even accept that we have been forced back in time, how are we going to get back? You can bet your bottom dollar I'm not going to stay here. Come on Josh, let's get going now, and go back to outside the fortress where we arrived. Perhaps that'll show us the way back."

In saying these words, she realized it was tantamount to admitting she accepted the mess they were in no matter how crazy it seemed. "The one thing I've learned from my father is the importance of action." '*Action. Get to work.*' she could hear Geoffrey Pinkman shouting now. Okay Daddy, she answered mentally. I'm working as fast as I can. She wanted to go back to the future, to her own bed. Even the hard, lumpy mattress in her kibbutz room was better than staying here. With Pinkman determination flowing in her veins, she stood up.

"Right, let's go."

Neither man moved.

"Come on, Josh. We need to go." Sam picked up the chalice from the hand built table and looked at him. He still hadn't moved.

"Sam, we can't. Yigal and I aren't quite sure how we get back."

"We do know that it has something to do with the chalice." Yigal interrupted. He took the chalice from her hands. "We have to work out the inscription. This, I believe will be the key to your return. And the reason you arrived is directly connected to your return, of course." He looked at Sam. "Providing you want to return of course."

Shocked, Sam couldn't believe her ears. "Of course we do. Why wouldn't we?" She saw doubt cross Josh's face as he hesitated to reply. She poked a finger at him. "Now you look here, Josh Ben-Sion. I am not staying in this primitive place. No offense to you Jan, I mean Yigal," she amended. "Josh, you got us here. If you hadn't ..." Her words and thoughts trailed off as she remembered the kiss and Josh's strong arms as they embraced her. She colored. "Well, if you hadn't interrupted me down in the crypt, I would have gotten my photos and would have been back at the dig and in bed before that little earth tremor. Let's get home, Josh. This may all be very exciting, but we have to start being proactive, thinking of ways out of here."

Perching on the bottom rung of the rough wooden ladder that led to the upper mezzanine, Sam leaned forward, resting her chin in her hands. Her mind whirled with a crazy merry-go-round of ideas. Nothing made any sense at all. "Designer clothes, photography, party organization, that's my expertise. Not time travel," she whispered quietly.

Although her mind accepted what seemed to be a ludicrous situation, there was no way she wanted to stay in the past. A thousand and one ideas on how and why they should go raced through her mind. Now. Not a minute later. But her thoughts were interrupted as the same doe eyed girl re-entered the room, carrying a tray laden with an assortment of fruit and cheeses.

Eyeing the food, Sam's stomach reasserted itself, rumbling loud enough for the Emperor in Rome to hear.

Yigal ushered them to the table. As Sam took her seat, she absentmindedly thanked the girl in English, gasping, annoyed at her stupidity. Yigal had warned her about speaking English.

"You're welcome," the maid replied, a sheepish smile on her lips as she left the room as silently as her entry.

"English! I thought you said no one here spoke English. This is a joke isn't it? You two have been having me on all the time. I might have known it." Hope fluttered in heart, that the entire episode was an elaborate hoax.

"No, Sam. I admit Rachel does speak English, haltingly. For some reason, at one point, the girl was able to travel time too. She went to the future, spent a number of years there and returned, to meet her own destiny. She didn't fit in. Perhaps she had an intuitive inkling that she didn't belong there. So you see, Rachel does appreciate your predicament. Been there, done that. Isn't that the saying?"

Deflated, she sat in silence, her dim hope and last vestige of optimism that their nightmare was just that—a bad dream—gone, destroyed by Yigal's explanation. Although she continued to eat, all joy at seeing food for the first time in hours had completely vanished. It could have been cardboard.

She was very scared. Unable to hold her tears back any longer, the hot, salty tears dripped down her cheeks.

"She needs sleep, Yigal." Josh said, aware of Sam's desperate clutching at false hope when she heard the English words spoken by the young maid. His heart wept for her pain and anguish. "I've got to get us out of here Yigal. Somehow..." Or he would die doing it if necessary. Scooping Sam up he followed Yigal to an alcove and placed her onto an unfurled straw mat and drew a coverlet over her. He gazed down. Sam was overcome with sleep and lay curled in a tight ball, huddled under the cotton cover. "Sleep, Pinkie," he whispered.

Retreating downstairs, Josh sat back down with Yigal. They had a great deal to discuss. "So, what do you think?" he questioned.

The old man's gaze shifted to the mezzanine where Sam slept. "About Sam?"

Josh nodded, brows furrowed with concern.

"I think she has accepted the truth, the fact that you have both traveled through time. Though I dare say she is struggling with it. It is imperative, Josh, that you don't let her speak English out in the streets, nor here in front of the servants." There was a stark warning etched in his pale eyes and signaled the deadly serious nature of his words.

Grasping the chalice, he held it up to the light. It glistened in the halo of sunbeams shining through the small window.

"You're expert in ancient languages, Josh. What do you make of the inscription?"

Josh squinted, looking directly at the markings, roughened with age, but not nearly as ancient as it had appeared in their time, after all.

The chalice in this century was only one hundred years old. He pointed at the markings. "You're correct in saying it has to do with love, hate and war. These markings here tell us this much. Do you have paper?" Josh chuckled, realizing he was about to request paper and pen. How easy to take things for granted. He smiled ruefully at Yigal who had also anticipated his unsaid request and was already reaching for a sharpened piece of charcoal and a scrap of parchment.

One by one, Josh silently deciphered the sonnet, until he thought he had their true meaning. In a low voice, he began reading it out loud.

"Today is tomorrow,
The future the past,
From far lands, they must see
In love, hate and war the two are entwined.
Holy of holy, city of gates
Towering fortress, soldier to pass
Take thy chalice, complete the circle
For…eternal circle enflamed.
Past to future completes the journey."

Silent, Yigal stroked his long white beard; absorbed by Josh's powerful words. He nodded in conclusion. "Young man, you have a difficult task ahead of you."

They talked for many hours, the sun their only sense of the passing time. Now, as it slowly began sinking into the horizon, Josh heard Sam's footsteps as she entered the room.

Rising on creaking bones from his bench, Yigal walked over to her and ushered her into their midst. He wrapped an arm about her shoulders, smiling benevolently. "Feeling better now you've had a restful sleep?"

She shrugged. "I see we're still in this nightmare." She turned and talked directly to Josh. "Sorry, I don't mean to be grumpy, but I'm scared," she admitted.

"Yes, Princess, nothing has changed." Josh eyed her. "I understand." He stepped to her, staring down into her green eyes, wide and full of worry. "I promise I will protect you."

The corners of Sam's mouth quivered and she smiled tentatively, looking up at him through the heavy veil of her lashes. "You don't seem nearly as frantic as I feel," she said ruefully. "In fact, Joshua Ben-Sion," she said laughing, "you're acting as if being flung suddenly into the past is a school excursion."

Josh could only grin. It was utterly true.

"Okay, you two, what have you devised? Have you found our way out of here?"

"Take a seat dear," Yigal interrupted. "Josh has been hard at work with the chalice while you slept."

Knots twisted in Sam's insides at the calm words. Yigal telling her to sit down made it sound like there was bad news ahead. She was exhausted from a restless sleep full of crazy nightmares, dreaming that the Wizard of Oz, who suspiciously resembled her father, had waved a wand and a puff of smoke enveloped the stone dwelling and lifted it up in a tornado to plop down in the middle of the kibbutz where they had magically returned to the future. Too bad it had only been a dream. It obviously mirrored her hope that anything, crazy as it may seem, would get them back home.

She sat slowly, eyes peering suspiciously at the pair.

"According to my reckoning, this is a riddle of sorts. They were very popular as a form of entertainment during this time period, families passing down history, a sort of Boy Scout campfire thing," he chuckled. "From what Yigal has told us it has to do with love, hate and war and we know it was because we were both holding it and touching each other when we were hurtled back in time. The words love, hate and war are mentioned in the riddle." Clutching the chalice tightly, Josh read the inscription to Sam.

She understood the part about love and hate. She had already admitted to herself that at times she hated Josh Ben-Sion. Big mouth. If only she had kept her words to herself, then maybe they wouldn't be in this predicament. Mind you, did Josh have to hate her too? She squirmed at the thought, not liking the idea of him hating her at all. "This is like reading poetry, trying to understand what the writer really means," she said. "So how does city of gates and the rest of the riddle help us get back?"

"Holy of holies, city of gates," Yigal interrupted. "I think it refers to Jerusalem," Josh said. "A holy city, city of seven gates, excluding the sealed golden gate. Don't forget, Sam, we entered through Zion Gate, now, a towering fortress. The only thing I came up with here is the Antonia Fortress. It must mean we have to get inside the fortress."

"How many miles is that and what bus do we catch? I don't think they have local service." The swell of panic choked like a noose around her neck. "It'll take us days, if not weeks to figure out a way to get in. I'm not good at this first century stuff, Josh."

One, final, desperate hope took hold. "It's worth a try." It made about as much sense as anything else. She stood up and clicked

her heels together three times, murmuring. "There's no place like home."
She closed her eyes and waited.

One eye opened tentatively.

The second opened.

She sighed with disappointment. "Well it was worth a try."

Both men stared at her with blank expressions. She shrugged.
"You obviously never saw the Wizard of Oz? Great movie. Saw it
tons of times as a kid. Maybe that was a preface to time travel," she
smiled wistfully at Josh.

Neither Josh nor Yigal replied and Sam slumped back onto the
bench, defeat raining down on her. "Come to think of it, neither of you
resemble a Scarecrow or Tin Man."

"We need to solve the riddle," Josh instructed.

"And fast."

"I haven't been able to figure out what it means by 'soldier to
pass' either. Hopefully it will become clearer."

Sam knew he was trying to sound positive, but it wasn't
helping her much.

"It does talk about completing the circle on the chalice. There
is a bit missing." He pointed to the gaping hole directly in the
center of the metal.

Sam could see the worry etched across Josh's face. "This
is like a jigsaw puzzle," she said. "Do you mean to say that
we're relying on a two thousand year old jigsaw puzzle to get
back home? We'll need more than a Wizard of Oz, or anyone
else to get us out of here."

"Sam," Josh whispered, a hand caressing her cheek. "The
army doesn't train for time travel, only combat. We'll get out of
here. I promised you before. I'll keep it. I failed Avi, but I won't
fail you too."

# Chapter Ten

Another day dawned, and still they hadn't found a way home. Instead, they'd holed up in the small stone house, Josh pacing the floor for hours as he came up with one idea after another, discounting them all. All her suggestions ended up the same way. She wondered what events would transpire that day. While Josh hoped they would find a way home, Sam knew he was itching to go out and see the sights this magnificent city contained. He acted like a little kid in front of a candy store being offered the run of the place. He couldn't wait to see everything for himself.

"So where to from here, Poirot? Remind me to watch a few more who-dunits before we time travel next time," she joked.

She saw Josh take a deep breath. Here it comes, she thought.

"I've been thinking. Since we're here, why don't we take a look around? Sam, you'd be able to really see our history. Won't your father want you to do that? Besides," he confessed to her with a sheepish grin, "I want to take a look at the Temple."

"I knew it. Now you're suggesting we wander around the place. Maybe you want to book us on a sightseeing tour, lunch included. Josh, all I want to do is go home." Sam turned to Yigal, but the old man's blank expression told her she wasn't going to get any help from that direction. She continued. "My father might be overbearing at times, but that seems a minor problem in comparison to this time warp we seem to be stuck in. Are you nuts, Josh? Why do you want to play Charlton Heston? We're in 69AD. This place isn't safe. Didn't you see all those Roman soldiers, the slaves? Don't forget the filth. We could get the plague in this place." Sam stared at Josh incredulously. "It's foolhardy."

Yigal interrupted. "Well, now, Sam, you're not quite right there. The plague. No, I don't think so. There's no plague at this time. Later yes, but not now, not here."

"Blast it, Yigal, it's not clean; we could pick up all sorts of disease. People died like flies back then, now. Oh, whatever." Sam snorted in frustration. How could she get through to Josh? "All you can see is the opportunity to visit and learn if all the theories are correct. What about the prospect of danger?" Sam turned back to Josh. "You had military training. Maybe we have to attack this time travel problem the same way you would a military battle. We're doing battle with the first century." Sam paced back and forth, head bowed in concentration. "We need to use twenty-first century know how here. How about... nope that won't work," Sam frowned and continued pacing. Her heartbeat pumped erratically as her mind whirred. "What would Daddy do? Pinkman's always figure it out," she murmured.

"So you accept our predicament?"

Sam said nothing, but heard Josh's heartfelt sigh from behind her.

"I admit my burning need to see and discover first hand everything I've studied for years is overwhelming," Josh admitted. "So much so, that I can't ignore it. Sam, please." he pleaded. "Just a couple of days. It's an archaeologist's dream. One day is all I ask. It's my dream. Please."

Josh's jet dark eyes stared at her, beseeching. She looked away, knowing she would bow to his entreaty. How could she refuse the wounded puppy dog look? Blast the man. "Oh, all right. You think you're Indiana Jones. Go ahead. Play games," she gave in, despite the churning in her gut and the raw bile that rose in her throat as if a dire warning. "One day only, Josh. No more. This is too serious."

Grinning widely, Josh immediately turned to Yigal. "Can you get us some clothes? No way can Sam go out like this," he said indicating Sam's still bare legs.

"Absolutely, dear boy," Yigal's enthusiasm was rising. "I'm rather excited with the prospect of taking this young scholar to examine his dreams," he advised Sam. "The Temple, that will come tomorrow. First we will make a small excursion around the streets of the walled city. An entree of what is to come, so to speak," he advised.

One day. He's already increased it to two, Sam realized, but said nothing, knowing it would fall on deaf ears.

Yigal rustled up worn clothes from his maid Rachel. The black haired woman shyly helped Sam dress in the simple tunic.

Before they left, they had to come up with a plan for Sam who was unable to speak Hebrew, let alone the ancient tongue, although she did speak some Latin.

"Sam, we should pass you off as a Saducee girl, recently returned from Rome, if need be. It will explain why you can't speak the language. Everyone says you have a regal bearing, Pinkie," he advised. "It'll be enough to convince everyone you are upper class and get you through if no one examines too carefully." Josh also dubbed her Sara for the duration of her visit.

Dressed in a cream colored tunic nearly to her ankles, Sam trailed behind Yigal and Joshua who tugged at her hand impatiently. He wore an earth colored tunic to his knees and dark chocolaty leather sandals with the myriad of inch wide criss-crossed leather straps, not dissimilar to the ones nicknamed *nimrod* sandals worn by modern Israelis were on their feet.

Within minutes they were surrounded by the first century and a bubble of excitement welled inside Sam. It was as if suddenly her senses went into overdrive. Sound, smell, touch, were all heightened—the mixture of odors, the gaggle of languages, shouting, calling, haggling over prices as they passed through the *shuk*, was overwhelming. She gripped Josh's hand tightly, terrified of losing him in the crowds swarming in every direction, while her photographer's eye observed every little detail.

Not far from Yigal's home, Josh began to sniff the air. The foul odor of burning animal flesh permeated.

"Joshua." Sam stopped dead in her tracks, worried about his odd behavior. All around them, a loud, noisy commotion rose. Mothers shouted after children. Traders hawked their wares at narrow stalls like the shuk in the Old City they visited several days before. Thick dark smoke filled the air. Onion, garlic and rank oil reeked in the narrow alleyways. Sam's nose wrinkled. "Something is wrong. Perhaps we should take another route," she suggested, wiping the stinging smoke from her eyes. "There's a fire and it stinks." She stood with her arms folded over her chest the way she saw Josh stand when he made a firm decision. A spiraling sense of disaster unfurled in the base of her gut.

Josh bent to her ear. She could barely hear him above the shouting going on all around them. "Don't worry, Pinkie. Jerusalem isn't very large, not like in our time. Smells," he grinned down at her, "spread quickly. It's the Temple sacrifice you smell. We must be near."

Sam clearly saw the ecstasy reflected on Josh's face. His eyes glittered like candles burning in a dark night.

"In our time, prayers are said in synagogue three times a day reflecting the times of the sacrifices in days gone by. This is one of those sacrifice times. Don't forget," Josh added, "most cultures around are still sacrificing humans. At least animal sacrifice is more enlightened."

With an increasing feeling of dread, Sam followed Josh down the narrow lanes. "Sightseeing in the first century. Who would have thought it? And sacrifices to boot." She would never, ever have believed it. Now she had no choice. It was perfectly clear to see.

Sheep, cattle and humanity from all over the Roman Empire thronged the cramped streets, while armed men moved among the crowds, making Sam shiver. She was nearly sure this was the same place they bought ice cream just a few days before. What she could do with an ice cream cone now!

Yigal halted and whispered quietly to them. "The Temple can be a dangerous place today. You know the history, Joshua. Zealots against Romans, Pharisees from the lower classes against the Saducee upper class. The less you say about yourself the better." He led the way through the crowd.

Heart sinking, Sam trudged behind the others, feet shuffling over the cobbled streets.

"Princess, look." Josh's command made her lift her downcast head. She stood dumbfounded, eyes wide, mouth open.

A golden roof stood before her. Pillars of white marble spread into a sort of porch paved with stones of various hues. In a daze, she followed the others down through rows of pillars, until the loud shouting, much like the hurly burly of the marketplace they passed through, interrupted her fanciful reverie. Birds in wooden cages beat their wings. Sam briefly remembered a trip with her father to Hong Kong and their visit to the Bird Market. She jumped quickly over a pile of fresh pungent animal droppings dropped by a beast about to be sacrificed. She followed the two men into a second court. Her mind reeled at the immense size of the complex. The one crumbled western wall where she had left her wish for a family like the Ben-Sions between the cracks was all that was left of this magnificent splendor. Sam wondered whether the other part of her wish would come true. Would Josh ever find something admirable in her? She hoped so. Perhaps if she could sort out the riddle on the chalice, then…"

"No foreigners may enter the Temple precincts." Yigal whispered. "No women may enter during their menstrual period." Silver-gray eyes studied her questioningly.

Flushed, she shook her head vigorously.

"You can enter as far as the Court of Women." Beckoning her, Sam followed; eyes wide at the sight as they climbed the steps and entered the enormous double doors surrounded by the gold and silver covered entryway.

"Remain here, Samantha. Don't talk to anyone," warned Yigal in an undertone. She was going to be left here among the throngs of women beseeching the Lord. All about, men's voices rose in song and carried through the court.

Josh strained on the balls of his feet to listen. Instinctively, he pressed forward to the huge gate leading from the Court of Women on to the Court of the Israelites. He climbed the steps at the western end of the courtyard to a platform. Yigal remained outside, forbidden to enter unless he was a Cohen, a priestly descendant or Levite, a traditional Temple guard. Joshua ben Reuven, being HaCohen, son of a Cohen, he edged forward to watch the ancient sacrificial rites of his people, in awe at the unfolding events. Somewhere, he realized, hidden from sight was the Holy of Holies housing the Ten Commandments given to Moses on Mount Sinai. The High Priest entered the sanctuary once a year.

He gazed at the rite of sacrifice, noting when the animals were led to an altar. It reminded him of the origins of the Jewish people and the sacrifice God asked of Abraham with his son, Issac, here on this very place. "Sacrifice," Josh murmured. "It is the key to understanding God's stubborn obstinate people." But even as he said the words to himself, no one around him took any notice, all eyes on the sacrifice and intent on their own prayers.

Everyday, sacrifices were proscribed by the rabbis to set God's people apart from others. Sacrifice of the comforts of the Diaspora to live in a Jewish country. The sacrifice of young lives like Avi's to keep them safe, Josh thought sadly. He couldn't take his gaze from the ritual and watched the rest of the ceremony in a dreamy daze. The hide was taken from the dead animals, the fat and organs tossed on the fire and the removal of the tithe due to the priests.

In another time, another place such as this, Joshua realized he could have been performing the sacrifice himself. Son of a Cohen. He was entitled to the priestly tithe. However, he kept this information to himself as the sacrifice came to an end and his fellow watchers began to shuffle out in the direction of the outer courts. Josh followed, lost in thought over the incredible events he had just witnessed.

# Chapter Eleven

Grateful that she hadn't had to watch the spectacle, Sam's senses reeled at the stench of blood and fat burning that permeated the inner sanctum and into the women's area.

"Yigal, we need to get back. Now," she suggested with urgency. "We need to get him off the off the streets before something awful happens." She glanced over at him and saw the wonder mirrored in his dark brooding eyes. But she couldn't fend off the sick feeling in her heart. Josh was heading towards some disaster and taking her along for the ride. It was unnerving, like a sixth sense. She might want to ignore it, but couldn't.

Once home, Josh paced up and down the small room. The visit to the Temple had disturbed him deeply. All the way back, he muttered about sacrifice and from the descriptions she'd managed to drag out of him, it must have been absolutely revolting.

"Sit down and eat Josh, I insist," she instructed. When he failed to respond, she grasped his hand firmly in hers and led him over to the table. Laid on the rough-hewn table were several wooden plates and crude spoons.

"You're acting like a kid with a new toy. Stop fiddling and talking to yourself," Sam chided, though she couldn't hide the concern in her voice. "You have the cheek to say I'm a blabber mouth." She piled a plate with cheese, coarse buckwheat bread and eggs. A curious sort of lentil dish completed the modest supper. "Start eating," she commanded.

Josh glanced up at her, as if he'd only heard her for the first time. There was a bleak look beneath his thick dark lashes. He looked back at his food, but did nothing.

Sam pouted, frustrated, concerned more and more every minute. "Honestly, Josh, you're like a caged animal when you get worked up. At least, for a change, I'm not the cause of it." She brightened and a small smile lit her face at the comforting thought.

Rachel entered carrying a clay jug. She stepped up to the table and leaning over poured the sheep's' milk into a drinking vessel. "Some things never change, do they, Joshua Ben Reuven?"

Her voice was a whisper. She continued pouring the drinks, dark hair falling over her shoulders as she went about her tasks calmly and efficiently.

Josh's body jerked alert and he swiveled on the stool and stared after the maid as she disappeared from the room as if seeing a ghost. He shook his head, unable to believe what he thought he heard. *Some things never change.*

*The maid, so similar in mannerism, soft, nurturing and caring like Rachel Alon.* This Rachel reminded him so much of his old friend. He went through school and army service with her. She was his first girlfriend. An innocent sort of platonic thing, remaining friends until Rachel disappeared on a trip to the Judean desert and was never found. He remembered her parents' heartbreak.

Josh's mind filled with memories. Memories he really didn't want to face, or own, but had no choice. Rachel was the field operator and clerk for the unit the night Avi died. Wrought with guilt, he had hovered as the medics tried to revive his dying friend, pacing up and down.

An old habit, Josh realized, thinking how Sam had just called him a caged animal as he'd paced Yigal's small quarters.

The maid's words scored his brain and his nerves jangled, thrusting him to the edge. How could a serving maid two thousand years in the past know of Rachel in the future? When would the guilt of his friend's death leave him?

Josh bent his head and began to eat, glancing up at Sam. She stood in the dim glowing light from the oil lamps. He detected an expression of triumph, her rosy lips curled upwards with satisfaction.

"Good, you're eating. Nice to have someone jump to my orders for a change," she laughed. "Just like they do for daddy." Her hand rested on his shoulder. "You'll feel much better once you have eaten."

"Women. They always want to be right," he muttered under his breath. Josh watched as Sam sat quietly, the play of emotions flickering over her face. Her increasing sense of control and the determination he had seen in her as she had become more comfortable at the kibbutz was empowering. For both him and her.

"I'm determined to find our way home," she said quietly. "I've been contemplating possibilities, none of which makes the slightest sense, but then again, neither does our situation."

Josh continued to eat his meal as the three of them discussed the possible reasons behind the time travel.

"I know I'm not too bright sometimes," Sam grinned, "but this happened for a reason. If we figure out the reason, we get to go home." She faced Yigal. "You said there's always a purpose. That's what we need to figure out for our one-way ticket. The sooner the better. I mean this is a great day trip, but enough is enough. Between being spat at and these clothes." She lifted the rough textured garments and scratched at her irritated skin. "It isn't that I don't appreciate your fashion sense Yigal, but honestly this stuff is starting to make me itch. Wouldn't it be nice if there were a convenient Victoria's Secret just down the road. Underwear would be a nice addition," she admitted with a rueful grin.

"Shame you didn't bring that flimsy stuff you had at the airport," Josh teased, a mischievous glint in his eyes.

Sam's cheeks flushed pink. "They're hardly a basic extravagance."

"Perhaps a minor matter of history must be set right," counseled Yigal in a quiet voice. "You can't change the large events. This city will come under siege and burn. The Temple will fall. You can't prevent that."

"But perhaps we can prevent a wrong. An injustice." Josh jumped up from the table, eyes ablaze with excitement. "We can set right a wrong. That's the reason. To correct a previous sacrifice." He started to pace again. "It's Avi. I have the chance to save him. Don't you see?" He almost shouted at her. "He died before, but here's my chance to save him. I have to find him. I can do this, I know I can." His deep voice rang with confidence.

Sam grasped his hand and caressed the side of his cheek with the other. Dark circles shadowed his eyes and she could see the pain and worry in their dark stormy depths. "Josh," Sam pleaded quietly. "I know you believe that the slave you saw is Avi. Even if it is, you can't save him. You have to accept some things are fate—*basheert*— isn't that the Hebrew word? Doesn't our faith tell us that everything in life is fate, in the sense that there are no coincidences, things happen for a reason? It doesn't mean you can understand the reason. Bad things happen to good people sometimes," she shrugged. "It's fate and you can't do anything about it."

But Josh pulled away from her and strode toward the small window, staring blankly out.

"All you'll do is get yourself hurt or," her voice dropped to a hush, "killed. Please try to apply your brains to a way to get us back home."

Josh spun round. "You don't understand. You can't."

"No, I don't suppose I can, but tell me one thing. What is this hang-up anyway? I have the right to know since you're so obsessed with it. Was Avi your lover?"

Stunned speechless, Josh gazed at her. Gently he took her by the hand and led her over to a wooden bench. "No, of course not, nothing like that. You don't understand. He was part of me, my best friend for life. I was the one who should have died. I never admitted that to anyone before," Josh blinked several times and his body sagged against the back of the bench. "I feel sick to my stomach every time I face his parents, knowing it should have been me, instead of him. Avi led the platoon when I should have. We swapped places at the last minute. If we hadn't, he would be alive today.

Don't you see? Here he is. I have to set things right. I can't fail him again." His voice burned with righteous zeal and he lifted his eyes skyward, as if in silent prayer. "I've never felt anything like that with Avi, not a physical love like you mean. It was a gentle love like that between a David and Jonathan. Nothing like what I'm starting to feel with you." His voice lowered and he bowed his head.

Sam slipped her hand inside his. Her fingers stroked his palms. "You mean that?" she asked, her eyes misting.

"Don't you feel it, too?" he asked.

Sam nodded her head silently. She hadn't realized until Josh said he cared, actually how much. She wanted Josh to care for her, the way she cared for him. She'd been too stubborn to admit it. Typical Pinkman, stubborn to the core. She hadn't stopped to think truly about her feelings towards Josh, only that she wanted to impress him. "You care?" Sam could scarcely believe she had heard correctly. "Even if I am stubborn and impulsive and do some dumb things at times?"

Josh reddened and ducked his head shyly. "Don't forget spoiled?" He laughed as she punched his arm playfully joining in her laughter.

"I was pretty awful, wasn't I," she admitted, blushing as she remembered how scathingly she treated Josh the day they met. "At the airport, treating you like a bellhop. Sorry." Reaching up, she gave him a kiss on the cheek, pulling back quickly as her own heart rate skyrocketed.

*Whoa! Slow down. Remember your history with men.*

Sitting quietly beside him, Sam contemplated her startling admissions. Her fingers stroked his palms, too overcome for speech and she wondered whether they would have admitted their feelings for each other if they had been back in their own time. But she wasn't to get the chance to analyze her admission as Yigal interrupted her thoughts.

"It's quite late. Rest and we'll discuss this more in the morning. You've both had a very long day. Josh, you and I will sleep in the loft." He nodded to Sam. "Follow Rachel."

Reluctant to leave Josh's side, Sam rose, kissed Josh on a cheek, stubbled with new beard, and slowly walked away. Halfway across the room, she stopped, turned and gazed back at him, feeling his eyes on her. "Sleep well," she said before moving to a corner where mats were already laid out on the floor for herself and Rachel.

Barely able to keep her eyes open, she was asleep within seconds of lying down on the mat. But it was short lived, as several hours later loud sounds above woke her.

*"Avi, Ani ba."*

Sam jolted upright. The room was inky dark. She cocked her head to one side and listened carefully, unable to understand the words. The sounds came from above. Hastily, she stumbled to her feet. A sound sleeper, Rachel continued her soft snoring.

Hands out in front of her, she struggled to find the rickety ladder in the darkness, tripping over a wooden bench on the way. She kicked her toe and yelped, hopping ridiculously on one foot.

"Samantha, is that you?" Yigal's soft voice called from above.

"Yes, I heard the most awful racket. What is going on up there?"

"Joshua's nightmares. Even here in the past he cannot escape. It seems what affects young Ben-Sion in his own time has followed him," Yigal announced.

Sam's brow furrowed. "What on earth are you talking about?" she answered, still half asleep.

But Josh erupted again drowning out Yigal.

Wide awake now, Sam groped at the wooden ladder leading to the loft. She climbed gingerly, unable to see where she was going.

"Where did I do this before?" she grumbled as she took the first step, remembering the ladder at the crypt and her stumbling to get out after the earthquake. She reached the loft and could just make out Josh thrashing around wildly. She pushed past Yigal, confident in her ability to soothe him. She stroked his head, already wet with sweat. "Shush it's over now, Joshua. Your Pinkie is here." She rolled him prone. "Do you have any oil?" she asked the hovering Yigal.

Yigal climbed down the ladder and returned shortly with jasmine oil. The scent filled her nostrils with its heady perfume. She hoped the odor would fade by morning or Josh would be furious at making him smell like a flower. As sparingly as possible, she poured drops of the oil onto his back and massaged him in widening circles. He groaned for a few moments, his body rigid, the muscles in the back of his neck corded. Although his lashes flickered briefly, his eyes remained closed. Josh was in the depths of his own nightmare, which wouldn't let him go.

"Settle now, Josh. I'm here and no one else. Time to sleep and rest your mind." She continued murmuring soothing words and working the tense muscles until she felt them give way beneath her hands and Josh fell into a quiet sleep, his breathing even and deep.

"I'll stay with him. He might need me again." Sam informed Yigal, surprised at the old man's easy, quiet acquiescence.

"You are the one who can lead him when and where he needs to go, young woman." He didn't give Sam time to ask for an explanation, giving her a brief smile, he turned and went back down the ladder.

Sam lay down next to Josh. Still sound asleep, he rolled over and put an arm around her. She snuggled into his embrace, grateful he had settled back to sleep. How awful for him. To think Josh suffered these nightmares for years. No wonder he was so obsessed with Avi. The only possible solution was to help him in whatever he believed his quest to be.

Accepting the decision was almost inevitable and made Sam feel better, her relief poignant when she realized she would at last be able to do something to help Josh and thereby, hopefully, help them all return where they belonged. Happy to have a loose plan instead of floundering, she settled quickly, eyes heavy with fatigue. "Goodnight, Josh," Seconds later she fell asleep for the second time that night.

# Chapter Twelve

Sam woke early the next morning to a soft rumbling next to her ear. Traffic. Must be the buses running already, she thought, still not fully awake. The rumbling sound shifted restlessly. Se propped herself up on her elbows.

Dark eyes smiled up at her.

"What are you doing here, Pinkie?" Josh asked her.

"You had another dream."

A slight frown creased his brows. "I don't recall, though its nothing new. My parents say I wake the whole house sometimes. I'm sorry if I disturbed you."

"Shush," she admonished, her hand stroking his. "It's nothing."

"Nothing? I don't think so. Funny. I feel so well rested. The same as when you found me in the kitchen at my parents."

Sam tried to give him a reassuring smile, but was overcome with a sudden, overwhelming nervousness. She was lying next to Josh!

"Breakfast," Josh interrupted her thoughts.

"I'll have coffee with no sugar, and half a grapefruit," she muttered, and snuggled under covers again, trying to hide her embarrassment.

With a soft laugh, Josh slid off the mattress. He climbed down the ladder and returned several minutes later with a clay drinking vessel and small wooden plate. Placing the dishes on the floor, he stooped and kissed her softly on the cheek.

"I know it isn't exactly a cappuccino," he twinkled, "but it's the local equivalent."

Sam groaned and leaned back, lifting the drink to her mouth. "Toothpaste and a toothbrush would be nice. My mouth feels like I've spent the night in the desert."

Josh handed her several chunks of cheese and an assortment of figs and dates. "Breakfast in bed."

"Thanks, I appreciate it. I'll never take anything for granted in the future. Simple things, like a washcloth, soft covers, sheets, even toilet paper, for goodness sakes –pure luxury," she grimaced, hesitating a fraction. "If we ever get back."

Josh kissed her cheek. "You look very tired. Sleep longer if you like. What do you get up to at night?" he chuckled, turning to climb down the ladder before she could answer.

Still chewing the fresh fruit, she strained to hear the discussion between Yigal, Josh and Rachel below. She smiled realizing Josh's voice was the loudest. A door banged shut. Startled, she suddenly realized what had happened and sprung into action, scampering down the ladder.

"Yigal?" she called.

The old man, seated at the wooden bench and looked up. Deep lines furrowed in his brow and dotted over his hands and arms were the brown spots marking his on-going years.

"Where did Josh go? Never mind," she said answering her own question. "Follow him. If he's gone to find Avi, he won't think clearly. Keep an eye on him, please, Yigal."

He rose slowly, his face masked with infinite patience.

It did little to calm Sam's raging anxiety. "Hurry, please. Before he is out of sight."

"I will do as you ask, Samantha, but Josh has a destiny to follow.

He has begun his journey as you will too," Yigal said turning toward the door. Sam looked out the window and up the street. She caught sight of Josh at the end of the alley.

"There is only one place Josh will be heading for; the fortress where he last saw Avi," Yigal informed her as he hurried out the door.

Time dragged and she paced around the room much the same as Josh did the night before, ignoring Rachel's amused glances.

"You are the same as Josh," she informed Sam. "Strong minded. Stubborn. Here, both of you will have the chance to discover yourselves, find new strength and destiny."

"How do you know?"

Rachel smiled. "Avi's death nearly killed Josh, isn't this so?"

Sam nodded her agreement. From what Jan had told her on her first day at the dig, it was true. "Even now, Josh is wracked with guilt, blaming himself because they'd swapped places."

"Josh believes this is his chance to set the wrong, right. Joshua will need you as his angel, Samantha, someone to watch over him and soothe him over the worst hurt. One day, he will learn to accept fate can't be manipulated."

"How do you know this?"

"I can be a guide, a translator, or servant, but neither Yigal nor I can do anything to change history." With a slight twist of her mouth, Rachel lowered her eyes and left the room, leaving Sam to ponder the woman's words.

But it was all too much. Fingers twisting in her tangled hair, she strode for the door. She couldn't bear any more. She darted out the door into the alley, followed quickly by Rachel.

"You can't go. You'll get into trouble and Yigal will be furious."

But she was unwilling to listen. "I have to go. I have to find out," she said, leaving a wide-eyed Rachel following in her wake. Sure enough, not five minutes later she was accosted by a legionnaire who began arguing with her in Latin. A large crowd gathered quickly around her. She saw their pleased looks as she traded insults with him.

"*O mores!* What manners!" she sniffed haughtily, hoping to disarm him when he ogled her. "*Odi profnim vulgus et arco.*" Sam searched her mind rapidly for old quotes Miss Madigan made them learn. She brightened. I hate the vulgar herd and hold it far. There, that ought to teach him. She just wished she could think of something useful to say.

The crowd snickered as the translation made its way through the throng. The angry legionnaire grabbed her shoulder, ready to drag her off, but the gathered crowed, emboldened by her insults, closed ranks and shoved against him, breaking his hold on her.

Struggling to find a way out, Sam spied Rachel. The girl whispered in her ear. "You are behaving like royalty instead of a simple Judean peasant." It made Sam realize her mistake immediately. She eyed the legionnaire. He was furious at her neat escape from his clutches. There had to be a way out of this. She carried on, only hoping her Latin would be enough. "*Sicus tollhouseus disintegratis,*" Sam muttered, trying to look knowledgeable and think of the correct phrase for crumbling cookies at the same time. Was there a word for cookie in Latin? Too bad, she hoped Tollhouse Cookies wouldn't mind the inference.

It seemed to work as the legionnaire, surrounded by the laughing crowd, seemingly lost interest. Within minutes she and Rachel arrived back at the stone dwelling.

Rachel shoved her in the door and locked it securely. "Yigal warned me to keep you out of trouble. I have failed. You have made a serious enemy insulting the legionnaire in front of the crowd."

Sam said nothing.

Rachel pushed a wooden chair over to the door and plunked herself down on it.

Sam glared back at her watchdog. "I didn't have to swallow those nasty comments he made. Nice backside and all that stuff."

Rachel didn't even bother to look up.

Hours ticked by with no sign of Yigal or Josh. No television. No walkman. Not even a book to read. Most of all, she craved her camera. If Josh longed to see the Temple, Sam was dying to photograph it.

Being without her camera was like missing an appendage. She felt almost naked without it.

"When I get back, I'm going to have a few things to tell those time travel writers about the real thing," she muttered pacing around again. "Maybe I can inspire someone to write a new series."

Dusk was falling with still no sign of either man. Even Rachel showed signs of worry. She opened the door several times peering furtively down the alley.

It was nearly dark when Yigal finally arrived home.

One look at his ashen face and Sam knew something was terribly wrong. She rushed up to him, clasping his hand in hers. "What is it? Where's Josh?"

The old man's lips trembled. His voice quavered as one tear fell down the worn cheek. "Joshua has been arrested. He saw a legionnaire beating Avi and killed the soldier. He's been taken to the slave camp."

Sam bolted for the door. But she wasn't quick enough and Rachel darted after her, pulling her arm, trying to hold her back.

"Let me go!" she pleaded, desperate to free herself from Rachel's determined grip. "Let me go to him. I have to help him."

But Yigal and Rachel shook their heads. "You mustn't run off blindly into the streets. You will only succeed in getting yourself into trouble, too." The older man's voice was so calm and certain; Sam relaxed in Rachel's grip.

"What can we do, Yigal?" She dared him to explain his plan.

He said nothing.

"Hmm. Exactly what I thought. No idea what to do." Sam's mind whirled furiously. "Thank goodness for Daddy. I've watched him in action enough times to get a germ of an idea."

Yigal and Rachel both stared at her.

"My father would say the best way to get what you want is to march right up and demand it. I have a plan," she announced. "We're going right to the top. No fooling around with soldiers or lower ranks. We go straight to the commander of the place. I'll demand my property back and you can accompany me as my servants. The one thing I know how to do is act like a silly, spoiled petulant girl. Whoever thought it might be useful one day?" She grinned.

"Common sense, my girl," Yigal confirmed.

Sam beamed. "It is, isn't it?" Quickly she explained her plan to the pair, noting as Rachel's face clouded with uneasiness.

"Do you understand Joshua is under threat of the death penalty? You know what that is here?"

Crucifixion.

Sam shivered at the thought of Josh agonizing for hours in an excruciating, tormented death. Romans crucified thousands without batting an eye. No, she wouldn't fail. Her face shone with steadfast determination. A Pinkman is obstinate and stubborn, if nothing else. "Leave it to me." She stood ready to march out the door again.

Yigal put a worn, mottled hand on her forearm. "Let Rachel dress your hair and tidy your clothes as much as possible. You won't impress the Roman commander looking like a peasant," he noted.

Although itching to race after Josh, Sam reluctantly agreed. *Geoffrey Pinkman said you have to look the part to get what you want. Image and first impressions are everything.* She slumped down again and allowed Rachel to pile her hair on top of her head fixed with a wooden comb. She disappeared out the door, motioning for Sam to wait.

Sam thought she would go mad with impatience as Rachel slipped into the room several minutes later carrying an indigo tunic and a small wooden box. Nimble fingers helped Sam change into the tunic while Yigal politely turned his back on the women. The maid tied the tunic around Sam's waist and drew back to examine her appearance.

She opened the box revealing several tiny brushes, a red dye and a dark one. Quietly Rachel motioned her to close her eyes while she applied a sort of eyeliner from antimony and red ochre to her lips.

Yigal studied her appearance, walking around her in a slow circle. "You don't look as elaborate as a true Roman, but you'll pass as an upper class Judean who accepts some of the Roman practices."

"Let's go. And for a change, leave the talking to me." Her voice carried an implicit warning. She didn't need to warn the two. If she failed, they could all be arrested. After all, she was masquerading as a person that didn't exist and they were aiding her in the performance. But, she determined, with an upward tilt of her chin, Josh needed her. That was all that mattered.

Head held high, shoulders squared, Sam strode defiantly through the streets of the city, her faithful servants trailing behind her. Fear and worry knotted in her stomach, but as they neared the fortress she switched into autocratic mode. Tossing her head high, she looked down her nose as she passed the peasants in her path. As they approached the fortress, Sam went into her act with the soldier on duty.

"You people have my property here. I demand to see the commander immediately."

Geoffrey Pinkman couldn't have been more threatening and demanding.

The soldier eyed her garments and hair.

Sam knew her speech was a bit odd, but she did at least speak Latin. She hoped and prayed the guard would think her an upper class woman. If time hadn't been of the essence, Yigal and Rachel could have coached her, but they had no time. She had to get Josh out of there, before they threw him to the lions—literally. Or crucified him. She had to rely on what always seemed to get her into trouble, her spoiled ways.

Seconds later, Sam breathed a sigh of relief when he opened the massive gate, motioned to another soldier and whispered in his ear. The second soldier openly studied Sam as she tapped her foot impatiently.

"Come now. How long does it take to arrange a simple matter? You have a slave that belongs to me and I want my property back. My family is very important here and I wouldn't wish to have to contact the procurator."

The two soldiers conferred together while Sam worked herself into a fine temper. Hands on hips, she bellowed a command. "Get the commander of this place here and now. You can tell him," she hesitated, trying to remember who she was. "Salome, daughter of the House of Pink," she mumbled the last part, hoping they wouldn't challenge her, "wants her property."

Princess Pinkie couldn't have done it better. Sam stamped her foot in annoyance, having a tantrum in front of the wide-eyed men. She saw the fear in the guards face and preened internally. The man was obviously afraid that to deny her entry would cause more trouble in the already rebellious province, and with what he thought was an important family, too. One of the soldiers led her into a building at the far end of the courtyard. Sam shot the astounded pair following respectfully behind her, a triumphant look.

"Piece of cake," she muttered. "Leave it to a Pinkman," she said, pleased with her act. So far so good.

They passed through a sort of vestibule and into a hall. A small shrine to the gods stood in the center of the room. A series of rooms appeared to lead off the hall. Surprisingly, a small garden containing roses was hidden at the back. The soldier led the trio to the garden and indicated with a wave of his hand for Sam to sit on a marble bench.

As soon as he left, Sam whispered rapidly to the two. "Yigal, find out where Josh is. Tell him we're here to help and not to despair. Rachel will stay with me. Hurry. If anyone challenges you, you tell them Princess Salome wanted a personal assurance from a trusted servant that her property wasn't damaged." She only hoped that there wasn't another Princess Salome alive at that precise moment. "Could get tricky," she muttered under her breath.

Yigal, however, hesitated. "I can only marvel at your ability to take charge of the situation and bark orders like a general."

Sam managed a slight smile, in spite of the nauseous tension gurgling in the pit of her stomach. "The one thing I possess in abundance is the ability to appear haughty, snobby and cold." She turned from Yigal, determined to concentrate on her mission. As she wandered idly around the garden, stooping occasionally to sniff the roses, her fingers twisted in the folds of the tunic betraying her anxiety. She started and straightened her shoulders at the sound of approaching footsteps.

"Princess Salome, our commanding officer is currently away in Cesaria until tomorrow. His adjutant, Remus, will be happy to discuss the matter of your missing property with you."

Pasting a haughty, cold smile on her face, Sam turned and locked eyes with the legionnaire she had royally insulted only that morning.

*Coincidence? Or basheert. Fate.*

# Chapter Thirteen

Dark brows shot up in surprise. "Princess Salome," the adjutant said sarcastically, his thin lips spreading into a cold, cynical smile. "How nice of you to take time to traffic with the vulgar herd," he hissed using her own expression from the morning.

Inwardly, Sam cringed, fighting the urge to scream. Something else seemed disturbingly familiar about the man, but she couldn't put her finger on it. In some ways he reminded her of Rob, the photographer. Was it dèjá vu?

However, this man was powerful. One false step and they'd all pay for it. She tried to think what to do. What would her father do? Action creates reaction. She wanted the legionnaire to react, giving her Josh. Pulling Audrey Hepburn out of her repertoire, she tried being gracious. Crazy thoughts danced through her head. After all, I saw Roman Holiday ten times. He's Roman, maybe it will help. She swallowed hard. She was desperate, using extreme ideas. But, it might just work. She hoped so.

Sam smiled at the irate man, letting her dark lashes flutter flirtatiously at him. She felt his eyes rake over her body boldly, returning to her breasts and gulped, fighting off the hysteria building up inside. "Now you wouldn't hold my silly words against me, would you?" she whispered caressing his forearm, revolted at having to touch the man. She was determined to free Josh, and knew her hasty action, running off half cocked, had not been a good move. Now they were all in the man's den and it was up to her to get them out of it, whatever it took.

The legionnaire continued his creepy leering and rubbed a calloused finger over his stubbled chin. *What will I do with you?* he pondered, though not actually speaking to Sam.

She refused to react and stiffened her spine, clenching her jaw as she withered inside under his lustful scrutiny. It made her skin crawl, but she didn't dare break eye contact with her foe. It would be tantamount to an admission of defeat, and a Pinkman never admits defeat. It was not a word she would allow in her vocabulary. Not now. Not ever.

"You claim we have property of yours. Perhaps we should discuss this over some wine." He clapped his hands and a servant appeared with a glass jug and drinking vessels.

The scent of roses wafted under Sam's nose. Rose wine. She sipped it slowly, hoping she wouldn't get drunk and lose all sense of what she was doing here. "You have a slave my father bought for me. I want him back. It's simple enough. He doesn't belong to you. He belongs to me. Joshua Ben Reuven."

Sam shivered as the legionnaire's mouth tightened. Raw, white fury flickered across his ice-cold eyes.

"Your slave killed one of my men. He can save himself only if I decide to allow him to fight unto death with another condemned man." He folded his arms over his chest.

Sam knew he was awaiting her decision. Bile rose in her throat. What if the opponent turned out to be Avi? Sam knew Josh would go down without a fight, rather than kill the man he believed to be his friend. He considered himself responsible for Avi's death in their time.

To do it again, here in the past, despite the fact that Josh was a modern day warrior trained for combat, would destroy him.

No matter how Sam tried, she couldn't find a way out, but accepting the challenge at least gave her some time. "Accepted," she agreed, a sweet smile on her face. "I do love a challenge," she added, feeling sick at heart.

Yigal slipped into the room and nodded.

"I would like to see that my property hasn't been damaged," Sam said. *At least we can see Josh* she reasoned silently.

"There are conditions."

*The evil pig had her in his clutches and he knows it.* "And what might they be?"

"You remain here overnight with me. You can send one of your servants to inform the House of Pinkus."

Having no choice, Sam nodded in agreement. She exchanged wild looks with Yigal and Rachel. The dark haired girl's jaw hung open. Yigal signaled frantically with his finger. No. Sweet Audrey Hepburn would do no good now. What would Sharon Stone do? Hoping she did a credible imitation, Sam shot the man a sly look. "You should have told me before what you wanted," she whispered in a silky undertone, forcing herself to smile as she ran a finger over his shaven jaw.

"You may rest for the afternoon. I guarantee a busy evening. Your maid will dress you accordingly." He turned quickly and strode away.

Yigal scurried to her side quickly. "Do you have any idea of the trouble we're all in now?" His worn face was a mask of anger.

"Never mind that. Did you find Josh?"

A nod of his head made her sigh with relief. "Is he safe?"

"He's been beaten with the lash, but he's alive. He's with the man he calls Avi. Avi is very sick. Maybe dying."

Footsteps in the hall made Sam and her cohorts cease all discussion. They followed a beckoning servant down the hall into a room. Small but elegantly furnished with a high-backed sofa, several chairs and tables, it seemed the height of luxury after the modest dwelling in the poor Jewish part of the city. Smoky, olive oil lamps lit the room. A crimson tunic and peculiar undergarments resembling a bra and panties were laid out on the sofa and pins and combs for an elaborate hairstyle were scattered on the table. Clearly the man wanted an elegant beauty for his seduction. At least he believed her to be of the upper class. Only wealthy women in Roman times had access to such garments.

"Well Rachel, you might as well get to work. If he wants a sex symbol, we better give the man what he wants."

Silently, the girl began dressing her unruly hair into an elaborate, contrived set of curls that framed her face.

"You appear calm and serene." Yigal shook his head in admiration. "Do you truly intend to sleep with that animal?"

Sam gave him a sad smile. "Of course not. I have no experience with men. I'm going to kill him. Make sure I have a knife handy." So calm and collected was her statement to Yigal and Rachel, it took several seconds for her words to sink in. Even Sam was astounded at her own cool composure. Eyes closed, she sat as still as a statue waiting for Rachel to finish styling her hair.

Feeling like a sacrificial offering, Sam paced around the room. Sacrifice. That word again.

Dressed in the flowing tunic with her scarlet tresses coifed like a Roman lady, she thought long and hard. Sam shuddered at offering herself up to the commander as the price of Josh's freedom, or, at least a chance at freedom. She had never dreamed that her virginity would go to a Roman legionnaire who was a creep.

Sacrifice.

Josh talked about sacrifice. If he were willing to surrender his life, as she believed he would if made to fight Avi, then she'd have to be as willing to surrender her virginity. If it meant she would have to seduce the revolting man to be able to plunge a blade between his shoulders, then she would find the strength to do it. Blanking out the horror of her situation, she remained determined. She rubbed her palms together, working out a plan.

"Yigal, fetch a platter of fruit and a sharp knife to peel it. Wine too, and lots of it. We want him good and drunk." Determined to give herself every advantage, she instructed Yigal, but two sweating men straining under a sofa and a mattress interrupted their discussion. A sweet, cloying scent permeated the room.

A bed of roses.

The big bad wolf sent for a rose stuffed mattress. A bed of roses for the sacrificial lamb.

Sam felt a quiver flutter up and down her spine. Her instincts were confirmed when she turned and saw her nemesis freshly shaved and bathed, eyeing her from the threshold. He nodded in approval at Rachel's handiwork and motioned her out of the room with a nod of his head. Rachel hesitated, but Sam nodded her agreement.

"You too," he indicated to Yigal.

Yigal looked to Sam. She gave him an encouraging smile.

Frowning, Yigal however obeyed the Roman and shuffled out of the room.

Sam turned to the Roman. "First I want to see my property," she demanded. She poured a large glass of wine and handed it to him, a smaller one for herself.

Dark eyes studied her face. "For a price."

The legionnaire pulled her to him and his hard, wet, lips touched hers. It made Sam ill. She fought the urge to vomit and forced herself to respond, fingers caressing his smooth cheek. "My property," she whispered, insisting gently. She took a step away and as casually as she could manage, played with the folds of her tunic, exposing more cleavage, giving him a look at what he desired. Her fingers brushed over her nipples and she gave him a saucy smile, teasing him mercilessly.

He clapped his hands. "Bring the new slave here."

Despite their war of words, playing for more time, Sam couldn't help but worry about Yigal's task. She was anxious to free Josh. He was in sorry shape according to Yigal. She only hoped he would be able to cope with the demands about to be placed on him.

# Chapter Fourteen

Half unconscious from the terrible beating he endured in the morning, Josh lay in his cell. A cold draft fluttered over his inert body. Time seemed to disappear. Lying prone on the scratchy straw covered floor, the dank smell assaulted his nostrils. Groggy, he tried to roll over, but the agony was so overwhelming he slumped back onto the stone floor, thankful for the coolness it offered as a relief to the searing throbbing across his back. He reached up to brush away a strand of straw from his face. His fingers traced the welts across his cheek.

He remembered.

The dead soldier.

Blood, screaming voices, pain.

Avi was being beaten. He couldn't just stand there watching the lifeblood flow from his friend. Enraged, he struck out at the soldier, killing him instantly. That had been his misfortune, and Avi's. Hearing the commotion, soldiers rushed from all directions, armed with swords, the razor sharp blades slicing his back. The pain of his arms being yanked behind him, tearing him apart as they tied him with strands of animal hide. The sting of sweat, mingling with the blood.

Josh closed his eyes for a moment, wishing away the memory and pain.

It remained. Just as the memory of Avi.

They were dragged away immediately, Avi barely alive. The last Josh had seen was Yigal rushing after them.

A rat scuttled over his legs and roused him, its sharp teeth scraping across his sandals. Josh kicked out sharply at the pest; pain racked his entire body.

Sitting up, he struggled to get his bearings His prison cell was barely fifteen feet by fifteen feet. With solid stone walls at least two feet thick, there was no chance of escape. No file hidden in bread would get him out. He had better start thinking or he would be housed in a coffin.

The cell was bathed in dim light streaking through a portcullis at the top of the towering stone. Straw covered the floor and two benches. He looked over at the other bench, finally realizing he wasn't alone. Another long, bony form lay stretched out, face down on the stinking straw.

Avi? Ignoring the searing pain, Josh crawled as fast as he could toward his friend. "Avi, Avi are you alive?" He drew the bucket of water towards them. Dipping a handful of straw into the water, he used it as a cloth to bathe the oozing sores on his friend's back. Whip marks criss-crossed Avi's back, the welts seeping blood and pus, a sure sign of infection. "Little wonder," Josh mumbled. The air was thick and heavy with a rancid stench. Despite his continued efforts to bath Avi, sweat trickled down his back, mingling with the suppurating sores.

His own body was a mass of constant torture, but he had no time to worry about the horrendous pain he himself felt. He had a job to do. He had to save Avi. His misery and fear meant nothing. Avi was uppermost in his mind.

Josh leant forward and listened for the sound of breathing. He could hear nothing and was filled with desperation.

"I was to blame for his death. Now I have a second chance. *Tsuvah.* Repentance. Setting things right. I want to make it right. Help me." Josh bowed his head, resting lightly against Avi. "I can't do this alone." What should he do? Josh was sure if he couldn't save his friend in the future, at least he could redeem himself in the past. He began to pray. There was nothing left, but prayer. He prayed silently, mumbling the words, beseeching the Almighty.

Soft moans from Avi woke Josh from his stupor.

"Water, I need water." Josh deciphered Avi's ancient Hebrew.

Josh quickly re-dipped the straw in the pail bringing it to Avi's parched lips, hoping to at least lessen his thirst with a few drops of water.

"Thank you, friend." the ailing man croaked, his clear blue eyes reflecting pain.

"Friend. You called me friend. So you remember, Avi. You remember." Relief seared Josh. His friend remembered him. At last his chance had come. For hours Josh bathed Avi's wounds as gently as he could. He was in pitiful shape, not one inch of skin seemed to have missed a beating, the flesh a variety of colors. Josh seethed with hatred for the Roman Empire. This was the glory of Rome—battered, bruised and helpless men. At least Pinkie was safe. He vowed to kill every soldier he saw in revenge.

He heard noises in the distance. Shielding Avi with his body, he tensed as the sounds came closer. The clank of the lock opening seemed to echo around the small cell.

Yigal rushed in. He whispered in hushed tones in Josh's ear. "Don't worry, I'm here to take you away. Say nothing, do nothing. Follow me."

Relief. He was saved from this hellhole.

Yigal pulled under Josh's shoulder, supporting him to stand on shaky feet. Josh nearly fell. His head spun from the exertion. "Avi, I can't leave him. Not now. Yigal, we have to save Avi." Josh struggled and resisted with what little energy he had left.

"Josh, be quiet. Do you want to ruin everything? I promise to return for him." Yigal looked over at Avi. "Do you understand the extent of your friend's injuries? I'm not sure the poor man can survive another twenty-four hours," he murmured.

Josh let Yigal pull him away, surprising him at the old man's strength. Yigal shoved him out the cell door. "So far so good. Now we have to see whether Princess Salome can fulfill her part of the plan."

"Who the hell is Princess Salome?"

A quirky smile lit Yigal's tired and worn face. "Wait and see, lad. Wait and see."

# Chapter Fifteen

Sam flashed a brilliant smile and poured more wine. "I do so love rose wine," she whispered, motioning Remus down on the mattress. She held the glass and offered him sips as his hands played over her body, stroking lower. She allowed him to caress her neck, his lips brushing lower as his hands crept up her smooth thigh. An octopus. He has hands everywhere. She drew back from him, terrified when she looked into his glittering eyes.

"Salome, sweet princess," he mumbled, pressing his lips to her neck. One hand pulled back the folds of her garment, exposing a round, firm breast. His large, rough hand cupped it, thumb and index finger kneading the nipple, making Sam shiver in revulsion. As the door opened, Josh was shoved into the room; Sam pulled back with a start and jumped with a cry, forgetting her exposed condition.

Already covered in filth, his feet were manacled. Similar chains bound his wrists. Dried blood stained his cheek where a whip had caught him. She rose in a dream and walked around him, sick at the sight of caked blood on his back.

Sam would never forget the loathing in his face as his eyes darted from the legionnaire to her, staring pointedly at her exposed chest.

"I know what I'm doing," she mouthed. Silently she pleaded with him and she thought she saw the realization of her intentions in his horrified expression.

Taking a deep breath, she turned her back on him. She couldn't do this and look at Josh's hurt face at the same time. His cold rejection of her was harder to bear than any physical pain. She had to make him understand she was doing it for him, to save him. Would he believe her?

"You could have been more careful with my slave," she said.

"I would have, had I known he was yours," came the silky reply. A large hand grasped her and pulled her down on the mattress again. He motioned for Josh to leave.

Sam shook her head.

"Do you think to amuse ourselves with an audience?"

You bet, and this is the opening and closing night of Pinkie and the Pervert, she thought. Sam pressed herself against the man's chest. "And where is the key to the chains?" she whispered, licking his ear.

Remus grinned. "Find it."

Sam gulped. I can do this. For Josh.

Sacrifice.

She grinned and groped under his tunic. The rat had a pocket under the folds. He edged away, teasing her, forcing her to search again, crawling after him. Her fingers explored as he moved slightly, causing the key to slip out of her grasp again. Sam searched again, knowing what he wanted. She gritted her teeth and stroked the erect organ, eyeing his satisfied smile with a grin of her own.

"My prize," Sam whispered, deftly snatching the key and holding it in the air playfully. "More wine for both of us." Still holding the key, she walked to the table and poured it. The wine sloshed on the floor. "Silly me." She skirted the puddle, quickly slipping the key behind her back to Josh. Pasting a smile on her face, though her heartbeat thumped erratically in her chest, she walked slowly, hips swaying toward the aroused Remus lying on the mattress. She handed him the wine, taking a small sip of her own to steady her frazzled nerves. Putting her cup down, she surreptitiously wiped her sweaty palms down the sides of her dress and forced herself to sit down in front of him, lifting the folds of her dress like angel wings to block his sight of Josh.

"Now turn around Joshua, this is too naughty for you to see," she said, teasing the Roman, feeling the scorching heat of a blush scolding her cheeks. Sam twisted her head and with a slight nod indicated the knife. Facing Remus again, she lowered the top of her tunic, exposing both breasts.

Please let this be over.

Rising panic and embarrassment nearly choked her as Remus's fingers groped roughly under her tunic shoving the material aside. A finger entered her. She wanted to die of humiliation.

"A virgin. What fun to deflower a virgin. After that, my men will all have a chance to enjoy themselves. There's no princess named Salome here. You're an imposter, so enjoy the fun while it lasts," he sneered. "Herod's niece is long gone."

Sam reached behind her for the knife.

*Gone.*

Panic spread through her like lightening. Suddenly, Remus collapsed into her arms, a loud scream echoed around the room as his head lolled on her exposed chest.

Josh stood behind the dead man, hands bloodied from the deed. "That was a pretty good seduction. How far were you planning on going?" His voice was cold and distant.

"As far as I needed to free you," she whispered, dying to fall into his arms.

But there wasn't time. A guard flung open the door and took in the scene. He rushed at Josh. Sam wrenched the knife from the dead man. That it slipped out easily went through her mind for a fraction, before she bolted toward the soldier, the blade still wet with warm blood. She leapt at the guard and stabbed with both hands. Eyes, wide with shock, he sank to the floor without a sound, Sam next to him in a hysterical heap.

"Pinkie, stop it. We have to get out of here."

Hot tears gushed down her face. "I killed a man, I killed a man." She moaned like a broken record.

Josh pulled her to her feet. "Would you do it again?"

She brushed the tears with the back of her hand and nodded.

"Then don't regret it. Go get Yigal."

Sam walked to the door and beckoned the anxious pair inside. Rachel's eyes widened at the two dead bodies. A ghostly white face questioned her.

Sam indicated the soldier. "I had to," she said simply. She turned to Josh. "We have to get out of here. Now."

Josh shook his head. "Avi. I can't leave Avi."

Stubborn. So stubborn. Sam breathed deeply. What to do? "Yigal, get a guard and have them bring Avi to us. Make up any story you want. Tell him we want to be entertained by the two or something. Get him here, even if you have to drag him." With a sense of urgency, the old man scuttled out the door.

She turned to Rachel. "Help me shove these two into a corner behind the mattress. Get the clothes off the guard. They might fit Josh. It's dark outside and we'll be hanging all over each other," she instructed Rachel. "They won't look that carefully. Let's hope not, or we all die," she added. Rachel dragged the men to a darkened corner and worked with frantic fingers to strip the guard.

Sam strode over to Josh who was leaning against a table for support. He stared at her. "Where did this organized, commanding manner come from? The spoiled princess is gone," he said. "Even I wouldn't dare to disobey you."

Sam bottled the urge to argue with him. She wasn't sure if he was joking or not. But now wasn't the time to argue. "Josh, it's going to hurt, but we have to clean those cuts. I'll have to use the wine, it's the only antiseptic we have. Try not to scream." You too, Pinkman, she told herself, bracing at the sight of his back. She gritted her teeth as she worked at the bloody material adhering to raw skin. Josh winced but never made a sound as she cleaned the wounds as best she could. Just then, Yigal entered shouldering a barely alive Avi.

So this was the man Josh believed to be Avi. Scrawny, filthy, covered in foul, oozing sores. Sam's heart filled with compassion for the poor soul. He looked very ill. Taking him would put all their lives in jeopardy. Nevertheless, she admired Josh's determination not to abandon the man. Faithful to the end, that was Josh.

Two thousand years of being faithful.

She tossed the key to Yigal so he could undo the manacles.

"Josh, you'll have to be a guard. Keep your face hidden as best you can. We'll give them a good performance to distract their attention. Avi is going to have to try to walk, at least as far as the gate and beyond it. Explain to him. We'll be caught if he can't do that much. I won't stand for jeopardizing Rachel and Yigal. I'm the killer, not them."

Josh towered over her. "What a woman. Who knew you possessed such strength?" he said with admiration. "Where has the change in you come from?"

Sam preened momentarily under Josh's homage, but one look at their motley band and the desperation of their situation struck home, hard. "We'll pass him off as Josh, my slave, released to me for favors offered."

Quietly, Josh explained to Avi. Sam saw the understanding flash between the two men and surprisingly, Avi willed all his strength and stood erect.

"Rachel, walk with him. Don't let him collapse. Let me do all the talking. Josh, I want you all over me as we approach the gate. Blow out all the lamps in here now. It will give us more time in case we're discovered."

The party set off, following her instructions. Fear pounded in her heart as the gate and the evening guard came into sight. Josh bent over her, his hands stroking her body, mouth buried in her elaborate hairstyle. The two guards guffawed and looked away.

"Open the gates," she ordered with a giggle. "My father wants the slave brought home tonight. I'll be back as soon as I can sneak out again, hmm?" Sam's hands stroked one of the guards on the cheek, struggling not to vomit as she caught a whiff of his unwashed body. She averted her face slightly. "Wait here for me," she whispered seductively. "I won't be long. I'll get rid of those blasted servants and that slave that caused me so much trouble. I'm entitled to some fun as a reward."

Willing herself to stay calm, she led the party out of the gate, giggling loudly for the two legionnaires to hear. She continued until they disappeared behind a corner. At that moment, Avi sagged against Rachel. Josh and Yigal lifted him and she and her band began to move, grateful for the dim light of the moon to guide their way as they made their way down alley after alley. They had to move fast, but were hindered by Avi's poor condition. Josh faired not much better, each movement sending stabbing pains shooting through him, though he remained silent. They crept toward Yigal's dwelling, the sense of urgency making Sam sweat with anxiety even in the cool Jerusalem night, but she knew they couldn't depart without the chalice.

It seemed like hours until finally the last corner they passed brought them to Yigal's residence. Sam made to start down the alley and was pulled suddenly back into the shadows.

"Don't be silly, girl. You did enough. We can't go down there now. The sunrise has begun. Remus found out you were an imposter, he may have told others. He may have found out you came from this district."

"We have to get the chalice. Josh and I can't return without it." Sam voice shrilled. "What are we going to do?" She couldn't hold back any longer. She quivered, shaking from head to toe. They had to get it. They couldn't go home otherwise.

The reality of truth struck terror in her. Not see her father, ever again. Accused of murder. To live life as a fugitive. She looked from one face to the other. All stared blankly at her.

"I will go."

She turned towards the quiet voice of Rachel.

"Let me. It is my destiny to help."

No one uttered a protest. Rachel was the only one of the group who stood a chance. Quiet, unobtrusive, she was like the invisible woman. The risk was too great for Josh, Yigal or herself, lest they be seen. Standing in the gloom provided by the darkened alley, Sam watched Rachel walk casually to Yigal's house, glancing to either side as she entered the door.

Tension knotted in her stomach as she waited and, despite the coolness of the night air, sweat beaded her brow. She wiped the back of her hand across her forehead, seeing that it was shaking. Not wanting to give in to any hysterics, she crossed her arms in front of her, holding each hand tight.

Seconds ticked, seemingly long and drawn out, but in reality only moments. Then she saw Rachel's silhouette as she exited, a bundle tucked under her arm. Sam let out a heartfelt sigh. "Where to now?"

"We have to get out of the city before dawn. They'll discover those bodies and comb the entire place. The only safe places I know that have no Roman garrisons are Machaeurus and Masada. Both far away in the Judean desert." Josh informed her.

Sam shivered. Even she knew the Zealots spent three years in their mountain fortress under siege. They died slitting each other's throats rather than surrender. Was that how it would all end? What choice did they have? Any other town would have Roman patrols searching for the redheaded killer and her slave.

"To the desert," Sam said decisively.

As the golden and pink rays of the sun streaked over the city of peace, she and her ragtag band moved off down the road, a fancy word for something that was little more than a dirt track leading towards Bethlehem.

\* \* \*

Despite her feet being covered in a mass of blisters, she wearily trudged on as the merciless sun robbed her of the little strength she possessed and burnt her delicate skin. It should have been a day's journey to Masada, certainly no more than an hour and half from Jerusalem with a car, but for three days they toiled on. Josh's infallible navigational sense served them well as they traveled in as circuitous a route as possible to avoid Roman patrols.

"I'm sorry," Josh would repeat daily. "But if we go the main route, we'd be fodder for the Roman patrol. This way we stand a fraction of a chance to survive."

"Better tired, and worn out, than being dished up for the Roman's entertainment." Sam shuddered at the thought. "You in the lion's den and me in some Roman legionnaire's bed."

Rachel and Yigal approached homes to beg for food, gleaning any information they could. It was too dangerous for her or Josh to beg. They might be recognized. Rumors of rewards for the capture of the redhead and her accomplice heightened their danger daily.

By the third day, Avi was so weak he needed to be carried by the others most of the time, despite his valiant efforts to walk. He was failing. Even though untrained in medicine or nursing, she could see it. Josh, too, was still weak from his lashing, but he never complained.

"How much further is it?" she questioned, as the third day wore on.

Josh shrugged in reply. "I might be able to tell better tonight. Impossible during the day."

Sam gazed around. Deep wadis and soaring cliffs slowed their progress. It was all sand, rock and stone, with hardly any sign of life anywhere. Despite the hardship, danger and fear she was still able to appreciate the stark beauty around her. The sheer size and color of the rock cliffs created a dramatic landscape against the azure sky, a photographer's dream. For the first time in ages, she wished she had her camera here. We have to get home. One day, she vowed silently.

Survival had been her only thought in recent days. Their rag-tag group's daily task was simply one of staying alive as they endured the relentless perils of the desert and fear of Roman retribution. Now, as she allowed herself to think of home, silent tears trickled down her face.

She reached inside the bag tied around her waist. The last of the dates scrounged by Rachel were still inside. She nibbled at the fruit absentmindedly. She was filled with admiration for the quiet, dark haired girl who nursed and soothed Avi. Her gentle touches and patience seemed unending as she comforted him whenever he thrashed and ranted at night, hallucinating with fever. Somehow, Rachel instinctively knew how to settle him with a quiet word and her palm on his forehead.

"We'll rest until the sun starts to set," Josh decided. "We can't go on in this heat." Gratefully, the party moved into the shadows of a cliff, the water shared sparingly among them.

Sam stretched out, her back braced on the cliff wall. "Put your head in my lap, Josh. It's still sore; you can't lean against the rock." Her fingers stroked his thick hair as he obeyed her orders.

"Pinkie?"

"Hmm?" Sam was already half asleep in the blistering heat.

"I owe you my life. I never saw anyone as cool or quick thinking as you were. If you didn't come to my rescue, I would be rotting in that cell. Thank you."

Sam opened her eyes and gazed down at him. He was covered in sand and soot and mosquito bites dotted his arms. His face and hair were gritty and filthy. Sam thought she had never seen a more handsome man in her life. "I found something I was good at after all. Murder." She laughed, almost hysterically. The sound echoed in the deserted canyons.

"Stop it." Josh sat up and shook her roughly. "You said it yourself. You can't change the past. Live with it and move on. You said you would have done it again given the choice. You did what had to be done to survive and showed incredible strength and courage, Pinkie."

Straggling hair fell across her face. She looked at him through the veil of tangled strands. She tried to smile, and failed. "High praise indeed from the man who recently thought I was a spoiled brat." She spoke in a quiet, low tone. "Avi's in a bad way. Probably dying. Are you going to spend the rest of your life blaming yourself for it? In this century and in another?" She put a hand on Josh's arm. A warm, earthy tingle of heat shot between them. Her gaze caught his, filling her with an overwhelming yearning to be in his arms, to be cradled and held, touched and soothed by him. Most of all, she wanted him to kiss her.

But he did nothing and Sam pulled back, embarrassed and the moment passed. To one side was Rachel her arms around Avi. Yigal dozed a few feet away, his bearded chin on his chest. "At least I know I did the best I could," Josh answered finally.

"You did then, too. Simply too pigheaded to admit it."

As Josh settled his head on Sam's cushioning lap once more, Sam reflected on their conversation.

Forgiveness.

It was time for Josh to forgive himself. Could he?

Surprisingly, even during the worst of the heat, Sam managed to sleep for several hours. Towards dusk, they all rose and continued their journey. In the distance over another of the endless series of cliffs, a turquoise shimmering sea appeared, and the further they trudged on, the smell of sulphur increased.

"I know where to find some fresh water. Can you walk a short distance?" Josh asked.

Too exhausted to speak, Sam nodded. Avi groaned but pushed himself along with the others down the steep trail through the wadi known as Nachal David. Finally, Josh lifted Avi over his shoulders, wincing in pain as Avi's body made contact with his still unhealed flesh.

As they trudged around yet another sharp, tortuous bend in the path, Sam came to an abrupt halt. The sight of the fresh water tumbling over a rocky preface caused her to burst into tears of relief. She ran for the pool and tore off the grimy dress. Her Roman underwear seemed like a fashionable bathing suit to her as she plunged in. Josh entered more carefully, floating Avi on his back. The sick man let out a small groan of pleasure; his fevered eyes fluttering open.

While Rachel and Yigal slipped into the cool water, ducking underneath to wash the filth from their heads an invigorated Sam swam up and down the pool like a happy child.

Happiness, however, was cut short. The sound of voices in the distance echoed up through the canyon.

Silently, Josh motioned everyone out of the pool and into the brush that grew near the water. "A Roman garrison from Ein Gedi might be patrolling nearby," he warned.

Sam watched, fearful, as Josh crept toward the narrow crevice and the sound, his stance a panther-like pose ready to pounce on the intruders. Head cocked and strained to hear the words. Hebrew. He visibly relaxed. The sounds grew louder. Men. Two men. He darted a look over his shoulder at her. She gave him an encouraging smile, though fear rose up in waves from the pit of her stomach.

Sam choked back a warning as Josh strode forward to intercept them as they reached the entrance to the rock pool.

Two men with faces burned a deep bronze color rounded the corner. Both were bearded. One carried a bow over a shoulder; both carried small daggers in their belts.

The men were Hebrews, Sam was certain.

"What are you doing here?" they asked in unison.

Their hands rested on weapons, but Josh opened his hands, palms up and their grips released on their daggers.

Sam let out an audible sigh of relief.

"I'm with a party of refugees from Jerusalem wanted for the murder of two Roman soldiers." Josh informed them, dropping the top of his tunic to show his own scars, still forming from the lash.

The two men exchange glances.

He continued. "We have two women and one very sick man freed from a slave camp." The men glanced over at her and the others, but Josh's eyes never once left the new arrivals.

Their daggers went back in place. "You're welcome to come with us. We live as free men. On the fortress known as Masada," said the tallest of the pair introducing himself as Eliezer and his compatriot, a skinny, dark eyed man as his brother-in-law, Shlomo.

They followed Josh to the group, their speculative gaze on her and the others. Quickly, she donned her tunic as Rachel fussed over an emaciated Avi who lay on the bank of the pool. Yigal, stood beside her. Sam couldn't take her eyes off the newcomers.

"It's all right. They're friends, not foe."

Quick introductions were made all round. Josh filled his band of refugees in. "They're from Masada. We're very close and can make it in a few hours. We'll be safe. No one will be looking for us there."

Relief flooded Sam.

Safe.

Masada.

This was where they were heading. Maybe this was the fortress that the chalice meant for their return home. Whooping with joy, she did a little dance. All her prayers were answered. Home wasn't far away. Everyone, apart from the new comers joined in her enthusiasm, grateful for safety and help.

The two men stood beside the group, shaking their shaggy heads, obviously wondering what madness they had come upon. Sam smiled at them, hoping the fact that they were Hebrews, and that they had said they had killed Roman soldiers, would increase their chances of assistance.

"*Habita*. Home, Home. We can go home." Sam looked at Josh's dark eyes, crinkling with laughter at her infectious joy. Rushing at him, she flung her arms around him, kissing him with reckless abandon; thankful Josh didn't turn her away. His closeness made her burn for more and her body ached for his touch.

A cough diverted her attention momentarily. Josh pulled away, holding her around the waist, while her arms still rested on his shoulders.

The newcomers stood, weight shifting from foot to foot, obviously eager to keep moving. "This is dangerous territory, dangerous times," one of the men said. "No time for dilly-dallying, especially not with women."

"Therefore, we should be on our way." Yigal suggested. Josh Ben-Sion has met his match. A woman as passionate as he is. Which century do they truly belong in, he wondered. He suspected their place was the time they came from, unlike himself, who flitted through the centuries as a catalyst to unfinished tasks. Or Rachel, he reflected, glancing over at the woman who cared for the slave. She traveled as a helper, fulfilling her own deep needs to rectify being unable to help Avi and Josh. Yigal believed Samantha and Joshua should return when their tasks were completed, once they had learned the lessons of insight and self-discovery. But that moment had yet to come. They had a long journey ahead of them.

His annual visits to Israel almost always included a journey through time; a secret reason for his desire to work on archeology digs. Being physically close to the time period gave off vibrations only he could feel. He felt the earthquake rumble as the innocents began their time travel.

As the motley band set off, each forward step made Sam's heart lighten. They were so close. As dusk began, they settled down for a meal sharing the fruit, coarse bread and dried meat. Dinner at the Waldorf was never more gratefully eaten than this modest offering. Nothing could dampen Sam's spirits. She was clean, had a full stomach and was nearly home. It amazed her that she had previously felt she couldn't do without so called luxuries. She and Josh would soon be able to return home.

Sitting near the fire, poking the embers with a stick, Sam watched the sparks fly. It was almost like being back in summer camp again. Desert nights were cool and below sea level as they now were, their ragged clothes were totally inadequate. She held her fingers out toward the flames, enjoying the warmth it afforded. Rachel knelt beside her.

"So you are nearly home. I am so glad. Joshua Ben-Reuven refused help in his own century. I tried. He wouldn't listen. He needed to seek the past, to free himself from the fortress around his heart."

Rachel's words took a few minutes to sink in. What was she trying to say? Rachel tried to help once before. Confused thoughts whirled through Sam's exhausted brain. "What do you mean, you tried to help?"

"It was my destiny, you see." Rachel stared blankly into the embers, turning her palms to the warmth. "Joshua, Avi and I, we were school friends. We joined the army together. We had such fun and adventures." A dreamy smile spread over her face, iridescent in the moonlight as she remembered her past and future combined. "Try to understand, Sara Bat Chaim."

Sam gaped at the use of her Hebrew name, a name she never used. How did Rachel know her father's Hebrew name? She tried to digest this remarkable statement.

"Joshua and Avi were inseparable. They loved each other as only best friends could. You know Avi took Josh's place the night he died?"

Sam nodded.

"Avi was always full of adventure, probably more so than Josh. He was a risk taker, while Joshua was more cautious. He thrived on adventure and was happy to take Josh's place. There was gunfire. Avi was shot. Severely wounded. Josh crawled to his side, dragging him across his back, to safety. You must understand that anyone would do that. We're trained to never leave a wounded comrade, but Avi was like his brother. But it was too late." Rachel fell silent, head bent, the silky strands of her hair fell forward. "When they arrived Avi was almost dead. He died shortly afterwards." Silent teardrops flowed down her cheeks.

Sam's mind whirred with her words. It wasn't the death of Avi in the future that was news to her ears. It only confirmed what Jan told her before. This Rachel, a girl in the first century CE described events that she shouldn't know anything about. "You. Here. Now. You're Rachel. You said you traveled through time. You were there. How?" Incredulous Sam stared at Rachel in disbelief.

The girl silently nodded, her head still hung down. "When I was a child I wandered away from my family's tribe in the Sinai desert. My next memory was being adopted by a childless couple named Alon in Jerusalem. I was the child of their dreams. I grew up with Avi and Josh as friends, always tagging along, wanting to join in," she smiled tentatively. "They always let me. I didn't fit in with many other children. When Avi was killed, Josh was so distraught. I couldn't help him. He wouldn't let me close." Rachel's eyes filled with tears and she hugged her arms across her chest. "I was Josh's first girlfriend, you see."

A soft gasp escaped Sam's lips. But Rachel patted Sam's forearm gently. "There was never anything physical between us. It was only a sweet, platonic love. The same as he felt for Avi. With you, it's different. Surely you must feel it. I knew it was not my destiny to help, at least not in that century."

Groping for words, Sam reached out a hand, resting it on the young woman's shoulder. She desperately wanted her to continue. It was beginning to make sense, in a strange way.

"Josh and I argued. He seemed to forget I had lost a best friend too. Avi was my true love. We had been going to announce our engagement. I lost the man I loved in a way Joshua couldn't understand. Maybe with you, he begins to realize what it means to me." Rachel's tear stained faced looked up at Sam and a sob tore from her lips.

Reaching over, Sam pulled Rachel into her embrace, trying to understand the loss the girl must have felt. Thoughts of the possibility of losing Josh flitted through her mind. She shuddered at the horrible thought and drew a deep breath. Nothing was going to happen to Josh. She had killed to protect him and if she had to, would do it again.

Soft hiccups punctuated Rachel's words, but she lifted her chin, a determination glittering in her dark eyes as she continued. "Josh wouldn't give up. He blamed himself. He felt guilty and kept haranguing himself and everyone else. He hated anyone for living but most of all himself. I couldn't take much more. I lost Avi. Then it seemed I was losing Josh to hatred. I left the city and went to the desert. I always feel comforted in the desert, perhaps because I come from Sinai. I walked and thought. Finally, I fell asleep in a cave, not far from here. When I woke shepherds surrounded me. I was in the first century AD, back where I belonged. I had come home." Rachel became silent.

Sam tried to absorb all Rachel had said. Rachel was the same person, but in different times, the same as Jan and Yigal. Each was able to cross the barriers of time to fulfill their destiny. It was no wonder she couldn't contain this information any longer. She rushed towards Josh. "It all makes sense, Josh. It does, it does."

Startled by her outburst, Josh stood up holding his arms up to stop her hurried footsteps. "Hey, hey quiet down will you? We never know who's out there. What big discovery did you make now?"

Regaining her composure, Sam looked around at the faces around her. "Rachel told me. She's your Rachel. Rachel Alon. Jan really is Yigal. It's their destiny to be here."

"Slow down will you. You don't make sense." Josh held his hand up to her, trying to get her to calm down.

Quietly Sam explained everything she learned from Rachel. About the destiny of the pair to be there to help, unable to move, until the next time they are needed to help someone. "Their will is not their own, but a higher being that sends them to aid a traveler's journey of discovery. Josh don't you see? You were seething with anger and hate. Hate for yourself, anger that you weren't able to save Avi in the future. You were so angry. Rachel couldn't help you, not then."

"If that's the case then, why are you here?" Josh questioned.

Sam was stopped short. She shrugged, but smiled, joyful she'd begun to understand. "I haven't figured that bit out yet. Give me time, Josh. I know I'm right."

"Go on, then, explain."

Sam sighed. She stared up into his dark eyes, willing him to accept it. He has to, she thought; otherwise we won't get back, her instincts screamed. She carried on. "Josh, you have to listen. Open your heart, your ears and your eyes. Your anger was destroying you. No one could help you. You needed a second chance and this way you got it. By being sent back in time. Everyone has a time, a place. Didn't you ever see people that somehow, no matter how they dress and talk, don't fit in? They belong in another place too. Rachel, for instance. Think with your heart, not your mind."

Josh nodded. "I remember the girl of my youth, her laugh, her smile. The way she always made sense. Gentle, quiet," he whispered. A smile crossed his lips. He turned toward the silent Rachel still kneeling at the fireside. "It's not so much the physical resemblance, but the quiet, calm manner, going about her business, helping others without being asked. That is the similarity."

"Please, Josh, please." Sam's eyes searched his, pleading, hoping desperately he would understand.

Josh slumped down, head cradled in his hands. "I am a soldier. I'm meant to protect, and here you are finding answers I haven't been able to even yet understand, Pinkie."

Pain tore at her heart. She squatted down beside Josh and embraced his massive frame as tenderly as she could, trying not to hurt his still scarred back.

She said nothing. Instead, she sat in silence, wishing she could ease Josh's suffering. Anything, to take away the hurt.

# Chapter Sixteen

Several hours later, Josh lay staring aimlessly at the night sky. Sam was right. He knew it in his heart. Exhausted, physically and mentally, he couldn't sleep. There was nothing new about that. Everyone else around him had long ago gone to sleep and a variety of snoring sounds echoed in the still night.

Sam lay quietly beside him, her gentle breathing warming the side of his cheek. She had solved the riddle of why he was here. Her ability to see beyond the superficial, even though she admitted it was something new, even to her, had helped her fathom his reason for being sent back in time and to begin to peel off the layers of hate, self-doubt and self-loathing. She was giving him a second chance. Josh didn't think he could have done it without her. In fact, he knew he couldn't have even started the journey of discovery without her.

From across the other side of their camp, a stirring Avi moaned softly.

Quietly, Josh went to him, wondering how long his friend would last. Although his external injuries were dissipating, it was the probable internal injuries and utter exhaustion that would kill him. Avi was going to die. Again.

Josh sponged his friend's fiery skin as best he could. His temperature had obviously risen during the day. Sweat poured from every pore of his body. In the quiet way that the feverish and dying sometimes achieve, Avi's eyes opened with utter clarity. Lucid and calm, he stared directly at Josh.

"Friend. You're a good friend. Thank you."

Such simple words, they brought tears to Josh's eyes. "What are friends for, if not to help in time of need?" Josh tried to brush off Avi's gratitude. He looked away, struggling for composure. He'd failed him, but still the man was thanking him. He'd had a golden opportunity to save the man who so resembled his friend, but he'd blown it, just as he had failed to save Avi in the future.

Avi's hand reached out for his.

Josh mumbled on. He had to say it. Had to get it all out. "Avi. I'm sorry. I really tried. The rocket-propelled grenades were too thick. I couldn't see through all the smoke. It was so fierce." He talked on and on about their past, their childhood, their friendship. He hoped for forgiveness. To save his own soul, to assuage his guilt and as the sun's rays edged above the rocky mountaintops, he finally sat in silence, grasping Avi's hand, staring blankly out, and seeing nothing. Stirring sounds from Avi broke his reverie. Josh looked down at his friend.

"Joshua, my friend. My brother." Avi spoke. "You saved me. I understand. It doesn't matter when. From the depth of my heart, thank you. Friends forever," he whispered, jolting Josh to the core with their clumsy four-year-old oath. Friends in person, in spirit. "Go in peace. Shalom." Avi was dead.

Josh's piercing scream echoed through the silent morn.

It took all Yigal's might to pry him away from Avi. "Avi must be buried as soon as possible according to Jewish tradition. Besides, it is dangerous if Avi is found by the Romans. They might connect the escaped slave to the wanted killers and then everyone would be in jeopardy," Yigal advised.

Unable to function, Josh left it all to Yigal. He found a small, empty cave; the whole area was dotted with them. With no tools to dig, it was the best grave they could provide. Josh tenderly lay his dead friend down. A Cohen, he should never come into contact with a dead body. Surely, the Almighty would forgive him this once? Avi was his brother in spirit, if not in name. In a low voice, he mumbled the words of Kaddish for the departed.

"Magnified and consecrated," he whispered, the words praising the Lord at the moment of loss barely audible, though he determined to keep faith, even in the worst of times.

Lost in private thought, Josh stood with his small group of travelers at his side around the burial site.

"Come on, get going. Now, everyone move," yelled Eliezer, rushing into the camp. "Romans. They're on the way. There's a patrol nearby. Our search was not in vain. We all have to leave now," he instructed with urgency.

Josh looked down at the burial site, knowing instantly it wasn't over.

"I'm sorry," Sam whispered. "I know you need more time but we can't afford to stay. Not unless you want to be Roman fodder."

He looked directly at Sam, knowing the danger they faced in Roman hands. Especially Sam. But he was torn. He couldn't leave Avi, not to feral animals. Not like this, but with the advancing patrol everyone's life was in danger. They were wanted criminals.

Sam. He had to save Sam.

He couldn't save Avi, but he could still save her. "I'm sorry, Avi. I know you understand. Thank you for your forgiveness." Wiping a jerky hand across his eyes, Josh made to lead his band away. Commanding officer, Ben-Sion. What a unit he led this time. An old man, a spoiled girl who turned out to have more strength and valor than any unit he ever led, and a girl who was a time traveler.

Beside him, Rachel stopped in her tracks. "I'm not going. Not this time. I've fulfilled my mission and now you must continue on your own." Her voice rang with certainty.

"You can't stay, Rachel. You're in as much danger as we are. Come on," Josh implored.

"No, Joshua. No. You are forgiven. I must tread the path of my destiny. I am no longer needed here. My job is done. I will finish the grave. Avi's earthly remains will not be desecrated and then I will leave." She rested a fine long fingered hand on Josh's forearm. "I will be safe. Don't worry. It is my time to go." She turned and refused to talk any more with the others.

There was nothing else he could do. Sam pulled Rachel into her arms. "Thank you, from the bottom of my heart. You saved him. He is whole again."

Rachel shook her dark head. "It was you who made him see. Made him open his heart again. Open to love, not anger. Josh can love again. Look after him."

Listening to Sam and Rachel, Josh stood rigid. There were so much he wanted to say, but couldn't. His gut contorted in pain and indecision. He hated to leave the girl behind, but they had to leave. Rachel spoke so much about destiny; surely it was destiny for them to reach Masada. He prayed it held the key to their return to the future, but had no time to ponder Rachel's words. No time to think. Only to run. Run for safety.

# Chapter Seventeen

As the party continued their journey through the eastern edge of the Judean desert, surrounded by the gaunt landscape, Josh eyed Sam with concern.

She wiped her tongue over parched lips. "Iced tea, cold diet sodas full of ice, freshly squeezed orange ice. Mmmm, tastes good."

Liquid, any liquid, Josh thought, desperation eating at him. Sam was rapidly dehydrating.

"Oh, Josh, look. How lovely." Sam excitedly pointed to the rocky summit three and half miles above them. "Isn't the snow gorgeous? I didn't expect a ski resort in the middle of the desert." Her body swayed as if performing a lilting dance to music only she could hear.

In one quick action, Josh lifted her in his arms, his back still too raw to sling her like a sack of grain. Sam was hallucinating in the same way she did at the dig. She was in sorry shape. He motioned to the men eyeing her strangely. "My wife needs water badly." Making Sam his wife seemed the safest thing to do. She might be grimy and dirty from their flight, but she was still beautiful. Besides, she could only get into trouble if some man made a play for her, no matter how innocent.

One of the men handed him a skin. Josh shook it. There were only a few drops of water. No help at all. He dripped the precious liquid on Sam's cracked lips. His heart broke as he watched her savor the few precious drops of moisture.

The party moved on, climbing the same "snake path" Josh had climbed as a youngster with his family and later on school excursions winding around deep ravines and sheer cliffs. At times the narrow path turned back on itself like the snake of its name. Josh shuddered as his eyes gazed down. It was like walking on a tightrope—best to look ahead. Sam moaned in his arms, babbling about ice cream, a mishmash of broken Hebrew she had picked up and more insults in Latin.

*"Glida shokolat, brutus,"* she mumbled incomprehensibly. "Chocolate ice cream, stupid."

The men eyed Joshua with suspicion, expressions stony. "Your wife speaks the tongue of the Kittim a bit too well."

"She was forced to live among them and forget her own language," he replied. Josh prayed they wouldn't decide he and his party were spies.

At the top of the agonizing climb, they crossed through a limestone wall more than eighteen feet high containing soaring towers. Even with his eyelids drooping shut from fatigue, he was able to marvel at the sight of Masada. He remembered the moving ceremony years before, when he swore his own oath of allegiance to defend his country after climbing the summit at dawn. The colors, the starkness of the terrain. Who would have dreamed he would see the place as it existed and not fanciful reconstructions from excavations? He soaked up every detail he could.

They passed through a ring of chambers, past an incredible palace. Great water tanks were cut out of the wall in many places. A sudden quietness surrounded them and his barely contained fear coiled in his gut. He could see their guides were still suspicious about them. "My wife needs water," he repeated and stopped at the tank. They drew a curious crowd as he tenderly cooled Sam's burning face.

Her eyes flickered open. "Gold, all around," she muttered. "Are we in Jerusalem again?"

A woman silently offered an earthen mug.

Josh dipped it in the water and coaxed Sam to drink, slowly dripping the liquid between her lips.

Once partially revived by the few drops of water, he continued into Herod's palace. As new arrivals, they were taken to the commanders. A rag tag gang of children and adults followed. Josh made out their furtive whisperings about Sam and her Roman attire. The comments weren't positive.

So these were the Zealots who would make history, hold off the Roman siege for three years and rob them of their victory by killing themselves. Josh prayed they would be accepted into the community; if not, they would all die of dehydration in a few hours.

They came to a halt, surrounded by the community. A tall, wide shouldered man, flanked by several others, directed the questions. Intelligent grey eyes assessed him and his motley group. Hunched over a writing table in the corner was a younger man, not more than his early twenties, a parchment and writing implements at hand. Josh thought he might be an Essene, one of the sect who kept himself aloof from others. The sect had little use for women except for procreation and spent lives in prayer and contemplation.

"I am Joshua Ben Reuven of Jerusalem. We are fugitives from Jerusalem and seek sanctuary."

The men whispered together for several seconds.

He took a deep breath and continued. "I killed a Roman soldier and escaped a slave camp."

Broad smiles lit the men's faces in approval of his deed. "And the others?" the leader asked.

"My brother, Avi, badly wounded from his time in the camp died below the summit." A quick glance over to the two guides accompanying them, confirmed his words.

"This is my uncle, Yigal."

"I heard that the Roman commander of the city was killed by a redheaded man."

Josh hesitated. "A half truth," he muttered.

Sam stirred in his arms, pulling herself as upright as she could. She turned to the leader and stared boldly. "Wrong. The killer was a woman."

Jaws dropped wide at the pronouncement and Josh nodded confirmation.

Agog, the scribe noted the statements rapidly, fingers flying over the parchment, black ink staining his fingertips.

"You are welcome on Masada."

At first Sam wasn't bothered by the whispers. Within days, word spread rapidly across the plateau's community and the gossip about her was rife.

The redheaded killer wanted for the murder of the soldier in Jerusalem was none other than Sara, the wife of Joshua Ben Reuven. How remarkable. Young girls thrilled at the thought of Sara freeing her husband from captivity, whispered quietly behind their hands. "They say she put the knife in the man's back as he tried to kill her husband," they whispered together, eyes dancing with excitement. A heroine, right in their midst! But heroine or not, Sam's inability didn't always find favor.

The older women were less delighted and eyed her with doubt. A brave heroine she might be, but they scowled as she passed, muttering about what they considered her odd, and even eccentric habits.

Prompted to help with the cooking, her attempts caused even more uproar. Everything she touched, burned, upholding her claims she knew nothing about cooking.

Some thought it snobbery. Acting like a princess. Sam knew everyone needed to work on Masada; it was a forerunner to the kibbutz movement. Sam was exhausted from their arduous journey and although she tried her best, it never seemed enough. Terrified that her lack of domestic ability might give them away, she was afraid of disgracing herself and Josh. Life in New York had not trained her for first century life. As she sifted through a cache of over-cooked, burnt to a crisp meat, aware all eyes were on her efforts, Sam sighed. "If only I had a microwave," she grumbled, annoyed at ruining the food.

Although she barely understood the whispered words from the older women around her, she knew what they were saying. Their tone was enough to confirm her suspicions that they were complaining. She stiffened her back, aware of the scathing looks in her direction as she bent over the fire. A thin trail of acrid smoke from the burnt offerings wafted up. It stung her eyes, but her tears weren't from the smoke. She so much wanted to succeed.

Try harder, she advised herself quietly.

Sam brushed away the smoke, tucking a strand of hair behind her ear. She straightened up. A child playing in the dust, pushing a plaited ball with a twig smiled at her, innocence and unconditional acceptance in his eyes. Sam smiled back, suddenly feeling stronger. She swallowed hard. She would find the fortitude. After everything she and Josh had been through, she could withstand the social ostracism. No matter how difficult, she would do it. She would try harder, harder, harder. She would succeed.

Okay, so her Hebrew was atrocious. She spoke the language of the Kittim. Sam mused about her most recent incident.

Sent to work helping a new mother, she horrified the woman when she insisted she needed to put a cat on the infant.

*"Hoo tsarech chatool,"* she claimed again and again.

Vigorously the mother shook her head at Sam and clutched her baby. An older woman with a disapproving frown shouted at her as she emerged from a chamber in the casement wall.

"Ingrate. Forget trying to help anyone here," she muttered walking away from the other women. Explaining to Josh wasn't much help.

"Looks like you mixed up your words again."

Sam stared open mouthed.

"You've confused the word for diaper with cat," he chuckled.

For the first time since their arrival Sam found herself laughing as she thought of her mistake.

But now, the end of the day drew near. Unable to do more, she wandered off to an area she hadn't yet explored, and found what she wanted the most.

"Where was he?" Sam paced, dry dung colored dust flying around the hem of her tunic. In the distance she saw Josh coming through the arch. Shaking her wet hair, she ran to him and hugged him. "At last you're here. Josh, they have the most fantastic swimming pool. You should come in with me and have a swim. The water is perfect," she urged pulling him towards the building. "You wouldn't believe it, they even have a wading pool for the kids. It's like some first century resort."

But Josh wouldn't budge.

"Come on. We'll play water polo."

"Stop it, Sara." He spoke gravely.

Sam halted and frowned. "What's wrong now? All I want is a bath. This is great. Who would have thought—our own pool."

"Hush," he commanded. He reached out and pulled her firmly to his side. "Be quiet and listen. That's a ritual bath, not a swimming pool. The small pool is meant for ritual immersion of objects like cooking implements to make them kosher. The whole building is meant for ritual immersion and you've managed to offend every woman in the community." Josh looked from side to side.

Sam suddenly noticed the sharp-eyed stares coming her way.

"I'll do what I can to rectify things, although I don't know how," Josh sighed heavily. "Don't you know what a *mikveh* is, Sam?"

Sam shook her head.

He slammed a hand against his forehead. "I don't believe it. It's such an ancient practice, even if you've never visited one, being single..."

Sam bit her lips, trying to stifle the coming flood of tears. But when he pulled her into his arms, she savored the feel of his hard body against hers, comforting, soothing.

"It's okay, Pinkie. Don't worry. I know how much you want a bath. We both could do with a good wash." Josh trailed a hand down her hair, twining the long strands between his fingers. "Despite all your bravery, they still pegged you a Sadducee princess."

Sam lifted her chin and blinked away her tears. "I do try."

"I know you do. It's hardly your fault for not knowing about a *mikveh*."

For a few minutes Josh was silent. Sam could feel his deep breathing as she rested her head against his chest. His arms wrapped around her were a cocoon she didn't want to leave.

"You know, Pinkie, there is one good thing about this. Having you next to me at night, albeit sleeping platonically," he grinned sheepishly, "is very comforting."

"You can't be serious. This is absolutely ridiculous." Fire glittered in Sam's green eyes, but Josh's remained stonily serious. "I can't believe you would actually agree to this nonsense."

He shook his head. "It isn't nonsense. It's the ancient way and the way observant couples still behave. You can't sleep with me, touch me or anything else with me while you're *niddah,* and they all know that you are since you asked for ..." his face reddened, unable to complete the words.

"Well, pardon me if I forgot to slip a box of tampons in along with a few rolls of toilet paper for the trip. I'll be sure to have the travel agent warn the next tour group that comes through to be prepared." Sam stamped off to a corner of the tiny chamber they were assigned when they arrived weeks before. "Stuck on Masada. No idea how to get back home, and now this! It is too much for words,' Sam wailed.

Josh towered above her, his face lined with concern. "You've managed to offend several of the women by accident."

"It wasn't on purpose."

"No, I realize that," Josh conceded. "But this your history, your culture. It isn't meant to be punitive. It's meant to allow you some privacy and give your body a rest and, well, it's supposed to allow a couple to develop other sides of their marriage. And," he acknowledged, "I guess it really allows desire to build up tremendously for the time when you can touch again." Josh swallowed hard.

Sam eyed him. He looked so controlled, whereas she was a bundle of aching need. Build up, he'd said. It was building up now. If only Josh could touch her. She wanted it so very much, but they slept side by side, not touching. She was aware of his fear of disobeying their ancient rules.

A dog barked in the distance and brought Sam up sharply. She flushed, hoping her thoughts didn't show on her face. She gazed at Josh's rigid back. A burning desire flamed inside her and an awareness and urgent need coiled in the pit of her stomach. Built up, she repeated silently. It was a raging inferno. This is agony. "What kind of religion is this anyway?" It's bad enough now. How will it be if I can't even touch his hand?

Afraid of causing more trouble, Sam sadly kept away from Josh. She settled to sleep several feet away from him, shivering more from the lack of comfort than the cold. Finally, she couldn't bear it any longer. Quietly, she rose and drifted out the door of the room, wandering near the campfire where people were still talking and arguing. She shrugged. Some things never change. Israelis argue all the time too. They must have perfected it after two thousand years.

Intuitively, Sam felt the clear blue eyes follow her as she paced around the summit's perimeter. She came face to face with Leah.

A bright grin lit the woman's face. "So you're *niddah.*"

Sam blushed. "How do you know?"

"I heard you asking for a pad, making another ridiculous mistake, yet again."

"Okay, so I got it wrong," Sam scowled. "Just don't get any ideas. I've seen you in action before," she said cryptically as she walked away from Leah. And she had. *"Yesh li vered,"* she had insisted when asking for help. Who cared if she had a rose? Finally, the idiot woman made it clear what she wanted and was handed a linen cloth. She couldn't go anywhere near her husband who might be interested in some comfort and Leah was acting exactly like her roommate in the future, Sam realized. Lindsay would have leaped at the prospect of a night with Josh as quickly as her predecessor. Here we go again, Sam thought. Although not the same person, they held the same characteristics.

As Sam wandered away, Leah chose her moment. With a furtive glance around, she slipped inside the visitor's quarters. Leah quickly followed her. Josh was thrashing about on a mat, screaming his head off. Leah stood speechless at the sight, Sam right behind, shocked at seeing the intensity of Josh's nightmare.

As another of Josh's scream rent the air, Sam bolted into action. "What do you want?" she screeched at Leah as she shoved past her. She knelt beside Josh. The nightmares. They were starting again. She put out a hand to touch him and stopped, glancing quickly up at Leah. Maybe Leah was the *niddah* patrol. She'd report to someone that Sam broke the laws and they'd be thrown out of Masada.

"What is it? A fit of some kind? Leah asked, wide-eyed with shock. The woman's gaze swiveled to the corner of the room. Glittering under a single moonbeam that shone through the small window was the chalice.

"What are refugees doing with an expensive object like this?" she asked pointedly. But Sam ignored her and thankfully concentrated on Josh.

What should she do? She couldn't touch him. Fumbling around she found a small stick and poked at Josh's chest with it. She felt like an idiot. "Joshua. Wake up. I'm here now. Everything is fine. You're safe. Avi is at peace."

Dark eyes flickered open. "You appear like an angel," he muttered. He went to touch Sam's face and stopped.

"I know you can't," she whispered. "We'll talk. You're safe now. We'll talk as much as you want. Whatever you feel in your heart."

Leah turned to leave and called out over her shoulder. "Joshua Ben Reuven, you are as odd as your peculiar wife. I thought maybe someone new like you would be fun to have around, bide my time with, but I have no need of an affair with a lunatic. There are plenty of men on Masada," she snorted.

Sam sighed at the retreating woman. Leah, like her modern day counterpart Lindsay at the dig, flitted like a butterfly from one casual fling to another. No matter what century. The woman was the same in each. Whether a Marrano in Spain or in the Venetian ghetto of the Middle Ages, some things, like habits, personalities and characteristics never change.

# Chapter Eighteen

"Do I really have to do this?" Sam protested.

Josh stared into her downcast eyes. Their color deepened to a stormy, dark green like the Mediterranean on a wintry day. His body reacted with an intense ache. He wanted so much to touch her, but knew he couldn't. It was forbidden. "I know this is hard for you but you know how observant everyone is here. You'll be an outcast if you don't obey the rules of family purity. You asked for something to use as a pad when the bleeding started. They know you're a *niddah*. Five days bleeding and seven more days. You can't put this off indefinitely, not if you want to be able to sleep with me. I know these practices seem odd to you but they're still being practiced in our time."

Sam's wide-eyed expression indicated her doubt. "I don't believe you."

Josh's soft laughter rumbled in his chest. He was dying to pull her to him, but being niddah, she was forbidden to touch him. "I can't tell you about my own parents. It isn't the sort of thing they discuss with children. My older sister, Liora, you met her at lunch, remember? She married a fairly observant man and I know for a fact she went to the mikveh before they were married and I think she still goes. No one will know about this except you, the mikveh lady and me. It's very private and personal."

With a heavy sigh, Sam listened calmly to his explanation. He was thankful that she knew he was right and wasn't arguing. Everyone grumbled and referred to her as a spoiled, Saducee princess just like they did on the dig in their own time. Nothing had changed, she was still tagged a spoiled girl, though he acknowledged, she had in fact changed.

"You know where the *mikveh* is. You have to comb your hair and cut your nails. The *mikveh* lady will make you take a long bath. If you want to pray, this would be the time to do it. The lady will ask how you've prepared and she might examine you."

Sam's head shot up. "Examine?" she choked out.

Josh nodded. "Nails have to be short, absolutely no trace of makeup."

"Makeup," she parroted. "That would be nice."

Josh shrugged, but not unsympathetically. "I know you've missed those things, Sam. You'll also need to have your hair combed thoroughly, with no knots," he advised. "You'll go into the *mikveh* and it will be like swimming in an indoor pool. I worked on an excavation a few years back where we uncovered a *mikveh* identical in size to the modern ones. They have to have at least forty *seah* of water. That means about two hundred gallons, because Jewish thought believes it takes a fetus forty days to become human, forty days to become a spiritual and physical entity. It represents the womb, really. It has to be natural water and you'll submerge yourself completely three times."

"Why do I have to do that? Why can't I swim a few laps?"

Josh laughed at her naïve question. "*Mikveh* has nothing to do with being dirty but has everything to do with the meaning of the act. The water symbolizes the Garden of Eden. Women have the unique ability to bring paradise back into their families through their wombs and the creation of their families. The *mikveh* lady will tell you if the immersion is kosher and I'll be waiting for you outside."

Sam walked to the entrance lost in thought over Josh's explanation. Knowing almost nothing about Judaism and Jewish practices made her think the custom had to do with being dirty; a sexist attitude of an ancient religion. But Josh's explanation modified her perception. As she crossed the entryway, Sam eyed the woman attendant warily. The attendant's dark lashes flew open.

Sam stared at her.

It was Dr. Navon. Or at least someone exactly like her. She had the same disapproving glance, the same look that said *I'm waiting for you to do something stupid.*

Sam peered carefully at the woman.

Okay, it wasn't the pottery expert, but it was definitely the same expression of disdain.

Sam straightened, determined to perform the rite correctly. She followed all the instructions Josh gave her.

"Now or never." Quickly she ducked under the water. She recited the blessing. "Blessed are You, Lord of the Universe who has sanctified us with Your commandments and commanded us concerning the immersion."

She immersed herself two more times, walked out and accepted the cloth from the attendant. Sam filled with satisfaction. The sullen woman actually smiled at her!

She rubbed her damp skin, turning it red as she thought over what she had performed. "It's something holy between the two of us," she mused aloud. "Between Josh and me." We're not just leaping into bed together she thought silently, well, we don't anyway. "It's supposed to be a union of two souls."

Filled with a joyous sense of realization and thrilled with her discovery, Sam ran outside to Josh who paced impatiently a short distance from the building.

A radiant, secretive smile lit her face, as if she knew something no one else did. Sam ran toward him, and covered his bearded face with kisses. No longer *niddah*, she was permitted to touch the man she ached for. He lifted her in his arms, pressing her damp head against his chest. Sam curled like a kitten in his arms, her fingers entwined in his dark hair. She whispered quietly into his ear, unable to keep from stroking his face.

Josh nodded with a broad smile.

Thrilled with the pleasure of being able to touch again, she laughingly urged him to their room.

"It's the middle of the day," he teased. "What do you want?"

She smiled slyly at him. "I know exactly what I want." Sam only hoped it was the same for Josh and from the look in his dark, eyes, glittering with shameless intent, he did. "At least we've plenty of privacy," she purred, caressing his stubbled jaw with the back of her hand.

"Mmmm," he admitted, moving closer.

Across the quadrant, she spied Yigal retreating around a corner. She drew back slightly. "Why doesn't Yigal want to know us any more?" she asked.

"He's taken up with the *Essenes*, impressing them with his learning and abilities as a scribe."

"I suppose," Sam agreed. "But, well, I don't see why he can't be more talkative."

"I think Yigal enjoys the solitary life and has distanced himself. He said his task was complete, though I suspect he's keeping an eye on us, making sure we solve the puzzle." Josh explained. "But why are we talking about him. There's something else on my mind."

"And mine too," Sam admitted, heat burning her cheeks.

As Josh pulled her to him roughly, unable to mask the magnetism he felt, Sam saw desire burn in the depths of his dark eyes. A shiver rippled through her body as she pressed herself against him. Wrapped in Josh's arms, he led her to their room, ignoring the indulgent eyes that followed them. She supposed all the married couples understood how they felt.

The moment Josh touched her, Sam's pulse erupted and her heart thudded in her chest "They weren't kidding about desire building," she grinned. Heat curled in the pit of her loins, spreading down every fiber of her being as Josh's touch wrought an intense and delicious pleasure. Like a volcano ready to erupt, she squirmed under his ministrations.

His large hands cupped her face and he pulled her snugly against him, kissing her repeatedly. It was her undoing and she melted with an urgent need and hunger she could no longer contain. She went willingly, glorying in the pleasure as Josh's fingers trailed a fiery path down her cheek, and the curve of her neck, followed by soft, shivery kisses. Sam's nipples hardened under the weight of his body.

He drew back and gazed down at her.

She was in a daze. She'd been kissed before. Josh had done it. That was how they got in this mess to begin with. An idea crept across her brain.

"Kiss me again," she ordered him, the tip of her tongue playfully wiping over her already moistened lips.

He obeyed.

Sam blinked. "Nothing's changed," she said and couldn't hold back her disappointment. They were still in the first century. "Well, it was worth trying," she shrugged.

Josh frowned, but said nothing. Instead he lowered his lips to hers, covering them, teasing them apart. Sam let out a low moan of pleasure. It didn't matter where they were, she sighed. For now, there were other delights to explore. Josh continued his determined teasing, his roughened hands cupping her breasts, rubbing the calloused pad of each thumb across her nipples. Her breasts swelled under his sensual assault and her body shook as he trailed a sensual string of butterfly kisses down her neck and shoulders.

This was nothing like Remus or that idiot Rob. Both grabbers. Josh's touch was like a silken web spinning around them, stirring the embers of an internal fire that Sam didn't realize she owned.

"Josh. Josh, don't stop."

He didn't disappoint her, but pulled his tunic over his head and threw it on the ground.

Sam grinned. She eyed the dark wiry hair of his bare chest, the taut muscles and washboard abdomen. This is what she wanted, she purred.

Her fingers danced over his chest, stroking his skin, feeling the roughened texture of skin and the wiry dark hair. Her emotions whirled like a crazy merry go round, but when he turned, one glimpse of his scarred back nearly broke her heart. She squeezed her eyes shut, trying to blot out the ugly, thick scars that crossed his back—a permanent reminder of his efforts to free Avi. Bending forward, Sam pressed soft kisses down his spine, terrified of hurting him, but thrilled when she heard his groaning response. It wasn't pain, but a groan full of intense need and desire.

"Princess, do you have any idea what you're doing to me?"

"I think so," she whispered, feeling his hands caress her thighs. Funny, how it felt so divine when Josh did this. Shyly, she removed her tunic dress, her Roman underwear had disappeared in tatters days before. She quivered as his fingertips explored her hardened nipples, teasing her with a delicious, sensuous torture and when Josh eased her down on the mat, her open arms begged him to end the torment.

"Not yet. I've waited too long to end it so quickly," he whispered. Lips, parched and cracked from the desert sun, traced over her breast.

Sam arched closer to his mouth, her fingers pulling his head down lower. "Josh, there's something you should know," she began.

"I know, Princess. I can't hold back either. Next time, not now. I can't stand this." His hard body crushed against hers, fingers tickling her smooth thighs.

Sam gasped from the sweet agony Joshua Ben-Sion let loose from deep inside her as his fingers delved into her moist center. She felt him stiffen and he withdrew, gazing down at her.

"Samantha?"

This could only be trouble. He never called her Samantha. Heart sinking in despair, Sam wanted to die of humiliation. "You don't want a virgin," she blurted out. "I should have known." She shoved hard at him, pushing him away.

Heat scorched her cheeks and tears blurred her vision. She was a failure at everything, no good on the dig, no good at pottery, and no good even at the beach. The only thing she could do was get in trouble and commit murder. What a resume.

"You would have let that animal touch you?" Josh's growled, turning from her.

Not knowing what else to do, Sam bent over his back, her long hair tumbling over his shoulder down his chest. "I would have done anything to free you. I remembered what you said about sacrifice. I would have sacrificed myself for that. You're worth it. You were always worth more than me. You're right to call me princess, a spoiled silly brat. I don't blame you for not wanting me." Unable to control her pent up emotions, she burst into tears.

Josh turned to face her, pulling her into his embrace. "I want you the way I never wanted anyone. You have more strength, more courage, more anything than anyone I've ever met. I feel humbled and unworthy of you. Sam, you're like a perfect rose. You've blossomed, finding strength and courage, a true spirit. Think of what you have done and achieved since we've been here. You're so much more than I realized, passionate, strong, and loyal. I'm so proud of you Sam, so proud you want me."

Sam's response was a moan of relief. She pulled him down again on top of her feeling his hardness against her thighs.

"I can't promise you this won't hurt," he whispered, "but I can promise I love you. I was stupid and stubborn not to admit it to myself sooner. I can live without Avi, but I can't live without you." The minute Josh uttered the words Sam saw a sense of peace flood his face. "The nightmares return only when you're not at my side. Not your physical being but your soul. The very essence of you is what makes me well and whole." Josh buried his face in the tangle of her hair. "I do love you, Pinkie. If I had a medal, I would decorate you for valor in the field. Since

I don't, well, we have to improvise." Gently, his knee nudged her thighs apart.

Sam felt the heat from his body as Josh struggled to maintain a semblance of control. A soft moan escaped her lips. "Now, Josh, please. I can't stand the anticipation."

His hardness entered her slowly; desperate to hold back from hurting her, but her passion was beyond control as she pulled him tighter against her body. She felt him enter her, gritting her teeth to keep from crying out, shuddering from his act of possession. A quick thrust, a gasp and it was done.

Josh remained still and Sam blanketed the discomfort, until suddenly, everything changed and her entire body exploded in tiny undulating shivers of pleasure. As the sensation abated, Sam stared in awe at Josh. "Now you own me," she whispered, stroking his cheek with one finger.

"Heart and soul. It's like I told you, our souls are joined, not just our bodies."

Sam savored his words and turned on her side. She cuddled into the curve of his body. In the now dimly lit room, her gaze traveled around their small quarters. In the corner the chalice glittered, almost forgotten, but not completely.

Sam's lips curved upwards and she let out a deep sigh of contentment, pulling Josh's hands up to cup her breasts. His soft, whispering snore fanned her cheek.

# Chapter Nineteen

Sam awoke with a sense of unease again. This was the second morning in succession she had experienced a deep-rooted feeling of something about to happen. Turning to the empty space beside her, she rolled over and breathed deeply. Her senses filled with Josh's male scent lingering on the fabric.

As she lay on the mat, she tried to fathom the reason for her unease. It wasn't fear or worry for Josh who had left two days ago with a scouting party to see where the Roman patrols were lurking. She knew Josh was able to look after himself. Joshua Ben-Sion was doing what he was trained to do, serve as a soldier, protecting others. Her inexplicable anxiety wasn't actually even an unpleasant feeling, rather a sense of expectation.

Standing up, she went to look out the window. Brilliant rays of sun danced over the craggy mountain edges turning them rose, lavender and amber. Sam let out a wistful sigh. Oh, for a camera. What a book I could produce here. Twenty-four hours in the desert. The soft sweet smell of the early morning dew that settled over the camp. She inhaled deeply and smiled as she recognized the smell of the thin thread of smoke from a fire. Work, action, protection and reaction were a daily challenge for these people. She had formed a great admiration for them, despite their sometimes blatant disdain at her lack of culinary expertise. But she was learning. She was trying.

Looking around the room, Sam caught sight of the chalice. This was the key to returning home. They both knew that. Trouble was, they hadn't really figured out the solution to the riddle.

Picking it up, she carried it back to her mat. She cradled the object as tenderly as she would an infant.

"We don't want you breaking now, do we," she spoke aloud in the empty room. Her fingers caressed the chalice. It was rather a beautiful peace of workmanship. Bringing her knees up to her chest, Sam pulled the bedding up around her arms. The increasing autumn chill in the morning air made her shiver. So much time had slipped past. What would her hysterical father think? Geoffrey Pinkman would have detectives combing the entire country. He would demand a meeting with the Prime Minister. Sam sighed at the terrible trouble her father would cause blaming everyone for his missing daughter.

She could imagine it all now.

"I want the chief of police, the Minister of Defense and everyone else to drop everything and find my daughter! I'm a major donor to the United Israel Appeal." Sam could vividly picture her father pounding his fist on the desk of some cringing clerk, a veritable hurricane weaving a path of destruction in his wake.

Tracing the roughened engraving on the chalice with the tip of her index finger, Sam recited the inscription to herself. Although unable to read any Hebrew, and not very good at speaking it, she had learned the words by heart. It had almost become a talisman she recited unconsciously to herself, wishing for some insight that would return them home.

"Today is tomorrow,
The future the past,
From far lands, they must see
In love, hate and war the two are entwined.
Holy of holy, city of gates
Towering fortress, soldier to pass
Take thy chalice, complete the circle
Break the chains that bind the heart, the head
For…eternal circle enflamed.
Past to future completes the journey."

Sam understood the part about holy of holies, and the bit about the future and past. Even the words referring to a fortress were obviously meant to be Masada. What she didn't understand were the words about breaking chains. Apart from when Josh and Avi were in the Roman prison, chains hadn't really been part of this adventure. She wished Josh was here. He was far more analytical than she, but neither of them had been able to piece it together in any way that made sense.

"If only I could figure this out," she muttered in frustration. Sam admitted she hadn't really applied herself to solving the puzzle in recent days. It had become almost secondary, no longer the most important part of their lives. "Because I'm happy and fulfilled," she said out loud, taken aback at her revelation.

Up until a few months ago, she wouldn't have dreamed of accepting such a simple existence. Her former life was so superficial. Josh had told her the Jewish belief that everyone has a unique purpose in life. Idly, she wondered what hers was supposed to be. A sigh escaped her lips as she snuggled down deeper among the folds of the bedding, once again wishing for the man known to all as her husband. Nothing in her life was as important as he was now.

Wide-eyed, she sat bolt upright, shivering from excitement rather than cold. "That's it. That's it." Sam laughed out loud, hysterical giggles gushing out. The power to return was always with them. It had been there all along. Like Dorothy and the Wizard of Oz, she had to discover it for herself on a journey of self-discovery. Forgetting the morning chill, she reached over and clutched the chalice, once again reciting the riddle out loud. Her thoughts whirled at a dizzy pace.

Yigal had already said they were here because of love and hate. Blushing, she admitted to herself the many times back at the dig she swore her hatred of Josh. What a change! Sam smiled to herself, remembering the hours of tender lovemaking in recent days. Hated Josh? She was incredulous at her own naïve stupidity. She adored him. Her mind reeled at the thought as she forced herself to concentrate again.

Holy cities and gates are all reality. They arrived in Jerusalem, entered gates and left by gates.

"In love, hate and war the two are entwined," she recited out loud. Josh Ben-Sion, man of war. Josh hated himself for his failure to save Avi. Sam believed that Josh had at long last forgiven himself, and thankfully the nightmares had finally gone.

So why aren't we able to go home still?

"Two. Two are entwined. Break the chains that bind. How stupid, how stupid could I be?" A lightning flash seemed to rumble across her mind. She giggled remembering ridiculous cartoons where a light bulb would appear over a character that shouted, 'I've got it!' It was staring them both in the face the whole time. All these weeks it was there, but they didn't open their hearts, only their minds and didn't see it.

Love and hate. Hate and love. It was a full circle.

Scurrying around their room, Sam threw on her tunic, not caring how she looked. She needed to get to Josh. Home, home, home! She danced a crazy jig as she left the tiny chamber. The day was already beginning and Josh was nearly home. She had all the answers.

"You've finally flipped." Leah sneered.

Sam came to a halt. "Are you spying on me?" she challenged.

But the woman merely smiled, a secretive sort of smile. It sent a warning shiver up and down Sam's spine.

"Leah, get out of my way."

"You beat me once. But not a second time," Leah warned. "Be wary, redhead. I will have revenge. You thwarted me once, taking what I wanted."

Blustering, Sam shoved past the woman. "Not now, I don't have time for your theatrics," she warned. But inside, Sam was a bundle of nerves. Leah was a woman out for the main chance. Always on the lookout for something or someone that would make her life easier. Sam only hoped it wasn't at her and Josh's expense. The woman had tried to seduce Josh and failed. Surely, she wouldn't try a second time.

Revenge came quickly.

"Think you're smart, don't you," the would-be seductress sneered, blocking Sam's path.

Having no choice, Sam came to a halt.

Leah carried on. "I could have had him, or any man, anytime." She snapped her fingers in the air, a disdainful expression flawing her usually pleasant features.

The scornful boasting voice grated on Sam's already worn nerves. About to tell Leah to move out of her way, that she didn't have time for dramatics nor the inclination to give the annoying harlot the time of day, her heart lurched when she spied a familiar sackcloth tucked under Leah's arm. "Where did you get that?"

"Out of my way." A flicker of fear marred the young woman's face. She had realized her mistake, but it was too late. She tried to hide the sack behind her back.

Sam wasn't having any of that. The chalice was too sacred to her and Josh. It was their escape route, their only route home.

By now a small crowd had gathered around them, interest flared by a possible fight between the heroine, killer of the Roman and Leah. No one actually liked Leah. She had a reputation as a free and easy sort of woman, frowned upon by most of the community. A troublemaker if ever there was one.

Sam stepped forward with a boldness she didn't feel and blocked Leah's path. "I asked you, where you got that sack." Deadly menace glared in her eyes like a storm about to break. "You've been in our room, haven't you? You're nothing but a low down thief." Crimson with rage, she made a grab for the sack.

"Who do you think you are? Princess somebody." The shrill voice dripped with sarcasm. "I'll tell you. You're no one. Princess No-one. Why, I bet you didn't kill any Roman."

Leah hoped to intimidate her in front of the crowd. An old timer on Masada, Leah held the advantage over her. Sam was merely a newcomer. She also realized the woman disliked her because of her failure to entice Josh. She was a woman scorned.

Leah's brutal reminder of the horrible few hours in Remus's power cracked Sam's fragile façade of control and her temper snapped like an elastic band stretched to its limit. "How dare you. You know nothing. You have no idea what I went through. At least I don't flaunt myself like a harlot. You throw yourself at any man. You're no better than a whore!" Sam remembered the word *zona* from the woman who spat at her when they first arrived in the past. She spluttered with the same rage that the old woman used on her, calculated to infuriate the other woman. She couldn't let Leah leave with the chalice.

Leah yanked her roughly by the shoulder, fingernails digging deeply into Sam's shoulder. Sam retaliated, throwing off Leah's grip.

A deep intake of breath from those around alerted Leah to their audience and she glanced over her shoulder at the onlookers. Anger took hold of her. "You are a newcomer. You can't humiliate me in front of my own people." With a wild cry, Leah sprang at Sam, hands reaching for her throat, grabbing at her with full force.

Sam retreated, but not in time. Leah's reflexes were quick. Her hands and nails clawed Sam like a wildcat. She had no option left. She had to fight off the woman, or risk injury. Within seconds the two were rolling across the ground, dust flying in their midst. Enthralled, the onlookers came closer and closer, shouting encouragement, but no one dared break up the catfight.

Swinging her fist at Leah, Sam landed a punch on the woman's shoulder, stunning her momentarily. Wild thoughts reeled through her head as she eyed her adversary. Watching all those episodes of The Avengers was coming in handy.

*Emma Peel, eat your heart out.*

Her fist stung from the punch, but Sam used her advantage to crawl away. Too late. Leah snatched her ankles, hauling her backwards, Sam's nails dug into the raw dirt. Sharp jagged rocks scratched at her skin, the tiny lacerations bleeding. Leah snatched several stones, ready to rain them down on her head. She prepared to throw.

Desperate to protect herself from the coming assault, Sam raised her arms over her head.

"Stop. Stop now." An old woman scurried forward. It was the old lady from the *mikveh*. Her word was law.

Leah stopped in her tracks, an arm held high holding a stone ready for her offensive.

"Leah, how dare you attack one of our kind. What wrong has Sara done to you?" The old woman pointed to Sam curled in a fetal position to protect herself.

Leah refused to reply. She frowned sullenly. Sam knew the vindictive woman had no reasonable answer.

Beaten, Leah stomped off, skirts swinging behind her. She stopped and turned. "You might have won this round, Princess Sara, she muttered scornfully. "Watch your back." The threat hung in the air like electricity before a thunderstorm.

Sam slowly lifted herself off the ground, the old woman helping, uttering kind words in her ear. Sam would never have believed she would have won this woman's sympathy based on their few dealings. She generally avoided *Shulamit* like the plague, certain she was bound to do something wrong and irritate her. She gave the woman a tentative smile.

Surprisingly, it was returned. "Don't you take any notice of Leah. She's a troublemaker."

Perhaps she was winning a few friends after all, Sam mused. However, as she watched Leah flounce off leaving her stolen booty lying on the ground, Sam realized that Leah would never be a friend.

Rubbing an already swelling bruise on her arm, Sam picked up the chalice, hugging it to her chest. She breathed a sigh of relief that no damage had been done. Their path home was still safe. Thankful for the older woman's help, Sam made her way towards her quarters, aware of the smiling and nodding faces of the women in her midst as she went. One woman even went as far as to come up to her and give her a hug.

Things were looking up.

# Chapter Twenty

Josh and the other men crawled and walked through the desert for two days, child's play to the trained soldier who was accustomed to long, forced marches, advanced guerilla techniques and accepting hardships as normal. Several times they came across Roman patrols, able to listen to their talk. It was like a game of cat and mouse. Each looking for the other, playing hide and seek. It was not very different to his days in the army.

"Too bad your wife isn't here," commented one of the men. "She would understand their talk far better than we."

Josh shuddered at the thought of Sam on a forced patrol like this. Imagine the trouble Pinkie could get into on patrol. Either she'd injure herself or someone else. She might even be unable to control herself and start insulting Romans again. No, it definitely wasn't a good idea to take Pinkie. But, the thought of her made him groan with an aching need.

"Something wrong?"

Red-faced, Josh turned away from the men to hide his embarrassment. He hated being without Sam. It was more than physical longing; he craved her being, the essence of her as a woman.

The group trudged homeward, walking most of the night. Cooler and safer, they were guided by the light of the moon and stars that shone so brightly in this clean, dry and hauntingly beautiful land. They climbed the miles wearily up the summit and passed through the fortress gates.

Sam came rushing forward, her face alight with joy. Long red hair flew out behind her. Josh broke into a broad smile at the sight. He held his arms open to welcome her. The love he felt for her swelled deep within him,

Two nights away had convinced him. A reflective sort of man, he'd finally recognized that he couldn't survive without the woman he had called Princess Pinkie in loathing. He had far nicer names for her now. Angel. Sweetheart. He wanted and needed her in his life. Forever.

Sam leaped at him nearly sending them both sprawling to the ground. "Oh, Josh, Josh. I've got it. I've got it. It's solved." Sam's face was radiant. Her red curls tumbled all around her. In her haste to share her news with him, she forgot and slipped into English.

"How could you forget?" Josh gritted his teeth, annoyed at her carelessness.

Sam froze and her smile evaporated. She slammed a hand over her mouth, but there was a raw hurt in her eyes he couldn't bare to see. Josh pulled her into his arms, kissing her with an intensity that shocked even him. It didn't take long for the kiss to change. No longer was he kissing to silence her in front of the staring crowd. His need of her took over.

"Josh, we have to talk." Sam's breathless voice interrupted the embrace. She tugged at his sleeve pulling him towards their quarters. All around them, his fellow patrolmen guffawed as his wife dragged him toward their quarters. The men and woman all knew that "services" were required, immediately. Several furtive glances between other couples hinted at similar intentions as the party broke up.

Soundly shutting the door behind them, Sam turned to him.

He pulled her into his arms again. "That was quite a welcome, beloved. If that was the entrée, I'm more than ready for the second course."

"My news can wait."

Josh quirked a dark eyebrow suggestively, making Sam's body tingle. She breathed in the scent of him, still sweaty from the two days of grueling patrol. She licked at his dry, cracked lips, filled with wonder that she could find this so incredibly sensuous. Irresistible. The man was irresistible no matter how he looked, smelled or tasted. Her passion rose as Josh rained kisses over her face and neck. Both tunics dropped to the floor, their haste to be together all-important, to touch and hold the other.

Sam's heart swelled with love for this man.

Snuggling in the crook of his embrace, warmed by the heat of their exhausted bodies, she felt contented. This was all that mattered to her. This man and being with him. Nothing else.

"So sweetheart, what were you going to tell me?" Josh nuzzled in her ear.

The deep growling voice thrilled Sam. She would never get enough of him. "Good grief. I completely forgot. Josh Ben-Sion, you make me a witless, drooling idiot. I lose any sense of composure around you." Her laughter tinkled like music as she nudged him playfully in the ribs.

"Glad to oblige," he retorted. "Go on then."

Sam took a deep breath. She knew she loved Josh with all her heart. Did he love her? Deeply and truly. This would determine their journey's end. "We were wrong all along. We took the words on the inscription too literally."

Sam rapidly explained how some of the words could be taken literally and others figuratively. It was all a matter of which way they were interpreted. It's the difference between deep and superficial."

She bit her lip and cast her eyes down. This was it, now or never. "Love, hate, war, two entwined. Josh, we are those two. The two are also love and hate. You loved Avi with all your being, hating yourself when you couldn't save him in the future. You wouldn't forgive yourself, or others," she added, remembering Rachel's word by the fireside. "You had to come to the past, to be able to break your chains. Figurative chains. The chains binding you to hate needed to be broken. That was your second chance to save Avi. Once you had that chance, accepted that it couldn't always be the way you wanted, that fate and destiny are continual, you could break the chains that bound you to hate and accept love. You became free of the hate, Josh."

Was she making any sense? Josh hadn't said a word. Seconds, then minutes past. It seemed like an eternity. He lay quiet beside her, his hand idly rubbing a hardened nipple. She waited for a reply, terrified of the answer, frightened that he didn't love her the way she loved him.

"Sam," Josh spoke quietly, his voice a hushed whisper.

She held her breath.

"For two days and nights I walked with the other men, watching, waiting, seeing what the Roman garrison planned. The days were fine. We were busy, trying to stay one step ahead of the Romans. Not unlike my military days. The difference was at night. Nights without you. I knew deep inside me both nights that I was incomplete. The one person I couldn't do without because she makes me whole was waiting for me on a mountain fortress with a group of people who are going to mass suicide in four years time. Without you I would still be persecuting myself, hate being alive every hour of every day."

He took a deep breath. "I've never spoken like this before. Never let my heart rule my head."

She gave him a reassuring smile, knowing how hard it was for him. He was a soldier, used to bottling his emotions and getting on with the job at hand.

He continued. "Pinkie," he smiled down at her. Sam said nothing. The name that had been a thorn in her side was now a term of endearment during their lovemaking.

"The hate inside me is gone. Vanished. This journey gave me a second chance to live. Not as half a man, but fully and it's all because of you, Pinkie. Samantha Anne Pinkman, *Sara Bat Chaim*, I love you." He let out his breath in a loud whoosh.

Sam was sure she would burst, she was so happy. He loved her. He had said it. Hallelujah. Happy ending here we come. "Oh, Josh. I knew it. I knew it."

"What. That I loved you? Women always have to have the last word. Ask my mother when we get back, she's an authority on the subject." Josh laughed along with her.

Sam was jubilant. Now they could go home. She stopped short. She'd been saying it for so long she believed it. Now, she wasn't so sure. She'd fallen in love with Josh and their simple life here. If they went back, would it revert to their former emotions? Would Josh revert to hating everyone, including her?

She couldn't stand that. Would she be the same spoiled woman, feeling sorry for herself, under her father's protective cocoon without the inner peace she had found on this craggy mountaintop? She winced, acknowledging that she would rather remain at Masada, knowing what the future would hold for all these people, herself included, if it meant she could love Josh and have that love returned.

She studied Josh's expression. He was a strong man, reliable. Sam cast off her doubts. Whatever obstacles came their way, no matter what century, the important thing was to be together. He loved her, and her love for him was equally strong.

His hand still on her abdomen, he broke into her happy thoughts, calmly asking. "So, we know how my side of the bargain works out. What about you, Pinkie?"

There was a flicker of anxiety in his dark eyes. "I'm content here, Josh, whether we stay or go back to the future. Honestly, I really don't mind any more. All I really want is to be with you. Nothing else matters. Not designer clothes, not Paris. Nothing. Only you."

Surprise registered on Josh's face. Sam chuckled at the sigh. "Yes, I know. I wouldn't have believed it myself. At least, not a few months ago. I was pretty bad wasn't I?"

"To be truthful, in a word, yes." Josh jokingly agreed.

"Oh, you." She took Josh's agreement at her bad behavior in good grace. It was true. She had been a spoiled brat. Princess Pinkie was a fitting name for the Sam Pinkman of the past.

"The riddle talks about chains that bind. This morning I realized, my chains were the chains of my life, the way I was brought up. I never wanted for anything. Whatever I wanted, my father got me. Any problem, he was there to sort it out. He was the cavalry, always charging in and fixing things. He never let me try to solve my own problems, come up with my own solutions. Sounds dreadful doesn't it, especially when I see how people here have lived, never complaining, yet continually under threat. Even in modern day Israel, it's the same. The sacrifices people make for each other. I feel so ashamed. My journey to Israel, both in the future and here in the past has been the ultimate lesson in life. For that, I will be eternally grateful. Not only has it given me a new perspective on life, it has given me you."

Sam hung her head, a tear trickling slowly down her cheek as she tried to hide her embarrassment. "It's all about sacrifices, isn't it?" she said lifting her tear stained face to Josh. "What sacrifice did I make. Nothing," she groaned as another wave of raw, heart-wrenching sobs took hold of her.

Josh cuddled her closer.

She was grateful for his comfort, but she had to purge herself, the same as he had. Until she came to grips with her past, her future, her chains, they were bound in the past, never able to go back, whether they wanted to or not. She carried on. "I realize I don't need that stuff. I don't need things to make me happy. I can make my own happiness. Well, that's not quite true," she qualified. "I can make myself happy, as long as I have you. I need you, Josh and I'm not afraid or ashamed to say it."

The relief was enormous. Finally, she'd managed to say what was in her heart and her head.

"Josh, the two nights when you were away taught me one thing.

Joshua Ben-Sion, Ben Reuven, I love you, I want you and need you forever, wherever and whatever century."

Filled with happiness, she fell into Josh's arms, relieved they had finally come to terms with their demons, purged themselves and found a new life and love, within themselves and of each other. But most of all, they had done it together. They had found love together.

Emerging from their quarters, with Josh at her side, Sam ran the gauntlet of sly looks from both women and men. Snickering laughter surrounded them. She tried to ignore the tight, little smiles and hushed voices as she and Josh walked across the courtyard. It hurt to know that people disliked her, distrusted, her, but inside, where it really mattered, she knew Josh loved her and that she, without doubt, loved him. Knowledge that you are loved was a powerful drug. Holding her head high, shoulders back, her hand firmly wrapped in the warmth of Josh's strong grip, she was comforted by the fact that the prophecy of the chalice had been fulfilled. They had decided to try to return to the future, yet neither felt in any hurry to do so,

Evening came. The air cooled and all around them, pockets of firelight lit the air, as members of this mountaintop home prepared for their evening meal. Every now and then a few sparks would erupt, fleeing skyward. Sam stared up at the fireflies dancing into the midnight sky.

Sitting on the edge of a carved wooden stool, her fingers twining themselves through her hair, Sam's thoughts returned to Rachel when she served as her hairdresser before they faced the enemies at the garrison. She felt the prick of tears, and roughly wiped a bunched hand across her cheek. Where was Rachel? What time or place was she? She hoped that Rachel was safe. Perhaps the young girl was with Avi in another time, together safe in each other's arms, enjoying the same love she shared with their friend. The thought brightened Sam's melancholy. Leaving her small room, she went to find Josh. He stood outside, leaning against the clay colored wall of one of the small out buildings, arms folded across his chest, his smile broad, laughing. He looked very happy, and it sent a rapture of joyous contentment through Sam. Seeing her, he bade the men goodbye and joined her. The two of them walked towards Yigal.

But it was as before. Yigal was keeping his distance and as they approached him, he held out his hand to stop them. "I know already. You found love. Both of you. Hate, fear and chains that bind are gone. You have fulfilled your destinies," he said in a rush. His old face beamed at them, deep wrinkles like crevices in the wilderness below them lined his face and his silvery-gray eyes smiled his joy at their success. "I suppose you are going back now."

"To be honest, Yigal, both Sam and I are content. We could stay here forever. Knowing that she loves me and I love her is enough, but we can't choose to be selfish."

"For the first part," Sam interrupted, "there is Josh's family. They would be devastated if he didn't ever return, and as much as my father can bluster, he is, well, my dad," Sam smiled.

"We have had the privilege to live in the first century and have gained so much knowledge to share with others."

"Dr. Navon," Sam interrupted, her brows wiggling.

"We choose to return, although we leave a part of ourselves here. The hole in the chalice is missing, so we hope our idea works."

A bony finger pointed at Josh's chest. Like the other Essenes, Yigal was careful never to touch, especially women. "The hole may be missing, young man, but you know the word. You filled that hole in your lives. You both have found that word within yourselves."

Sam looked at Josh, then back at Yigal.

"You knew all the time. You knew the missing word."

"Yes, I did. It would have been no use telling you. This journey through time, through life, was your destiny, a journey you had to make to discover your destiny. Would you prefer to be the people you were before? For me to tell you how to return to the future straight away would have been pointless. You had to find out for yourselves what was important and what was not. Now you know, go. Go in peace."

Sam rushed up to Yigal wanting to throw her arms around the old man. She caught herself as she saw the look of horror creep across the wizened countenance. "I'm sorry, I know you have joined the *Essenes* for our protection," she gave him a rueful smile. "Thank you Jan," she said, reverting to his future name. "I'll love him and will look after him and I know he will look after me."

Yigal nodded. "I do believe you will," he said smiling. "There's a determination and gleam in your emerald eyes young lady that I haven't seen before."

"Like glittering jewels in the moonlight," Josh said.

Sam's jaw dropped. "How poetic."

He shrugged and gave her a saucy wink, turning back to Yigal and shook the old man's hand.

Together, she and Josh slowly walked around the palace, the storehouses full of food, and the soaring walls.

"How I'll miss this place."

Immersed in thought, Josh merely nodded.

"Most of all, though, I'll miss all the remarkable people here, unknowing that their bravery will echo down the centuries."

"High praise, Sam." Josh ventured.

"I suppose, but well, like Yigal said, it's a journey in so many paths, not solely the path back to our own time, but personal, internal and external at the same time, all entwined with each other. I mean, even the old lady at the *mikveh*, who is so like Navon in the future, warmed to me, guided me. I'll miss *Shulamit*."

Quietly she and Josh turned and went to their room, shutting the door soundly behind them. Sam's eyes widened in the darkened room. She stooped and threw their meager possessions frantically around the chamber.

"It's gone. The chalice is gone."

Cups, plates, a small cosmetic box donated by *Shulamit* along with their sleeping mat was ransacked. But the one thing they prized above all was gone and she knew who took it, too.

Leah.

Sam squeezed her eyes shut, blinking back the tears. Now was not the time. It could be anywhere now, even destroyed. Would Leah have destroyed it? The thought horrified her. The chalice was the one thing she treasured, despite her love for Josh, or was that because of it.

Desolated, she collapsed against Josh. Huge crystal tears gushed down her cheeks and her body heaved in sobs. Even his embrace and soothing words couldn't stop her hysteria.

'This is ridiculous. We said we were content here."

"Yes, but—"

"But what? It isn't here, we stay here."

He made it all sound so simple. "Josh, having the chalice here gave us choice. Like a woman who wants to have a baby, when she struggles with infertility, that choice is often taken away from her. The chalice is gone, our choice is halved. Besides, didn't we decide that our families need us too?"

A sharp knock sounded on the door. One of the men from Josh's patrol entered. Stern faced, it could only spell trouble.

"Come with me. Both of you." He yanked Sam to her feet.

Josh shot to his feet. "Keep your hands off my wife." he bit out. "What has happened to change you so quickly? We shared the camaraderie all soldiers share the past few days, now you glare daggers at us."

But the man remained mute.

With Josh's comforting grasp firmly around her waist, Sam followed the man into the palace. The same group of leaders that greeted them the first day, stood facing them, arms folded over their chests, glaring coldly. A cold chill went up and down Sam's spine. They were in deep trouble. She felt Josh's hand tighten on her waist. He felt it too.

The leader held the chalice in front of them. It glittered in all its glory. "Stolen property," he accused, tone sharp and strong, brooking no nonsense. "You stole this and brought it to Masada and kept it hidden. Everything is shared here; you knew it when you came."

Sam and Josh nodded in unison.

"Did you steal from wealthy Jews and think to bribe the Romans?"

Sam gasped. "You'd think that of us?"

"Did you ever kill anyone, or was that made up, too?" Hard eyes narrowed on her. Instinctively, Sam wanted to shrink from the accusing gazes that surrounded them. She took a sideways glance at Josh, and her mind was made up. She wouldn't cower. Not now. They'd come too far. Well, that didn't mean she couldn't squeeze up a tad closer to Josh. She did and he wrapped an arm around her, pressing her against his hard body.

The men in front were angry. The scribe ever-hunched over his table scribbling on the parchment as if this were some sort of trial.

"That's Eliezer Ben Yair," Josh whispered in her ear. "He is a remarkable man and will exhort 960 men, women and children to die at their own hands."

Sam watched the leader and could see in him a sense of strength of purpose.

"Their deaths," Josh continued, "is a symbol of courage. Rather than be taken as slaves they will prefer death as free people, than the chains of slavery. They will maintain to the end their belief in the Almighty."

She believed every word Josh said. The leader was like a rock, impenetrable.

"This is the key. The belief that has kept Jews alive for thousands of years while every other culture died out. Greeks, Romans, gone, but the Jews persisted," he informed her. "Things are happening way too fast here Sam. We need to come up with a feasible explanation." For a moment he was silent, then with a loud gasp, he smacked a hand against his forehead. "Stupid. Think in the first century, not the twenty-first."

"So how can modern technology help us?"

"I have an idea," he nodded toward the chalice. "Follow my lead, Sam. Will you let me do the talking?"

Sam nodded. "If you know a way to get the chalice back in our hands, I'm all for it."

Josh turned to Eliezer Ben Yair and called on his military officer training to hold him in good stead. "The chalice was not stolen," Josh's voice boomed. Everyone stopped speaking and turned to face him, interest obviously piqued. He continued. "The tale we told was true. My uncle can confirm that." His head inclined slightly to Yigal standing in a corner, whose worried eyes watched the unfolding scene. "We should have known Leah would make trouble. Jealous of you in the future, the same thing happened again," Josh whispered to her. "Leah stole the chalice and brought it straight to you with the story of theft."

Sam's heartbeat raced. What next?

Josh took her hand. His palm was sweaty. She gripped it. There was no way on this earth, no matter what the year, she would let go of it.

"Hold on tight, whatever happens. I want you to hook your other hand through my belt and keep it there," he whispered.

Sam's fingers twisted in the leather, tightening the grip. She held on fast.

"The chalice isn't stolen, but we need to go into the moonlight for you to see why we brought it here and why we kept it a secret," Josh announced. His words were firm and authoritative. The party moved out, a circle of men surrounding her and Josh. The group looked exceedingly doubtful.

Sam looked up at the sky. It was a blanket of stars, the air clear, clean. The moon-*Rosh chodesh*, heralded the start of another Jewish month. *Tammuz*. In another year, the Temple would burn and Jerusalem would fall during this dreadful time.

Leah, acting in her usual manner, sidled up to one of the men, a sly look on her face. A large circle of Zealots surrounded them as if to prevent their escape.

"Ready?" Josh questioned.

Sam nodded

He extended his hand for the chalice.

Reluctantly, Ben-Yair handed it to him, but kept his eyes focused on the motions.

"Sam? "I love you, for all eternity." Josh held her tightly.

"I know. I do too. I love you too."

Sam shook with fright. She shivered and Josh pulled her close. With Josh she could do anything. She couldn't help thinking of Dorothy in Oz again. She looked down at her faded leather sandals. No red shoes here. She placed her hand on the opposite handle of the chalice. Josh had the other. "We came here together, we read together," he insisted gently. They began to recite the words of the inscription.

"Today is tomorrow,
The future the past,
From far lands, they must see
In love, hate and war the two are entwined.
Holy of holy, city of gates
Towering fortress, soldier to pass
Take thy chalice, complete the circle
Break the chains that bind the heart, the head."

Staring at him, her heart burning with love and passion and the glory of their incredible journey, locked in unison, she continued.

"For love eternal circle enflamed.
Past to future completes the journey."

Josh bent forward to kiss her. At first Sam thought nothing had happened. Then it started. Just the same as in the crypt. Her pulse raced and the ground began to shake as a swirling mist rose up from around their feet, engulfing them. Flung against Josh, she felt his arm steady her. She held on tight, not wanting to go, not wanting to find out the truth.

Dazed, she blinked several times and wiped her eyes. Bare dirt walls surrounded them, a few rocks and stones still on the floor. "We're home. We're in the crypt, Josh. The future...it's returned," she screamed excitedly.

But amongst the mist on Masada, the people cringed as the pair disappeared from sight.

"What does it mean?" They ran to their leaders, begging for an explanation of what they saw. No one said a word, all eyes on their leader, waiting in silence, pleading for some explanation to the mystery they had witnessed.

Yigal stepped forward. "It means that the Lord is with us." He spoke calmly and convincingly. "Anyone can see that Sara and Joshua were different."

Heads nodded all around. He tried hard not to smile. "The Almighty sent his angels to us as a sign of his faith in us to behave according to the laws," he informed them

Angels.

A murmur went through the crowd. Of course. They could disappear. They must have been angered when they accused them of theft. Prayer was needed. The people beseeched the Lord to forgive them for their foolish conclusions and begged forgiveness as their scribe settled to record the remarkable event they had witnessed, something, he believed, some day, someone would read.

# Chapter Twenty-One

"Well, weren't you two the crafty ones?" Lindsay's voice echoed down through the opening of the crypt.

Sprawled on the ground, Sam's arms and legs were entwined tightly around Josh. Curious faces peered down on them. She looked at Josh. "Oh-oh. This will take some explaining. Tunics aren't quite kibbutz wear," she smiled trying to untangle herself.

"Pretty kinky, spending the night down there." Rob shouted down.

Sam winced. The man was thrilled to embarrass her in lieu of her rejection. She stumbled to her feet, pulling Josh with her and fumbled at the base of the ladder. "You don't understand."

Lindsay snickered. "Oh, yeah, right. I don't understand." Loud laughter echoed down from the entire volunteer crew.

Sam's face burned with embarrassment. "You really don't," she insisted. Her finger pointed to Lindsay and Rob. "We traveled through time. To Judea, two thousand years ago and you were there. And you."

The laughter increased. Jan's silver head appeared behind the younger faces.

"And you were there, too. How did you get back so fast?" Sam marveled at the speed of time travel. *He's more experienced than we are,* she reasoned. *Maybe he takes some kind of freeway while we take the back roads.*

"Wow, you must have given Sam some night," Lindsay joked. "She's half out of her head. Maybe she dehydrated again."

Sam gave the blonde a withering glare. "They don't believe me?" She turned to Josh, confused. She glanced down at the chalice, still clutched to her chest.

"Give me that before you break it, you foolish girl." Dr. Navon shoved her way past everyone and snatched it from Sam.

"What's my baby doing down in a hole in the ground?"

"Oh, no," Sam groaned. There was no mistaking a Pinkman bellow. This was just great. Things were bad enough. Everybody thought she was nutty and now her father turns up.

Geoffrey Pinkman's angry face appeared in the hole above her. "Baby, what are you doing down there and what the hell are you wearing? Get up here now."

Sam climbed up the ladder, Josh following. Dr. Navon brought up the rear with the precious chalice in her hands. At the last minute, the doctor stooped, picking up another clay object that caught her eye. As she turned it carefully, slithers of dirt and pottery fell away, exposing a worn parchment, ostensibly hidden inside.

Sam watched the woman whose face flushed scarlet with excitement, eyes like shiny beads as she turned the delicate parchment over and over "Out of my way, young man. There's no time. This, I believe," she beamed at Josh, "is an important find."

But, there was no escape for Sam. "What are you doing here?" her voice dripped with honey, hoping to waylay her father's interest. He had picked the worst time possible for a surprise visit.

"Who is that? He pointed toward an equally dirty Josh who stood at her side. "How dare you drag my baby down in that filthy hole all night?"

"Dad," she pleaded, but Josh interjected and spoke quietly at her side.

"Stop calling her a baby. She's no baby." Josh's dark eyes locked with hers and he gave her a small secret smile.

It was enough.

"So that's how it is? Shapira!" her father yelled at the top of his lungs.

The elderly professor came up and gave Geoffrey Pinkman a brief nod. "Well there she is and doesn't she look like she's getting right into the spirit of things. I told you sending her on a dig would be wonderful. She's dressed just like a first century Judean. You really should send that dress to the dry cleaners," he added to Sam. "Young Ben-Sion. The same thing." He turned to her father. "Now then, she's safe and sound. I told you he would take care of her and not to worry."

"Take care and not worry? What does he mean?" Sam felt her heart do flip-flops. She had a bad feeling in the pit of her stomach. Not back five minutes and trouble already.

"Joshua was supposed to mind you for the summer. You seem to have had a good time together," Shapira noted.

Sam turned to Josh, her face a mask of rage. "A babysitter. You were hired to be my babysitter. That's just great. And I believed all that stuff. I thought we'd gone past that, Josh. I believed you, every word." She laughed bitterly. "I thought I'd learned my lessons, not to fall for some unreliable man. Huh! Some lesson," she choked back.

"It was true, Sam. In the beginning it was my job; I was your minder. Make you happy, make your father happy, and make the university happy. Trouble was, it didn't make you or me happy."

"Then everything changed," Sam interrupted "I thought we had discovered a deep and abiding love that would last a lifetime, many lifetimes," she whispered. She glanced over at her father, who was still muttering under his breath. "Look at him, still protective." She turned back to Josh, her head high, shoulders back, but her heart ached so much she felt she'd crumble any second. She gritted her teeth, calling on all the reserves she could. "I've survived many things lately, Josh Ben-Sion, I can survive you. I don't need a babysitter. I needed an equal, a partner."

But Josh didn't move, didn't react.

"Okay, so I may have been useless at most things when I came, but I survived more than the dig. You know it, and I know it. We did it together. Don't try and deny it."

Josh cocked an eyebrow. "I wouldn't dare."

But things seemed to be spinning out of control. Her father pulled on her arm, pulling her toward a vehicle.

"It seems now we're back, it's all changed again, Josh."

Getting into the car, Sam averted her face. She didn't want Josh seeing her tears and she could hold them back no longer. Her father vented his displeasure at her side, but Sam ignored it. As the car began to move off, she turned back to stare at Josh momentarily. Dejected and forlorn, he stood like a lost little boy.

Sam could hold back no longer and her face crumbled in despair. Her lips parted as she was about to say something, but the car sped up and she lost sight of the only man she realized she had come to truly love.

Feeling helpless, she felt her heart break in two.

But if she thought that was bad, the next few days were the worst Sam ever spent in her life. Try as she might, she couldn't persuade her father to listen.

"I'm not a child, I'm grown. Independent."

"Yes, yes," her father muttered, but that was all she could get out of him.

Not hearing from Josh made it worse. It worried her sick and she hadn't been able to contact him either. Was it over? The question played like a continuous record in her brain. It frightened her far more than she cared to admit. Doubt was her undoing. She needed desperately to contact him, but it was as if he'd vanished.

She loved Josh with all her heart and she knew he loved her. However, based on her previous performance with men she could understand her father's frustration and without Josh by her side, where her father could see the kind of man he was, she didn't have a chance of explaining. Instead she was left to listen to his complaints.

"I might as well see something of Jerusalem while we're here," he grumbled

Playing the tourist guide, Sam trailed her father through the Old City. Instead of the crumbled Wailing Wall, her mind filled with visions of the splendor of the Temple in all its glory. She trudged over the ancient steps seeing the alley where Yigal dwelled with Rachel. The more she and her father saw, the more heartbroken she became. Listless and miserable, she ate only enough to keep going and dragged through each day. Had Joshua never loved her?

Finally, her father hit the limit. "Quit crying over some man," he growled Friday afternoon. "We're going to dinner with some old friends and I want you to get with it. Put on a nice dress and do your hair."

With a sigh, Sam rose to follow his orders. Deep longing for Josh seemed to have sapped all her energy and vitality. Where was the warrior princess from the past? Somehow she had to get back the strength she had at Masada. Today, however, it was easier to obey. She trudged into the bathroom to shower and change. Idly combing her curls, she wondered if she should pile it on her head the way Rachel did for her. She shrugged her shoulders. Who cared. Silently, she followed her father into the waiting taxi as the sun set over the city, bathing it in the incredible gold she loved to see so much. It brought a tear to her eye, but a warm glow to her heart. She had shared so much. At least she had memories, even if Josh didn't want to speak to her anymore.

As the taxi stopped in front of the Ben-Sion's house, Sam sat up with a start. She folded her arms over her chest and glared coldly at her father. "What are we doing here? I'm not getting out."

"Stubborn," her father sniffed. "A Pinkman through and through. Good luck to him. I hope he knows what he's getting."

Sam's mouth opened wide, but nothing came out.

Green eyes that mirrored her own twinkled down at her as her father led her through the gate and into the house. Sam gazed around in confusion. They were all there, the entire family—Chana, Reuven, the girls and their children and husbands. Even Professor Shapira. Little Keren's dark eyes danced with excitement.

And Josh.

He stepped forward hesitantly, taking her hand in his. "Princess, I was never your babysitter." His voice was firm and clear in the silent room. "I meant every word I ever said to you. I love you. I can't live without you. I can't eat. I can't sleep. I can't do anything without you. Samantha Anne Pinkman, Sara bat Chaim, would you please, please marry me and put me out of my misery?"

"Sounds just like Sam," her father mumbled. "She's miserable, too. Makes a rotten guide," he joked.

Everyone around her instinctively leaned forward. Sam noticed several sets of eyes misting in the romance of the moment. She caught her breath, but her heart beat an erratic and excited beat. She went hot and cold at the same time and goose bumps darted up and down her arms. She swallowed hard. "You meant every word?"

The dark head she loved so dearly nodded and Sam exhaled. She hadn't even realized she was holding her breath. She burst into tears as she flung her arms around him. "I love you too," she said dotting kisses all over his face. Josh's arms wrapped her in a deep embrace. "I've come home," Sam sighed and a sweet laughter erupted around her. She lifted her gaze. She'd forgotten all the spectators. Josh pressed her against him, kissing her with an intensity that left nothing to doubt. All doubts vanished—replaced by a true and absolute love as she surrendered to his teasing, sensual mouth.

Finally, breathless, Josh pulled away. He looked down at her. "Does that mean yes?"

She smiled.

A loud whooping and cheering went up around them.

Chana Ben-Sion walked over to Sam's father. *"Mazel tov,"* she said as she kissed his cheek.

"That's quite a boy you have," her father commented to Josh's mother, still caught in the spell of enchantment the pair wove around them. "Very convincing. Spent hours ranting and raving how he loves her, when I was ready to kill him."

Professor Shapira beamed. "I told you that it would be memorable for the girl to discover her Jewish roots."

"Sam, it's almost Shabbos. Would you like to light candles with us?"

Reluctantly, she withdrew from Josh's embrace.

"Wait, Ima. I have something I want to give Sam." He withdrew a small velvet pouch from his pocket and shook it carefully. His fist closed over the object, making Sam squirm with curiosity. "I don't have a lot of money," he explained, "and I warned your father that I won't live on his either."

Sam filled with pride at his words. So noble. So wonderful. She sighed with pleasure. Who needed money? She had learned the hard way about what really counted in life. Thankfully.

Josh continued. "Like I said, I don't have a lot of money and I don't imagine I ever will. I wanted to give you something that would express the way I feel, so I drew all my wages for the summer." His fingers opened revealing a small pendant, glittering with tiny rubies like a cluster of grapes. Sam blinked back tears.

"A woman of valor, her price is above rubies," he whispered.

She met his dark gaze. It all happened. No one would ever believe it, but it would be a secret they would always share. Carefully, Josh fastened the catch around her neck.

Chana beamed with pleasure and poked Reuven. "I told you so. Not his girlfriend. What rubbish he tells. I could have told everyone this would happen."

As dusk arrived the golden lights that shone over Jerusalem danced, covering the city in a halo of gold. Outside the birds bid farewell to the day, while inside, Sam had Josh at her side. She grinned at the man who was to become her husband. They were together, that was all that mattered.

Everyone walked into the dining room for candle lighting and an unforgettable *Shabbos* dinner. Reuven helped the awkward Geoffrey Pinkman bless his own daughter, his hand on her head the way he did with his own children. As he did, it filled Sam with a sense of satisfaction. Silently, she looked up. *You heard my prayers and answered. I asked for a family like the Ben-Sions, and you gave them to me. Something admirable for Josh to find in me. You did it all. Thank you. I'll try not to disappoint you.* The Sabbath candles flickered back at her

# Chapter Twenty-Two

Sam stood in her wedding finery, the best Pinkman's store could offer. A custom designed dress calculated to make her look like a fairy princess.

Princess Pinkie, she smiled to herself. She had asked the designer to make the dress in a tunic style, similar to the ones she had worn in the "past". Simple, yet elegant and covering her arms as convention decreed. He obliged her to perfection. This dress was no rough linen garb from the first century, though. Thousands of glass beads had been painstakingly sewn on, row upon row over the silk. Now, with the sun's rays streaming through the window, the beads glinted like a cache of diamonds. Around her neck she wore the ruby necklace given to her by Josh on their engagement. This gem was the most precious of all. More so than any ring. It symbolized their bond, the new chains of their lives, the ones that were to bind them forever in love.

Sam gazed at the mirror and barely recognized herself. The sun was setting over the city; crimson, orange and gold bathed the Jerusalem stone in the new as well as the old part of the magical city.

Earlier in the morning Sam had gone to the *mikveh* with Liora, Josh's sister insisting on doing everything right.

"You're glowing," her aunt commented as they left her room and headed toward the King David hotel lobby.

"I'm happy," she acknowledged. And she was. Very.

There was a small crowd of hotel staff and interested onlookers in the lobby to watch her enter a limousine. Inside, Sam felt her stomach do a somersault. Bubbles of excitement welled up within. She couldn't wait to see Josh. Forbidden to see him over the past days, she ached with desire to see his face, to touch him, to hold him.

The car sped through the streets towards the Hebrew University. She and Josh had decided to marry at the university synagogue, since the university and its dig unwittingly brought them together. Their reception would follow at the hotel.

It was a short journey, no time for contemplative meandering. The car drew to a halt and Sam was helped out and ushered into a room where her father, Reuven, and Josh were waiting with the rabbi. They were together to listen to the terms of the wedding contract. A legal contract and agreement. For the rabbi this was the most important part of the ceremony, but Sam only had eyes for Josh. Resplendent in a dark suit and tallis, dark eyes gleaming down at her, her groom took her breath away.

Terms agreed, the men left the room to escort the groom to the wedding canopy as Chana and Sam's dotty old Aunt Claire from Provence linked arms with her and led her into the synagogue to the canopy erected near the altar. Covered with roses, the canopy was a symbol of the home she and her husband would build together.

Sam walked towards Josh, barely aware of their family and friends all around. The prayer shawl around his shoulders made his bronzed skin stand out.

Everything passed in a blur. She stood still and listened to the terms of the contract as Joshua Ben Reuven HaCohen, Joshua, son of

Reuven the Cohen, agreed to marry Sara bat Chaim, Sara, daughter of Chaim. She exchanged a secret smile with him when the part about giving a wife satisfaction was read.

The rabbi indicated that Josh should lift her veil. "Look carefully, Joshua Ben Reuven. Is this your bride?"

"The one and only." His dark eyes filled with pleasure as he took out a small, simple gold wedding band. Silently, Sam extended her index finger as Josh placed the ring on it.

He intoned the words proclaiming that he sanctified her by the laws of Moses. Sam made the seven circuits around her groom binding her to him forever.

Sanctified.

The very same thing she told him at Masada.

The glass under his foot shattered, in remembrance of the Temple, more meaningful to them she realized than any other bride and groom. As the sound of the tinkling glass reverberated around the room, the entire room to let loose in raucous cheers.

"*Mazel tov!*" Crowds surged around to offer congratulations.

Sam smiled at everyone; thankful they'd been able to rush the wedding so that the team from the dig could all attend before flying home at season's end.

Lindsay was already making eyes at one of Josh's cousins. Rob offered to do a wedding portrait as a gift. Old Jan, smiling with deep satisfaction, sat at a table with Dr. Navon. Sam caught sight of her cousin, Nathan, the family geek and computer genius. He always seemed a bit of a misfit. Surprisingly, he was chattering away to Josh's sister, Ruthie.

Back at the hotel, the reception was in full swing, excitement rising as the dig team received a surprise.

Somehow, within a few short days, Sam had managed to create a personal photo album for each. The photos captured the character of each individual through her lens. There were pictures of the site with Jan patiently digging away, a fierce concentration on his face,

Lindsay leaning suggestively against a series of young men, Rob and his cameras leering at one of the young kibbutz girls. Even Dr. Navon was in the album, holding a broken piece of pottery. Sam believed she had encapsulated the entire summer in their faces.

"I thought I would offer a wedding gift, too." Professor Shapira said walking up to her and Josh as they tried to leave.

"But you already did," Sam protested. "You offered Josh a permanent job as your assistant now that he has a wife to support." She grinned and gazed up at her husband.

"I meant for you, my dear. I have a great deal to do with the Israel Museum. Perhaps you would like to produce a series of photos for a calendar promoting our work?" Sam beamed her delighted acceptance as her husband tried to tug her away.

"Just one second." Geoffrey Pinkman stood like a rock in their path. "Before you make your escape I want to give you this." He handed her a key.

Bewildered, Sam stared at it.

"So busy being in love, you had no time for practical matters. Were you planning on moving in with your parents?"

Sam stammered a response. "We're on a waiting list for married couples' rooms at the university."

"A waiting list." He shook his head. "Now, I remember your warning young man," he added. "Son, this is a wedding gift. Take it with love. It's the key to a new house not too far from your parents and not too near so you'll have privacy. It even has a darkroom all ready for use. Of course, houses come cheaper if you buy two." He chuckled, eyes twinkling.

"You bought a house too?"

"I might want to retire one day and spend time with my grandchildren. You'd better get started on that now."

Sam flushed.

"Thank you," Josh answered for both of them. He made a mock military salute at his father in law. "I hear that a Pinkman order is never ignored. Happy to obey commands." Josh grinned at her father.

Geoffrey Pinkman waved it off. "The man who loves my daughter is special."

"Can't argue with that," Sam nodded, smiling up at her husband.

"Son, that was some wedding ceremony," her father added, referring to Sam's quiet, wordless participation. "She was quiet for some time!" he joked.

"I'll take good care of Pinkie."

"Bensie," Sam corrected. "I'm Samantha Ben-Sion now. I like the sound of it."

"Me too," Josh responded as he led her upstairs.

# Chapter Twenty-Three

"**J**osh, it's getting late. You'd better bring Avi in and change him for *Shabbos*. They'll be here any minute." Sam Ben-Sion stood at the doorway and smiled at the scene in front of her. Her husband and son were busily playing in the sandbox of their backyard.

"Avi, you have to dig very carefully for artifacts." Josh took the shovel from the toddler who gazed up at him with the same dark eyes.

Sam giggled. Josh was burying plastic toys for Avi to dig, pretending they were on an archeological dig. The bewildered child could barely speak, but Josh had wasted no time training his son. Their child was named for her husband's dear departed friend. Just prior to Avi being born, she went to Josh's dead friend's parents, asking if they would be upset at their name choice.

Avi's mother burst into tears making her sorry she ever brought up the idea.

"You don't understand. Now his soul can rest. We would be honored if you would do this for our son. It isn't as if you knew him."

How could she tell them she had known Avi? Like everyone else, they would think her insane.

At times, she wondered if the Avi and Rachel she and Josh had met were somehow souls seeking peace. Anything seemed possible after their adventure.

Her father on the other hand, went insane at the birth of his first grandchild less than a year after the wedding. He not only flooded their house with enough baby clothes for ten children, along with toys, strollers, and playpen. He badgered the admissions officer at Hadassah Hospital and showered every mother that gave birth the same day with baby gifts. She laughed at the memory.

Now, as she watched Josh lift Avi to his shoulder and carry him inside, she gave up a silent prayer of thanks.

"Whoever would have dreamed you would be making dinner for the family on *Shabbos?*" he teased.

"Slightly better than the burnt food at Masada," she agreed. "You can thank your mother's countless lessons."

"It's given her hours of pleasure teaching you."

Sam agreed. Now she felt whole. Part of a family. She loved Shabbos and looked forward every week to the peace that descended over her city of dreams and her own home as the sun set. The first time she watched Josh place his hand over their son's tiny dark head, so like his father's, and bless him the way Reuven had done, she was moved to tears. Her eyes would always mist when Josh turned to her and recite A Woman of Valor.

As father and son played, Sam fingered the ruby pendant. She wore it as a constant reminder of their journey and the lessons learned.

She and Josh were content with their lives. Josh had finished his doctorate and was now an assistant professor. He planned to start the season's dig in the next few weeks with her as the photographer. She'd nagged him without mercy until he took her into the desert for a photographic shoot. The result was a book about to be published of her photographs. Postcards of her work sold at tourist spots around the country. Sam had fulfilled all her ambitions and was satisfied with the blessings in her life.

"I forgot to tell you what Dr. Navon came up with today. You should have been there." Josh burst into laughter.

Sam stopped stirring the soup bubbling on the stove and turned to him.

"She examined the chalice and scrolls thoroughly and came to the conclusion that they were prophesies of the future made by an *Essene*. In it, she decided they predicted the burning of Masada, the Roman soldiers passing through the gate, and the chains represent a refusal to go to slavery."

"And what does Professor Shapira say?"

"This is great," Josh slapped a hand on his leg, chuckling. "He says she's an idiot and got the whole thing backwards and that it's about Jerusalem. They had an absolute catfight over the stuff about angels in the scroll and how they disappeared."

"So that was how they explained our disappearance at Masada. I sort of wondered what everyone thought."

"Nobody figured out the flame is really you. Your red hair I mean. How it ever got to the crypt I don't know but there were a few survivors at Masada and I suppose they brought it. Who knows what surprises this season will bring?"

Sam's eyes danced with excitement. More than you bargained on, she thought. Certain she was pregnant again, she prayed for a daughter to name after Rachel.

"I nearly forgot," Josh said, "I had a letter from Jan. He'll be back this season. He wrote something about how his journeys are always pleasant ones. I hope he isn't planning another trip to the past." Josh bent his head over the boiling pot, sniffing the aroma of fresh dill. He closed his eyes. "Smells good. Just like a Friday night should. By the way, I heard Lindsay wants to come back, too. That makes a full crew, with Ruthie and your cousin."

Sam sighed. "Cousin Computer Nerd. Poor Ruthie. Nathan never gives up on her. It must drive her crazy the way he follows her around like a dog. He's even more impossible than I was. Then again," she said, "this is the land of miracles. Maybe he'll get one as wonderful as ours."

"Nothing could be more miraculous that what we have." Her husband took her in his arms, kissing her soundly, making their son gurgle with approval.

They were still kissing when the entire family walked in, ready for another Shabbos together.

~The End~

## About the Authors

As the New Zealand half of Janelle Benham, Jane Beckenham was originally encouraged to write by friends she met on the internet. A chance meeting on line with Sydney based Ellen found Jane co-writing with Ellen, although at the time neither had met. Jane tries to balance family life and writing, a hard challenge facing many writers. She wishes there were more hours in the day because her nights are spent dreaming up stories she is compelled to write.

Always fascinated by history EJ Ben-Sefer has been writing for years, primarily as an academic for scholarly journals, but also fiction. American born Ellen lives in Sydney, Australia, but spent many years living in Israel, visiting archaeological digs, useful research for their book—A Woman of Valor. Ellen is currently teaching nursing and has her doctorate in humanities and in her other life is a mother of two.